MYSTERY

A Death in the Family

Come Home and be Killed

Burning is a Substitute for Loving

The Hunger in the Shadows

Nun's Castle

Ironwood

Raven's Force

Dragon's Eye

Axwater

Murder Has a Pretty Face

The Painted Castle

The Hand of Glass

Listen to the Children

Death in the Garden

Windsor Red

A Cure for Dying

Witching Murder

Footsteps in the Blood

Dead Set

Whoever Has the Heart

JENNIE MELVILLE

A Death in
the Family

St. Martin's Press
New York

"A Thomas Dunne Book"

ISBN 0-312-11772-8

First published in Great Britain by Macmillan

First U.S. Edition: March 1995
10 9 8 7 6 5 4 3 2 1

A Death in
the Family

Whispers from the Past

A soft old voice was talking: 'Good girls don't have babies out of wedlock. Now you must always remember that, good girls don't have babies out of wedlock . . .'

Another voice protesting: 'The bairn's too young to hear that sort of talk. It's that book you keep reading; put it away, Granny Niven, and don't dwell on it. The child is too young for such talk.'

'Never too young for that. Tell the wean.'

Mary Ellenor, a gentleman's servant, debauched by an apprentice coachmaker. Hanged for infanticide.

Agatha Ashbrook, who was very stubborn and would not give any account of her life. (So she was probably a prostitute, or a bunter or a moll or mackerel, in the slang of the day.) Hanged for infanticide.

Chapter One

'She put her hand in mine as confidingly as if she
had known me since her cradle.'
      The Old Curiosity Shop, by Charles Dickens

Charmian Daniels drove home from Slough to Windsor
on the day in November that the castle burned. As she
moved across the bridge which spans the Thames at
Windsor that November afternoon, she looked out of
the car window to see the Castle blazing. Flames leapt,
dark clouds of smoke spiralled to the sky, she fancied
she could hear the roar of the fire as it took hold. It was
like Valhalla-on-Thames.

She had been thinking of death and murder, as who
would not who had been talking to a mother whose
child had disappeared. Gone through the door with a
man and never come back. The fire chimed in with her
mood, almost of despair. Things should burn, could
burn, must burn.

She drew the car into the slip path where she sat
viewing what was so clearly a tremendous confla-
gration; she wound down the window, she could smell
smoke and charred wood. In the darkening autumn sky,
with soft rain beginning to fall, she could see the yellow
and gold of the flames and the redness at their heart.
Too far away to feel the heat, she could imagine it. A
smut came through the window and fell on her hand,
she dusted it away. A bit of history there, she thought,
a burnt bit of Windsor Castle.

She sat there wondering if the fire was a symbol, that she was watching the House of Windsor burn down. Then she thought about the people who lived and worked in the castle like the Dean and clergy of St George's chapel, the Poor Knights of Windsor in their lovely terrace of ancient houses, the Constable of the Castle in his tower. Some of these people were her friends. She thought of Lady Mary Erskine who worked (as far as she could be said to work anywhere) in the library rubbing lanolin into rare bindings, and Canon Kerinder who preached so beautifully but with one eye on the clock because the Queen didn't like more than ten minutes, and General Bunty Binns, veteran of several wars and the first female Poor Knight. The Castle was a small town, where people lived and worked and died; more than just the home of a sovereign. Over the centuries since William the Norman had run it up on a contrived hill of earth and stone in order to hold down the English, it had been sometimes loved, sometimes neglected, and several times rebuilt. It was home to so many besides the Queen and her Court.

They'd be in there fighting the fire, she knew that much. Lady Mary would be carrying out the valuable contents of the library, she might be swearing at the damage to her hands and nails and protesting that she was due out to dinner tonight, please; and Canon Kerinder would probably have joined the Castle Fire Brigade, he was a practical man and had been an engineer in the Navy before taking Holy Orders and would have rolled up his sleeves and got down to it while still keeping an eye on the clock. What time was Evensong in winter?

Ahead of her lay the curving sweep into the town, behind which lay Edred's Yard, a tiny cobbled rectangle where Mr Madge, Goldsmith and Silversmith, sixth of his name, and successor to an even longer line of craftsmen going back to 1780 before the French Revolution had a shot at creating the modern world, kept his jewellery shop, still called Chs Tuscombe's, the name of the original owner. Mr Madge was a magisterial and enigmatic figure with a certain theatrical flair. In his shop she had reserved, awaiting the safe birth, a Victorian gold and coral bauble for a child about to be born, but whose birth promised to be hazardous. Charmian found the idea of this coral ring, which had belonged to an earlier generation, somehow gave security to the new arrival.

As she had stood in the shop, she had remembered, goodness knows why just then when she was feeling happy, a conversation earlier that day with the man she was going to marry. A memory and her own response.

He had telephoned. Early in the morning, when she was still in bed.

'Forgiven me?'

'I'm thinking about it.'

A typical understatement from her, she had thought about it all night, dreams and all.

There was more to the conversation but that was all she remembered at that moment. Thinking about it.

As she put the receiver down, a thought flashed into her mind.

I always wondered what went wrong with that first marriage of his . . . asked around but people don't tell you that sort of thing.

The urge he had to dominate. Irritation moving quickly into anger and something more. The hand on her shoulder, and her own instant reaction. Jerking away.

If there had been any violence, she had no doubt how instantly and hard she would have reacted. Nature and training would have made her respond.

Perhaps it's me, she thought, still standing looking over the jeweller's counter. 'I can be awkward, difficult, even to those men I like. Them, most of all. Perhaps I resent them or my reaction.'

'Miss Daniels?' The jeweller's soft old voice had recalled her to the moment and they had completed their transaction, and she left the shop.

She had followed the road down Peascod Street towards Maid of Honour Close where she lived. On her left would be the new Mother and Baby Clinic where a young friend of hers, her god-daughter, Kate, lay expecting her first child. Before that clinic, so modern and clean, there had been a children's home, and before that a Foundling Hospital, in front of which was a patch of open scrubby ground near the Barracks, known in the nineteenth century as a Baby Drop, where the unfortunates who bore a child outside marriage would place their babies to be taken into the Foundling Hospital.

Behind her, out past the district of Cheasey and in what remained of open country before you came to the industrial belt of Slough, she had left a weeping young woman. Biddy Holt was thirty years old, blonde, pretty, and very near despair.

'See her,' Mary Erskine had said to her yesterday, summoning her with an urgent telephone call. 'Just see her.' She added: 'Soon, please.'

'Look, you sent me a message, I came.'

'So you did, thank you.' Mary had sat back, she was not giving up.

'I can't do anything.' Not strictly true, she could if she so desired. For a couple of years now, Charmian had been head of SRADIC (Southern Register, Document-ation and Index of Crime), which meant she had access to all files on all important investigations, she could inspect at will. More, she had created her own small team to look into cases that interested her. Charmian had moved up the police ladder quietly and skilfully, beginning in Scotland, then moving to an English prov-incial force, serving in Deerham Hills, transferring to the Metropolitan Police, and moving to Windsor to head her own unit. In so doing she had created her own image, of a woman of force and charm, who could stand up to her male colleagues without losing her looks. She had red hair which was highlighted now with touches of silver, she was slim, and she chose her clothes well. Looks counted. 'I like the way you've done this room.'

Lady Mary had recently removed herself from the large elegant family house to a small modern flat over-looking the Home Park and the Castle itself. 'Still close to the Queen,' she had said cheerfully. She was tall, blue eyed, with golden hair, the classic English beauty with looks inherited from a great-grandmother who had been a Gaiety Girl and had married an earl. There had never been enough money in the family, but Lady Mary, a natural gambler, was always hard up even if the cards and horses were going her way; she was always in love, usually disastrously, but underneath remained faithful, in her fashion, to the impecunious soldier whom she planned to marry.

'It's the pinkiness that's so good,' said Charmian, 'that lovely browny pink that cheers the spirit without look-ing pallid. Lovely curtains.' They were of heavy corded silk of great richness but saving money never worried Lady Mary. Money she had not, excellent, expensive tastes, inherited from the great-grandfather who had known beauty when he saw it, she certainly did have.

'I had help, your god-daughter helped.' Kate Rewley had trained as an architect but now took a passionate interest in interior decoration. She had tried to lay strong hands on Charmian's own home but had so far been resisted. 'Don't change the subject,' Lady Mary had gone on, getting back to what really interested her. 'At least let her meet you. I spoke to Kate when I visited her in hospital yesterday and she said to speak to you, that you'd help.'

Thank you, Kate, Charmian said inside.

'But I'd have thought of you, anyway . . . She blames herself, you see. She let him go with the man.'

'Just a nameless man?'

'She was expecting a father, Harry Allen, to collect her on the school run, she had a phone call to say it would be a father. Perilla Allen rang, said she had sprained her wrist, and she couldn't drive. Harry would be doing the run.'

'But she didn't know the man who came?'

'No, never seen him before. She didn't know Harry Allen, either. But the child seemed to know him, went off as merry as a grig. It seemed all right. She had no reason to believe there was anything wrong.'

Not until the real father had turned up afterwards.

'You're not telling this story well, Mary.'

Lady Mary sighed. 'Doing my best.'

'What did the man who was supposed to collect the child say? I presume he was questioned?'

'Yes. Says he called, found no child waiting, rang the door bell whereupon Biddy had hysterics more or less. He knows nothing else.'

Charmian frowned. 'Lot of *No, nos* here. So many gaps. Was it unusual to have a substitute driver? Had it happened before? Who knew?'

Mary frowned. 'So ask her.'

'I'll ask you: what sort of a person is she? The sort of mother who will let her child go off with a stranger? And has she done it before?'

Mary seemed to have nothing to say, except: 'I think the detective, the police, you know, they came at once, did ask that sort of question.'

'They will have done. Who's handling the case?'

'A chap called Feather.' It seemed such an unlikely name for a man who was heavily built.

'I know Dan Feather, usually called by his initials, DF, he's good.'

'Good manners, anyway.'

'You've met him then?'

'Biddy asked me to be there. She hasn't got a husband, she needed someone.'

And Lady Mary, with all her connections in various powerful rich families and her perch in the house of Windsor, was a useful ally.

'I suppose she's a cousin of yours,' said Charmian, knowing the aristocratic network of relationships into which Lady Mary fitted where you knew your cousin back to the reign of George III of Hanover and England.

'As a matter of fact, she isn't. But we came out together and have kept up ever since . . . Not that Biddy was your average deb,' she added thoughtfully.

Charmian was diverted for a moment. 'I didn't know you were a deb, and did a season.'

'Of course I did. Everyone did.' —Everyone of a certain family connection, that is, Charmian added to herself. 'But it was yonks ago.'

Charmian went back to the missing child. 'What about the father, what part does he play?'

'He wasn't there. They don't live together. Never have.'

'You mean aren't married?'

Lady Mary was defensive. 'Well, that's no big deal these days.'

But Charmian knew that in the social class in which Lady Mary moved where there might be a title and an estate, a matter of inheritance, marriages from which an heir might spring were the rule. At least for the first marriage, afterwards you could choose. Property mattered.

'So he's married already? With children? Thank you, I'm getting the picture.'

Perhaps she had sounded a mite too disapproving, her Scottish puritan background did show through her surface sophistication at times. 'How's your love life,' said Mary aggressively.

Charmian ignored this question. When Lady Mary was bad tempered, it meant she was unhappy, and Charmian was sufficiently fond of her friend not to want to probe into this unhappiness. You didn't always cure a pain by lancing it. In any case, Charmian was planning to be married herself at Christmas, having at last got round to admitting it would make her happy, which Mary knew very well. Charmian was approaching the event with a mixture of hope and caution, she had been married once before, when much younger; it had not worked well. Better luck second time round, she would need luck, there could be a problem.

'How old is the missing girl?' she asked.

'Eight years old.'

'How long has she been missing?' But she had heard something of the case already and knew it was already too long.

'Seven days.' Mary added: 'Biddy rushed to the school, only to be told that not only was she not there now, but she had not been there for the last three days.'

'How strange.'

'It's because it's strange that I thought you'd be interested.'

Charmian considered. Her god-daughter's pregnancy had sensitized her to mothers and children. 'I'll see what I can do, but no promises.'

She knew Inspector D. F. Feather; she could go straight in, in an official kind of way, and get a polite but official kind of answer which would tell her as little as Feather could manage to get away with. But he could be approached. She had discovered that he started work early and that then he might talk as he drank his first cup of tea of the day. He had no wife and his work was both his spouse and his consolation. There had been a Mrs Feather but she had left the scene and no one knew where. Some of his more jaundiced subordinates said that he was just the sort to have her buried under the floorboards. But he was a good detective. There was a girlfriend, so she'd heard.

And when she walked in to his office early the next morning, and saw his tall broad-shouldered figure, thick fair hair, greying at the sides, eyes bright blue, a large hand dangling a teabag over a mug of hot water, she thought he did not look at all like a man who had killed his wife and hidden her under the bed, but very much like a policeman whose wife had walked away sadly because he hadn't looked at her, not really looked, for a long time. But life had given her several sharp knocks, perhaps they had softened her, because to her surprise she had discovered that she was now as capable of falling in love as any woman. 'I have become a romantic,' she admitted.

Feather looked up in surprise. 'Morning, ma'am.' He knew what to say, as Lady Mary had said: he had good manners. 'Like a cup of tea?'

'Yes, please.'

'It's about the Holt child.' She accepted the tea. 'Your case?'

'Yes, it is.' He frowned. 'One to handle with care on all sides.'

'Because of the mother?'

'In part, of course, but it's one of those complicated family backgrounds. She's divorced, but the girl wasn't Holt's daughter, she was the child of Peter Loomis.'

'Peter Loomis? Good Lord.'

'Yes, Peter Loomis, MP. He was tried for killing his wife.'

'But the jury couldn't come to a verdict.'

'That's right. The judge gave them a talking to and sent them back, but they still couldn't bring in a majority verdict. So they had another trial.'

'And the jury still couldn't agree?'

'Another judge, another talking to, so they went back in and came out and said he wasn't guilty. It was the nearest thing to Not Proven you could have.'

'So she's Peter Loomis' child.' Charmian considered the fact. Had Lady Mary known? But of course she had, and it explained some of her anxiety. She had known but said nothing. Must have realized I would discover, Charmian thought.

'That information hasn't come out.'

'No, not yet. But it will.'

'Where is he? Have you spoken to him?'

'He's at Chantrey House, that's the family house, National Trust property now, but he has a place in the grounds. He lives there with his mother. Yes, I have spoken to him. He's upset but had nothing to add that helped. Not so far,' Feather added thoughtfully. 'His mother tried to be helpful. Loved the child.'

'Is it a part of the case? I mean has it got any bearing on the child's disappearance?'

'I don't know. All I know is the kid is missing, and we haven't found her.'

Might never find her alive, but he did not say that aloud. All the same, the unexpressed words echoed round the silent room. Nor did he say 'And what is your interest in this, ma'am?' being too canny and cautious.

Charmian obliged him: 'The mother is a friend of a friend.'

'You know her, do you, ma'am?'

'No, never met her.' Although she might be interested in doing so quite soon.

Feather reflected. 'Pity, I would have liked your opinion of her.'

'Don't you trust her?'

Feather was thinking it out: 'It's more as if she doesn't trust me.'

'She's in shock.'

He nodded. 'Yes, that too. I accept that, and I went slow with her. But she didn't want to talk.'

'Some people are always distrustful.' Charmian frowned. 'But you believed her? She was telling the truth?'

'I believed she was telling the truth as far as it went. But I feel that there is more that she is not telling . . . I don't know if you'd feel like it, ma'am, but I'd be glad if you had a talk with her.'

You and Lady Mary, thought Charmian. 'I will.'

Feather hesitated. 'It's not quite over, either.'

'What do you mean?'

'Something horrible . . . A doll, left on her front door. I don't know if she'd tell you. Doesn't like to talk about it.'

'I'm not surprised.'

'And I don't know what to make of it . . . I'm not sure if she's telling me the whole truth.'

'About the doll?'

'About anything.'

'Have you seen the doll?'

'Yes, just an ordinary plastic doll. Forensic have it at the moment.'

As she moved towards the door, he stopped her with a word: 'She's dead, of course.'

Charmian stood frozen. 'What makes you say that?'

'Feel it.' He held his hands and stretched the fingers wide. 'Feel it there.'

As far as Charmian was concerned, this was Day One.

She had made a few enquiries and learnt that the affair between Biddy Holt, Driscoll, she had been then, and Peter Loomis was well known and that the birth of the child had preceded the murder of Peter's wife (for whom no murderer had ever been found). There was a suggestion that it was the arrival of the child that had precipitated the murder. But Lady Mary said that Biddy had got married quickly to Holt, a marriage of convenience, and withdrawn from the scene.

Charmian went through a routine day at her SRADIC headquarters, dealing with an average day's work, but her mind was thinking about Biddy Holt and her daughter. Under the influence of these thoughts, she left early, and made for home.

Home was Maid of Honour Row, her tiny Victorian house, where she was greeted with detached politeness by Muff, her large tabby cat, and by a note from her friends and neighbours the retired white witches, Birdie Peacock and Winifred Eagle.

'Taking Benjy for a dog-training class.'

Benjy was Charmian's dog but he lived with Birdie and Winifred.

'A friend of ours runs it for special dogs. We think Benjy will benefit.'

A training class for dogs run by a witch or a warlock? 'Better be careful, Muff,' she advised. 'Benjy may come back with a few anti-cat spells.'

Muff was undisturbed, but moved to her feeding bowl where she took up her position. Charmian knew what was desired: she fed Muff, after which she changed her clothes, putting on jeans and a sweater. This was not to be an official visit.

She took a last fond look at her house before she closed the door behind her. She had the idea she was stepping into strange territory.

'It's the doll.' She held the key in her hand. 'Just a little plastic baby.'

It was getting dusky because it was turning into a damp November evening of the sort that the Thames valley knows well. Charmian drove out of Windsor, taking the Cheasey road but avoiding that lawless area, which everyone did if they could. Beyond Cheasey and before Slough was a wedge of open land which was still country with cattle grids and what looked like several groups of dark, low cottages put together to make a house. As Charmian walked across the grass towards The Vinery, however, she saw that she was mistaken. Sunk in the earth, built of dark stone with a low roof, a house, perhaps even this one, had been on the site for centuries. It looked strong and solid and immemorially old, as if its foundations had known the Roman invaders and had outlasted them.

The Vinery was a house on which money had been

spent, the white paint was fresh, the thatched roof looked well groomed as if someone had taken a comb to it, and in the barn, which served as a garage, was a shining new Jaguar. This too was white so it matched the house.

She had parked the car on the grass verge, locking it carefully, since lawless Cheasey, home to many a skilful car-stealing family, was not far away. Her hand was raised to the antique brass knocker when the door opened.

'I was watching, I saw you come.'

'You were expecting me?'

'Mary said you might come; I've been looking out for you. On and off, you know, and hoping . . . Mary said what a help you always were. I'm Biddy Holt.' She held out a polite hand. She would always be polite, Charmian thought, looking at the small, sturdy figure in jeans and a white sweater. She had dark crisp curls, but her eyes were hidden behind dark glasses which could not entirely hide the puffy redness.

Recent tears, prolonged tears, probably, you got to know the signs in this trade. What you couldn't be sure of was the cause: straight grief, twisted guilt, plain anxiety, take your pick.

'Mary said that I was helpful?' Charmian felt both chastened and surprised by the judgement: she had not always been helpful to Lady Mary, more often sharply critical. Carping, she said to herself. That's what I've been more often than not.

'Are you on your own?' she asked the girl. Biddy looked no more than a girl with her light young voice and small, neat features. Probably very pretty when normal.

'Inspector Feather left a policewoman with me, but I

sent her away after a bit. I wanted to be on my own.'

Charmian nodded; she knew the feeling, but she was still outside the house, with Biddy holding the door. 'Can I come in?'

'Oh yes, sorry.' She led the way through to a long, low-ceilinged sitting-room with a huge stone grate in which a log fire burned; a small white dog of indeterminate breed lay before it. He stood up and gave a low growl as they approached. 'Quiet now, Tray . . . he's edgy with all the people that have been in and out. He's picked up the tension, dogs do, don't they? Coffee? Tea?'

'Nothing, thank you.'

Biddy hovered, looked irresolute and distressed, then she motioned towards one of the big sofas that stood on either side of the fire. The dog at once leapt up. 'Down, Tray. Miss Daniels, do sit down.' She led the way by sitting down herself at some distance from the fire. The dog crawled on to her lap and this time, she did not forbid him.

She told her story: 'We had breakfast together as usual, Sarah was a bit off her food, excited. Not ill, just a bit excited, she did get excited when she was going to school . . . she loved it, you see.' She paused before resuming her story: 'I was one of a group of mothers who did the school run, there isn't a school bus, it's such a small school, you see, it wouldn't be economically viable, so we take turns. We are all friends.'

She had got the message the night before that the father of a fellow pupil would be collecting the group, she didn't know him, the bell had rung, her daughter had rushed to the door with her, appeared to know the man who was calling for her, and had departed.

'And you didn't know him?'

'No . . .' But Charmian picked up the hesitation.

'You're sure?'

'I just have the feeling that I might have seen him.'

'Where? Where did you see him?'

'I don't know, I can't be sure . . . It might have been in a shop.'

'Selling or buying?'

'Oh, not selling . . . he wasn't someone who worked in a shop. No, he must have been shopping.'

'Can you recall the shop? It would be worth knowing.'

Biddy frowned but no illumination appeared in her face. She shook her head, her eyes going blank. 'Can't see anything.'

'Food shop? Clothes? Shoes?' What was there left? 'Flowers? Fruit and vegetable.'

'Might have been food,' said Biddy. 'Yes, could have been.'

'Small shop? Large shop.' Don't let it be a supermarket, no hope of tracing a stray man there. But even this was denied her. Biddy shook her head.

'I don't know. I can't get any further.'

'Keep on trying,' said Charmian. 'It's worth it . . . Why did you tell Inspector Feather that you didn't know the man who came for your daughter?'

'I thought I didn't.'

'But you thought your child did know him? And that was why you yourself accepted him? Your daughter went off cheerfully, even gleefully, you said.'

'You're putting the wrong gloss on what I said. She just seemed to accept him, she was placid. For instance, she put out her hand and smiled. I said: "That's all right?" And she nodded. Of course, I thought it was. I thought he was Harry. But don't read too much in to it. I didn't say she went off as if she was going to a party . . . I think that might have puzzled me. Alarmed

18

me, even. I'd have noticed that. As it was it all seemed so normal ... it wasn't till Harry turned up, late and full of apologies, that I panicked. Harry was upset too, I can tell you.'

'What did you do?'

'I rang the school and she wasn't there. That's when I learnt she hadn't been present for several days. Then I did go over the top. I remember screaming. Then I told the police.'

She's lying, for some reason, she has slightly, very slightly changed her story, the details are a tiny bit different; she might have seen the man, Sarah didn't eagerly greet the man but went off placidly, although she had been excited earlier.

'I'm telling the truth,' said Biddy quickly. 'Really, I am, it's just that when I was speaking to you just now, I suddenly thought, that, yes, perhaps I had seen him before. Perhaps he was watching, following me.'

'Do you think so?'

Biddy shook her head. 'I don't know. I don't know. Maybe I shouldn't have said that.'

Maybe you shouldn't, thought Charmian. A step too far.

She frowned. 'If your daughter was collected as usual each day, then she must have been delivered as usual even if she never appeared at the school. What happened in between? Did no one see her go off? Didn't you think it strange?'

'Of course I do, I think it's bloody strange, I blame the school.'

'Inspector Feather says they seem a relaxed outfit and that you yourself have often kept Sarah away without warning so they didn't think much about it, blaming you, but that they would have got in touch pretty soon.

It does sound as if whoever took your daughter knew the school. You haven't got any idea who that person could be? What about her father?' He was the obvious suspect.'

But Biddy was firm. 'No, no, he would have come himself, not sent a stranger.'

What stranger? Charmian thought. She changed the subject. 'What about the doll? You found it outside?'

'Yes, by the bay tree at the front door. Not hidden, I think it was put there so I would find it. Perhaps by Sarah, and that frightened me.'

'And it was definitely one of your daughter's dolls?'

'Yes, she'd broken the nose, I knew it by that, the Inspector took it away. I didn't want him to.'

Charmian considered. 'Yes, he'd want to do that. I'd like to have seen it.'

'I can show you the others.'

'The others?'

'Yes, she had a family of them.'

Biddy led her through to another sitting-room which was more of a child's play-room in which there were plenty of toys, Sarah had not been deprived of play-things judging by the rocking horse, the doll's house and the toy train. On a sofa, ranged side by side, were a group of dolls, some dressed, some completely naked. They were all of a size, just about four inches, small and made of pale pink plastic. The round faces and blank eyes stared at Charmian, a sad and sombre semicircle.

She turned to Biddy: 'They're tiny.'

'Yes, she'd liked little dolls, and of course being all the same made them more of a group. She gave them different names, the one that came back was called Little.'

Charmian picked up one naked object.

'That's Small.'

Charmian held it in her hands. Just a little plastic doll with no clothes on. Certainly not beautiful, hard to tell if it was much loved.

'Just an ordinary plastic doll,' Feather had said. But it wasn't ordinary. Not this one. Small had his or her left eye blacked out.

Charmian raised an eyebrow and Biddy answered: 'Sarah has a slight cross in one eye and she thought Small was starting one.'

'Ah.' Now she came to look again, it seemed to Charmian that several of the other dolls looked as though they had run into eye trouble. 'That can be cured.'

'Of course, it will be,' said Biddy quickly, but she looked away, not meeting Charmian's gaze. Charmian could see tears in her eyes.

'Why did you feel you wanted to see me?' she enquired gently. 'What was wrong with Inspector Feather? He's a good man.'

'He didn't believe me, I could tell. It was in his face.'

Charmian nodded. She had picked up a truth here. Policemen got that look, probably she had it herself. And as it happened, Feather had not entirely believed Biddy Holt.

'He seemed to think I could have told him more, that I was keeping something back. It was in his face, in his voice. And he didn't appear to be doing anything. No one was looking for Sarah.'

'Oh, they are, you can count on that. I saw Sarah's photograph on TV myself and your appeal.'

'Oh, yes, I appealed,' said Biddy, 'and that was when I felt how hopeless it was, how I was talking into the air and no one was listening.'

Charmian knew that a police sweep of all the open land and woods was under way, but when you were near Windsor Great Park that was some task. Other officers were calling door to door in Windsor itself. They would move on to Merrywick and Cheasey later. The search would then extend to Reading, Slough, and Oxford. London itself would be added to the list.

'I'll tell you what I'll do,' she said. 'I'll call in all the records, and then if I decide it is needed, I will send in my own investigating team.'

At the same time, she could hear Feather's voice in her ear: 'She's dead, of course.'

Biddy looked at her, she took off the dark spectacles and stared into Charmian's face. Her eyes were streaked with small red veins. 'I want her back.'

'You'll have to trust me.'

As she sat in the car, she looked back at that dark old house with the sad family of dolls inside it. A house that had known tragedies and mysteries in its time, the sense of the past was strong.

She drove towards Windsor with Feather's voice in her mind, the sense of unease was so strong that it was no surprise somehow to see the Castle burning.

Then, not on impulse, because it had been at the back of her mind all the time, the worry about Kate being so strong, she took the turn in the road that led her towards the Princess Mother and Baby Clinic where her godchild lay in bed.

It was a short drive so she was there quickly. Too quickly, because she wanted to think how to handle Kate. Kate in good health could be tricky, always loving but impetuous and spirited: sick, she was difficult.

The Princess Clinic was new, only three years old,

expensive, and full of the sort of modern technology that would have alarmed those earlier patients of the old hospital and before that, in the days of the Foundlings' Hospital, would have seriously surprised those even earlier sad souls who had borne their babies without benefit of clergy or midwives and laid the infants on the hard grass of Baby Drop land.

In fact, the wire and tubes which had been attached to Kate when last seen had alarmed Charmian herself. She took a deep breath while she prepared to face them again.

Inside the hospital was white and pastel, determinedly not frightening, but managing somehow not to be welcoming, not to be a place you would walk to unless you had to. It smelt of money, though. No one poor was delivered in the Princess Clinic.

'Dead already, dead already.' Feather's voice came with her as she went past the reception desk, took the lift, then walked through the corridor.

Kate was resting on a mound of pillows. Her face was very thin and white, the bones showing the cheeks, her eyes huge. She was, although no one had told her, yet she had probably guessed, very ill.

Charmian kissed her, carefully, gently, she was so fragile.

Kate sounded happy. 'I got up today, they let me go to the bathroom myself.' Off her pretty cell was an even smaller bathroom. 'And last night when I couldn't sleep I took a walk round the room.'

'Did you, dearest?'

'I was careful, a bit nervous. Silly, isn't it? But I didn't want to risk the baby.'

She was at risk herself.

'Of course, Kate.'

'Once you start on this baby business, you want to do it well.'

'Of course you do.' She was repeating herself out of want of better words of love and support.

'I want to be a loving mother.'

'I know that.' Charmian held Kate's hand, it was hot and dry.

'But you know sometimes I feel angry. Go away, baby, I say to myself. I wish you weren't here, I've had enough, there's not room for two of us. Go away and let me get back to being myself . . . Can you understand that?'

'Can't I just,' said Charmian, thinking of the love and resentment and violence that was growing up in her relationship with Humphrey.

Kate hung on to her godmother's hand. 'I could do with seeing more of my husband . . . but he's got a case.'

Charmian nodded. 'I know that.' As his boss, she had given him the case, and might be on the point of giving him the case of Sarah. 'He's tied that one up, though.' But she had this new case waiting in the wings.

'He telephones a lot and always comes in the evening when he's finished for the day. Only sometimes I'm asleep and they won't let him wake me.' Kate sounded resigned but sad.

I ought to go easy on Rewley, not give him the Sarah Holt business to handle, thought Charmian. I shouldn't put it on him. But she knew she would, she could be ruthless, work was work.

'But he leaves messages and books and flowers. I'm reading a lot.'

'Good. Anything I can get you?'

'No, just come when you can . . . You help.'

'I'm glad.'

'You get it right, how I feel. My mother doesn't, not even Rewley. Perhaps men can't, but you do.' She always called her husband Rewley, everyone did. 'He looks at me with love, too much love, it worries me, and Anny buys me expensive bedjackets and nightgowns' – she looked down at the trifle of chiffon and swansdown on her shoulders which had been her mother's latest gift, – 'and says why not get in a special nurse.'

'Anny's always had too much money.' Charmian delivered the judgement briefly. Anny was her best and oldest friend, and a fine artist, but money had let her get away with more than she should.

'What about your father?'

'AWOL,' said Kate sadly. Her father always absconded when family crises loomed, he loved his daughter as he loved Anny but sometimes he preferred to hide. With a bottle of whisky if possible.

'But you understand.'

They sat in silence for a minute, then Charmian said: 'I've been there, you know . . . I had to make a decision once, I made it, but I've never known if it was the right one . . . But it didn't seem the right time to have a child. Perhaps it never is. And the father . . .'

Kate looked at her. 'Not around? He didn't stay around?'

'You could say that.' He'd been dead, as it happened, but no need to go into it. Not a tragedy if you didn't make it so.

Her throat felt tight, pushing emotion aside, she walked to the window to look out. From this window in this sheltered room, she could see over the wall to the patch of rough ground that was all that was left of Baby Drop.

The area was larger than she had expected, stretching

in the dark towards a thick belt of bushes and trees beyond which it was lit by a row of street lamps.

She could imagine the flitting, nervous figures of the girls who had hidden in the shadows before they laid their baby down. Some just wrapped in rags, but others, so she had been told, nicely dressed with a little trinket or two about them, a necklace, a locket, or a tiny bracelet. She had also heard that one or two were buried under the loose turf. Not all deaths of the infants were natural. You could think of their ghosts out there, poor little creatures.

'I saw someone walking around there last night when I went to the bathroom . . . because it was so special being allowed to move round, I took my time. I stood by the window. I could see in the moonlight.'

Charmian frowned. 'This person . . . man or woman?'

'Couldn't tell. Huddled up in clothes.' Kate meditated. 'A huddle, it was.'

'Doing anything special?'

'No, just walking around.'

Charmian came back from the window, and stood looking at her godchild. She didn't like what she saw.

Kate said in a small voice: 'It's haunted out there.' Kate sat back against her pillows. 'I can feel it.'

'What you need is a strong-minded female friend.'

'Dolly Barstow is looking in.'

'She'll do.'

Dolly Barstow was a detective sergeant who had worked with Charmian: she had been seconded to another police force for a few months and was now back but doing a course in medico-legal studies which seemed to mean working in a hospital for part of the time, and then sitting at the feet of lawyers in King's College, University of London. Charmian, who had taken an ambitious route herself in the past, liked Dolly. Kate and Dolly had been close friends for some while.

Charmian hugged Kate. 'I'm off. Look after yourself.'

'They don't let me do anything else.'

She drove home to Maid of Honour Row, passing the Castle, which was still burning, with the smoke and smell of charred wood hanging over the town. Her own small house was quiet, the cat Muff met her with a soft sound which probably was a suggestion for food, this being the subject which usually drove her to communicate.

Charmian spooned out some food on to her special dish which had DOG on it in large black letters. Muff did not mind, she had been a cat for a long time and knew exactly who she was.

Charmian prepared and ate her own modest meal. Her marriage was planned for two months ahead and she was on a strict diet.

After she had eaten, she telephoned Inspector Feather at the Incident Room.

'He's gone home, ma'am.'

She could and did call his house, a woman's voice answered the telephone, to Charmian's surprise. So he's got someone, she thought. Not the wife, she would have known her, and this speaker sounded young. Pleasant. And she seemed to recognize Charmian's voice, to know she was someone you had to listen to, but to know also that Feather would not be pleased, and to be willing to say so. He was worn out with this new case, had been up most of last night while they dragged the river near the railway, and had now gone to sleep in front of his favourite television programme.

Charmian pressed her point.

'I'll get him,' said the voice doubtfully. Lover, house-keeper, sister, aunt, or just friend? Not aunt, Charmian decided, she sounded too young, but this left a wide choice.

'Please.' And when he came, trying to sound alert, Charmian began: 'About the missing girl . . .'

'Yes, I'm worried too. It's been a bad day.'

'Bad news?'

'No news, that's the worst sort. No witnesses, no sightings, not even false alarms . . .' He took a deep breath, and came quite awake. 'At least she's not in the river.'

'Plenty of other places.'

'We're looking,' said Feather grimly.

'I've seen the mother.'

'What did you make of her?'

'A bit puzzling . . . The story she told me was just slightly different.'

'Ah,' said Feather. 'We'd better compare notes.'

'But she did tell me about the doll, and showed me the child's collection, family of dolls.'

Feather said: 'I suppose the girl actually has gone.'

'What an idea.'

'Keeps coming into my mind . . . Only her word for it.'

'You don't pull your shots.'

'I've shocked you, ma'am.'

'No.' The shock that she was not shocked. 'It is something you have to think about.'

'It happens.'

'But you were convinced the child was dead.'

'Not incompatible,' said Feather heavily.

Charmian said: 'I just have a hunch, but search the open ground behind the Princess Mother and Baby Clinic.'

For this was Baby Drop territory and what had been a good spot for a burial might have lingered in folk history and been used again. Some sites did attract their own history.

Chapter Two

Mist from the river mixed with smoke from the Castle
which still smouldered, and the clouds hanging low over
the town, pressed the mixture down on the town and in
through cracks in windows and doors. Charmian smelt it
as she dressed and drank some coffee, Muff, as she
came in from the garden, had the smell of it on her fur,
and Charmian thought her own hair had picked up a
smokiness. She stood under a hot shower to let it wash
out. Her hair needed cutting, but Humphrey was on his
way home from China and he liked her hair long.

It was the first time that she had let what he liked
about her appearance influence her, consciously
anyway, and it felt strange. Looking back, her previous
strong determination to dress only for herself and what
pleased her now seemed arrogant and selfish. There
were others in the world, you loved some of them and
why not give pleasure if you could.

All the same, if shoulder-length hair had not suited
her, then she would not have worn it. No motives are
totally pure.

This thought refreshed her, restored the balance to
what was, she admitted, an astringent personality, so
she emerged from the shower in a good mood. It was

hard being a changed woman. For a long time now, she had thought of herself as being solitary, capable of having temporary attachments but nothing lasting. She had chosen to be like this, it seemed safer.

So it had been a surprise when tender, anxious love could come springing back. It was a spring, new and vigorous, as if the stream had been running underground all this time but had now burst forth.

An engagement ring, a vast blue sapphire flanked by diamonds almost as large, was even now being altered to fit her finger by Mr Madge, the jeweller. Mr Madge's shop, tucked away in a precinct called Edred's Yard, which must be pre-Norman as old and quiet as he was himself. As well as jewellery and gold and silverware, he dealt in antique objects, anything that took his fancy from fine delicate china to a suit of armour which stood at the back of the shop next to a large collection of objects of all sizes that might have come from anywhere, Germany, Italy, China, and ancient Rome or Babylon, anything in short that might have caught Mr Madge's or his father's eye, and the value of which was hard to assess. The dust thicker here at the back of the shop where the objects gave the impression of not having been disturbed since the death of the late King. But Mr Madge kept his old customers in the town, county, and Castle. Humphrey and Humphrey's ring were well known to him, as it had been to his father and his father before that. They had cleaned and reset it for several generations.

Charmian took a quiet, secret, half-ashamed satisfaction that her finger was more slender than that of the original ancestral Kent owner. It was one of those rings that wealthy landed families (gentry, they used to be called) keep by them for the engagement of the eldest son. No one but Humphrey was left now, he was only and all, heir to whatever there was left; a small estate in Dorset, some careful investments, and a good deal of old-fashioned jewellery.

He would probably telephone again today from Bonn or Peking or wherever he was, and they would sort things out. But he must never show anger to her again, however maddening she was, not direct, physical anger, or she'd be off. Probably having given him a black eye first. That was how she felt at the moment: strike first.

She towelled her hair and considered the day. Her task was to know about all the investigation of serious crime in her remit, to be informed, to make sure she was informed (not as easy as it sounded, all policemen liked to keep their own secrets if they could), and to undertake an independent inquiry when she saw fit.

She did not exercise this right too often, but her small inquiry team which George Rewley headed, and who was assisted by Amos Elliot and Jane Gibson, both detective constables, was beginning to be well known. And somewhat feared.

They were known for never giving up. She had recently sent them, like ferrets, into a fraud case where they were investigating the investigators.

She drank her coffee in the kitchen, wondering if Inspector Dan Feather had started the inspection on the Baby Drop land, or if he would give it low priority. She drank her second cup of coffee, thinking about Kate and looking absently at the dust on the shelves opposite which the morning sun made obvious. Someone ought to do something about it. She had a housekeeper who appeared twice a week to clean and polish but she was at present sunning herself in Morocco, enjoying what she called her 'winter break'. The widow of a policeman, she had a string of admirers, one of whom had gone on this trip with her. She had offered a touch of sympathy to Charmian for being about to marry again. 'You're better off on your own, dear, that's something I've learnt. Not that my Jim was a nuisance, he was a good man, but there's the freedom to pick and choose, and now I've got it, I mean to keep it. But there, this new one you've got . . .'

Charmian appreciated the force of the word 'got' here.

As Charmian was dressing, the telephone rang.

'Rewley here.'

'How's Kate?'

'Not too bad,' he said cheerfully. 'Uncomfortable and cross. If only her blood pressure would stop whizzing about.' There were other complications and hazards for Kate and her baby, as they both knew. 'But I didn't ring about that. I think we've got to the bottom of this business and I can leave Jane to wrap it up. Jenkins Junior did not do anything wrong himself but he fed information to Jenkins Major who was able to profit.' These were not the real names of the characters concerned. 'And Jenkins Major had something solid in Jenkins Super who was sent in to do the books . . .'

'A chain?' said Charmian.

'A chain. I've got some papers for you to sign.'

'That's good, because I want to speak to you. I've got a series of meetings. Come to the library about twelve.'

Her department had recently been moved nearer to the town and was now housed in an ancient building which the Police Authority had bought and promised to preserve without spoiling its character. The foundations of the building were probably fifteenth century, so Charmian had been told, on which an Elizabethan building had been superimposed, only to be replaced in its turn by a Queen Anne construction so that Charmian worked in a string of rooms that had ceilings and panellings from the very early eighteenth century. The floors sloped, the doors were warped, and every draught sped through the window-frames, but she loved it. She issued the invitation with some pleasure: the library was her own invention. On a tight budget, her own assistant there was a young librarian who came in three mornings a week. Otherwise, she was on her own. But in some ways she preferred it so, it was a place to work privately.

Only a small fund had been allowed her to set it up, but she had taken the best professional advice from the local university (from which the librarian came), so that she had a well-chosen library on criminology, forensic science, and pathology. In addition, she had three shelves of local history. Nice neat volumes, some in old calf, others rebound in strong red and blue by prisoners in the local prison workshop.

These were all on open shelves, to be used by the carefully chosen group who had access to the library, but in a locked cupboard she had a few files on cases she had been involved with, some of the material here was too inflammable to be made public.

'You're a historian manqué,' her friend Anny Cooper had said, when Charmian let her in to view the room. She put her hand on the row of local history books. James Henderson on Saxon Windsor and Norman Windsor. Mowett and Fraser: *The growth of Windsor under the Tudors*. Eliza Charteris: *Windsor in the Eighteenth Century*. Joseph and Mary Frost: *Windsor Traders and Craftsmen*.

'You know me too well.'

'I know you always underestimate yourself. You're doing it now.' Anny turned her head away. 'This marriage, don't let Humphrey call the tune.'

'He wouldn't do that.' Charmian tried to sound confident.

Anny shrugged, not answering.

'You don't like Humphrey.' It might be the time to question Anny about his earlier marriage but she couldn't bring herself to do it.

'No, that's not true, although all that family can be tough customers.' She didn't see Charmian wince as she turned towards her. 'I think I'm jealous, you get on better with my daughter than I do, and sometimes you seem to get on with my husband better than I do myself.'

'How is Jack?' asked Charmian with sympathy. Anny and her husband had a marriage that came to pieces every so often. Anny was rich, a talented artist, and Jack was neither.

'On a toot.' Anny was gloomy. 'He'll kill himself one day.'

'He'll come back when Kate's had the baby.'

'Yes, and I shall be glad to see him, it's always the same. I drive him away, then welcome him back. Take no notice of me, I admire what you've done here.' She took a book from the shelf. 'Prout on Local Buckinghamshire Customs, first edition too. I have it myself. Inherited, I didn't buy it. You're making a good collection.' She smiled, apologizing without words as Anny so often did. 'You know more about Windsor than I do, yet I've lived here almost all my life and you've only been here a few years.'

'Almost ten,' said Charmian, thinking that to know the district was her shop, and that she knew more than Anny guessed, even more about what Jack got up to than she let on. 'And you can't live in a place like Windsor without developing a strong sense of the past.'

She thought about this conversation almost every time she went into the library. Although she had countered Anny's words, her friend had put her finger on a worry that Charmian felt herself. She loved Humphrey, he loved her, it was a real emotion for them both, but he moved in a world she did not know. 'I'm a police officer, a detective, that's what I am, after all, while he, what was he?'

What he was in the world, she was never quite sure, a kind of diplomat who dealt in security matters. Yes, he touched her world there, but she never wanted to get too close to that subtle, two-faced, sinister world, her villains were more straightforward in what they did, like arson and murder.

She got through her morning work quickly, most of it today was routine, and let herself into the library, usually kept locked, with her own key.

The room was quiet, dark, and smelt pleasantly of polish. Books lined the wall from top to bottom. The bottom row was made of bound volumes of *The Times* of London, going back some twenty years. For anything earlier, a trip to London was necessary. The row above contained similar volumes of *The Windsor Gazetteer*, and here the coverage went back thirty years or more. All these volumes had been acquired by Charmian at auction and in some cases, she had spent her own money.

While she was waiting for Rewley, she decided to refresh her memory on the case of Peter Loomis. She pulled out the volume she wanted and spread the heavy book on the table.

The London *Times* was the best, first source for the case, later she would look in the local paper (the Loomis family had a house near the Castle as well as a small estate in Oxfordshire, or they had then, she had an idea it had since been sold, so the case would be covered), and then she might ask around, pick up the local gossip if people would agree to talk to her, they could be close sometimes.

It was as Feather had said: Edith Loomis, aged only twenty-four, had been found dead, her skull broken by one savage blow to the back of the head, she might have been bending down when she was hit. She had died in the family house, Chantrey House, on a hill overlooking the river at Windsor. She had been dressing for a dinner she was to have attended in a house in the Castle precincts.

She wore a silk slip and one shoe was on and one off, she might have been leaning down to put it on when attacked.

The prosecution had said that this meant she had known and trusted her attacker.

The defence said she was attacked by someone who crept up on her from behind and who was probably someone who had broken into the house.

There were no signs of a break-in but someone had left several windows unlocked, two of which were open.

It was possible since some jewellery had gone, family stuff of no great value.

The evidence against her husband was: first, motive, they had quarrelled badly; secondly, opportunity; and thirdly, there was blood of Edith Loomis' type on a tweed jacket of her husband's which was rolled up in a cupboard.

Peter Loomis had a good defence barrister, Sir Aldred Muir, who was able to prove that the blood was old blood, the flow coming from a wound when Mrs Loomis had cut herself badly when gardening.

He also produced Peter Loomis' mother, Lady Grahamden (she had married more than once, indeed, been widowed several times and divorced once, not a lucky family with marriage, Charmian thought), who asserted that her son had been with her most of the time when the murder had taken place.

Charmian raised her head from the pages. Well, she would, wouldn't she?

But Sir Aldred had in reserve a second witness, a family servant, who said she had seen Peter leave his mother's house.

All in all, just enough to unsettle the jury, and Peter Loomis had walked out of the court a free man, but one with a good deal of suspicion hanging over his head.

Charmian had had nothing to do with the case, and on the whole she was glad because it was one of those affairs that sinks reputations.

What would I have done?

Gone more deeply into that quarrel?

She flipped over the pages, reading again bits of the report with comment.

There was anecdotal evidence that Mrs Loomis either could not or would not have a child.

Charmian considered the dates: seven years ago. Sarah had already been in the world for some months.

So the child had been in the case from the beginning. In a way. If you saw it that way.

I wonder exactly where Biddy herself comes into that murder. Her name had not been mentioned, which was an interesting omission. She had married shortly afterwards. Where was her husband? I hate muddled families, they produce muddled crimes.

She was deep in the story when Rewley walked in.

'Oh, hello.'

'You'd forgotten I was coming.' He sat down in a chair by the fire. His face looked thin.

'No. Just thinking. You seem exhausted.' She closed the volume to give him a closer examination. 'Kate?'

'It's impossible not to be worried about her. She has no idea how ill she is. Or perhaps she has.' He shook his head. 'I don't know. I wish we'd never embarked on this business.'

Charmian didn't take the easy line: that it would be all right when the child was there, because no one could be sure what state either party would be in. In what she was coming to think of as Baby Drop time, the nineteenth century or earlier, mothers often died in childbirth with their baby. Even now these things could happen: Kate might die, the child might die.

'You have the reports for me to sign?'

Rewley produced his packet of documents from a briefcase. 'You'll want to read them.'

'Of course, give me a minute.' She moved herself to the other side of the table where the light was better. Although she liked the academic gloom of her library, there were times when a good lamp was needed. She adjusted the lamp so the beam shone directly on to the page. 'I hope the local Fraud Squad will be grateful.'

'I don't suppose so. Means more work for them.'

Charmian read slowly and signed the reports carefully. 'Yes, you've got it all there. I'll send it on, not to be gratefully received, no doubt. They dislike me in that department, can't blame them, but they are moral troglodytes. No wonder they have their offices in a basement, underground is their milieu and I keep digging up what they do and finding the roots all wrong.'

'They aren't lazy,' said Rewley judiciously of some of his colleagues in Fraud Office, Subdivision B. 'They just don't see things as clearly as they could do. And of course, they get very anxious.'

'They ought to act, and if they don't I'll put a bomb under them. Good work.'

She took her spectacles off, she had recently acquired

a pair, and gave Rewley all her attention. 'I'm as worried about Kate as you are. I won't say that work takes my mind off it, but I can work. What about you?'

'I'm not working well ... not efficiently.' He looked away as if he didn't want to meet her eyes. 'She didn't want the baby at first, she felt it was something she had to do. I shouldn't have let her.'

Charmian shook her head. 'You couldn't. Have you ever stopped Kate when she was set on anything? Has anyone? And now, I suppose, she thinks it's all her fault. Which it isn't.'

'No, it's nothing congenital or built in.' He sounded wretched. 'It's just an accident of fate that happened to Kate.' He explained: 'She has very high blood pressure that won't come down, she's had one tiny stroke, she could have a brain haemorrhage at any time ... In addition, the placenta is so placed that if she gave birth normally she would probably bleed to death ... So they will operate as soon as the child is viable ...'

'Then I'm going to tell you to take time off. Be with Kate. You won't worry less, but it's what you should do.'

'I'm not sure how much she wants me around, she's drawing more and more into herself.'

'Try it.'

'Yes, I will.' He was a bit surprised. His boss's usual line was to put in some hard work.

'And I may have something for you to think about.'

That's more like it, Rewley thought, that's the Charmian Daniels I know. 'I think I could make a guess.' His eyes fell on *The Times*. 'I saw what you were reading.'

'Sarah Holt— You made the connection?'

'Everyone does. It's all over town. But I didn't know you were interested.'

'Mary Erskine.'

'I might have guessed. She does drag you into things.'
Because of his marriage to Kate, he allowed himself a
certain ease in his conversation with Charmian when
he felt he was off duty.

His face had lost the drawn look. Charmian was
pleased at the reaction she'd got, she'd cheered him up.
Good. The only hearing member of his large and talented family, Rewley could lip read, which seemed to
give him a special sort of sensitivity, empathy. He picked
things up out of the air. Because he was so worried
about Kate, Charmian was the more worried. He often
seemed to know things about to happen in advance.

'She has a large circle of rakish friends,' admitted Charmian. 'But in herself she's straightforward and good. If
sometimes silly,' she added reflectively.

'So what do you make of it?'

'Not really informed enough. Yet.' She could pick
things up out of the air too, and what she read now in
his face was that he didn't want to think about it. Too
close to the bone. 'And what about the Loomis
connection?'

'Is there one?' answered Rewley.

'Seems as though there ought to be,' said Charmian.

'He's the child's father, that's common knowledge. I
can't see him abducting her. Why would he?'

'You never know in families.' Charmian spoke from
her sad knowledge of the murky depths to which family
relationships could sink. 'What do people think of
Loomis?' So often the hidden, secret underground judgement on a man that went around the flower-beds was
the true one.

'Everyone thinks he was guilty.'

'Except the jury.'

'The story is they didn't like the judge. Either time.'

41

'If he didn't kill the wife, who did?' There had been no answer at the time, and none now, but plenty of speculation.

'Biddy Holt? Her name came up.'

'I have been worried about her myself,' admitted Charmian. 'She's not quite what she seems.' After all, what a story: letting the child go away with a man unknown to her, and then later, thinking that 'perhaps' she did know his face. And the dolls? Was there really a doll left by the house? You could question everything.

'Or it might have been someone who hated all three of them in the past: Loomis' wife, Edith, she was killed after all, Loomis himself, and Biddy Holt. And who still hates them.'

Rewley picked up the reports she had signed. 'I'll go to see Kate, I promised Anny that I would telephone her. She doesn't go in much, she says she upsets Kate.'

'She always did.' Charmian stood up, grasping the file of *The Times*. 'Heaven help her grandchild.'

'It's a boy, by the way, did you know? They did a scan.'

'No.' Kate hadn't told her.

'Don't admit to knowing, then. Kate probably wants to tell you herself.'

Left alone in the library, she tidied the books and papers she had been studying, but she did not put them away. She wrote a note for her librarian asking her to leave them as they were since she was still using them.

What a mixed, confused story lay there, only partly told, all hate and violence, hidden in the dark, but what had happened was still working on life now.

As she walked out of the library back to her office, locking the door behind her, one thought ran round and round in her mind.

How the past does devour the future.

*

She was back in her office for barely five minutes when the telephone rang.

'Feather here, I'm speaking from my car. I am down at Flanders Road.'

'Yes?' Flanders Road, she recalled, was the road that ran parallel with the Baby Drop land, it was shielded by the trees she had seen from Kate's window. Benson Road was on the other side.

'We have a body.' He paused, someone seemed to be interrupting him, then he went on, but she could not hear what was said. 'I thought you might like to come down.'

'I'm on my way.'

She felt real pain. The child, the poor child. The past did not only devour the future, it ate it alive.

Chapter Three

' "It is time for me to go to that there berryin' ground, sir," he returned wildly.'

Bleak House

The smell of burning, made up of charred wood and scorched stone, still hung in the rain-laden air of Windsor as Charmian drove towards Baby Drop territory. Not the first time the Castle had burned, she speculated, the original Norman castle had probably been no more than a wooden stockade and they went up as a matter of course. She could see scaffolding already in place of the roof of one of the great halls but there was the building itself, substantial and still whole.

More than the usual number of tourists climbing up Castle Hill too with their cameras and guide books. St George's Chapel was open as usual and Changing the Guard was about to take place. The Welsh Guards today in their dark grey winter uniform. She was held up in the traffic as the new Guard marched in, band playing. It would take more than a fire to stop the Guards.

Inspector Dan Feather was waiting for her and met her by the grass verge. She had parked her car in Bowen Street, just out of sight.

'Hello, ma'am, thank you for coming. I think it was right you should.'

Charmian looked through the belt of trees and across the grass to where she could see the Clinic building, shielded by another fringe of trees, she could make out Kate's window. No one was standing there, which was what she had hoped, she didn't want Kate in her present state looking at this scene.

He looked tired and drawn, as if he hadn't liked what he had seen. There was earth on his hands with a stain of grass on the sleeve of his raincoat. 'Mind where you step, ma'am, all the local dogs seem to relieve themselves on the grass here.' His voice was gloomy. Never a cheerful man, as Charmian knew, he hated cases involving children even more than most police officers. 'I'll be glad when we've got this bit over.'

'Worse than usual, is it?'

'I can't say that, they're all bad, this sort of thing, but I've got a nasty feeling about this, and that is worse than usual.'

'Feel much the same way myself.' Charmian kept her eyes on the window of Kate's room as she crossed the grass. Feather had to take her arm at one point, with a 'Careful, ma'am'. She knew what was feeding her disquiet, anxiety over Kate, one misery feeding another, but what was up with him?

Memory dredged up some story of Feather as a young detective constable, finding a child that had starved to death, left behind by its mother. And there was something else as well, but at this moment she could not remember what it was.

No man is a cipher, she thought. He is a detective inspector, but behind that formula is a man.

'You're sure it's the girl?'

'Not sure of anything yet, haven't got that far.' He led her round the screen which had been set up around a hole in the ground. He introduced her to his sergeant and to the police pathologist who was standing by. 'We had an abortive shot over there' – he nodded to the patch of ground further away – 'because the grass had been disturbed, but it was just one of those ruddy dogs, and then we tried here. There were signs of deeper digging.'

Charmian looked down. The turf had been cut away, and the diggers had gone down a few feet, not far but far enough.

An arm could be seen, lightly covered with soil. A small, thin arm, the hand curled.

'You waited for me?'

'A pause seemed indicated . . . Professor Drake wanted it.'

Drake nodded at Charmian, they knew each other. He came from the University of Middlesex, they had worked together before.

'Photographs,' said Drake shortly. He walked around the area in a way that Charmian knew to be characteristic of him; he paced round till he came back to her side. 'Fairly unusual to see the arm sticking up like that.' He took a few more paces. 'Must have been buried like it.'

'Yes.' Charmian nodded. Her eyes met Feather's, they were both thinking the same thing.

'And therefore as stiff as board at the time.'

'Not dead long then, when buried.'

The uncovering went on. The arm had been supported in its position by the earth and stones beneath it.

'Stop here for a moment,' ordered the Professor. 'I want to do some measuring.'

She knew already that it was one of those days that take the skin off you, when even the objects round you, houses, trees, the roads, seem harder, edged with stone, clearer, larger, with a life of their own. Redolent of the past, right back to childhood, reminding you of incidents long past. A hell of a day, a day with teeth.

The professor was kneeling on the ground examining the arm, the angle of extension, and its relation to the shoulder muscle, a frown formed on his face.

A painfully thin arm, the muscles more obvious than Charmian had expected. Not clean, it looked worn, travel stained and bruised. She bit her lips. What sort of life had Sarah had to be as thin as that?

'Not long dead,' said the professor, the frown left his brows but deposited itself more thickly in his eyes.

'How long?' asked Feather.

'You know I can't answer that yet.' He stood up and nodded to the diggers who were gently and carefully removing the soil. 'Take it easy.'

'You can always try,' said Feather, which was surprisingly pushy for him.

'Just a few days, then.'

A small figure, wearing blue jeans and a jacket, the face still covered with a shroud of earth. The work on clearing the soil began again, careful, delicate work.

'Pick up anything that's there.' Feather knew there was no need to make this order, it would be done as a matter of course, but it was a mark of his inner tension.

Charmian looked at him and wondered: What does he know about this that I don't know?

Across the grass and beyond the trees to the road, a car was parked, with the engine running. Charmian saw the car without taking any particular interest in it, at this distance she could not see the driver who was a jolly-faced woman who was laughing, her face screwed up with merriment. Or pleasure. What Charmian could see was that the car was a bright, unusual yellow, but splashed with mud.

Slowly the shroud of earth that veiled the figure was being lifted. A small round head showed itself, the hair was blonde but dirty and matted with earth. They uncovered the crown of the head first, then gently moved down the features: brow, eyebrows, closed eyes, nose and chin. A small-featured pale face over which a brushing of earth still remained.

Charmian looked at the face, and frowned, her expression unconsciously echoing Inspector Feather's. The professor had put on his professional mask of detachment and the dark thought which had concentrated itself in his eyes had now moved down to his hands which were moving with delicate swift care.

On the other side of the road, behind where they all stood, and much nearer to the shrouded excavations, a small crowd of onlookers was standing. It must be raining, a woman had an umbrella over her head, but Charmian hadn't noticed what was falling. A dog was barking somewhere. Out of the corner of her eye, Charmian saw a rangy-looking mongrel, brown and black with a feather tail and a big jowl, burst through the crowd and run towards where they were digging.

Feather swore under his breath, a uniformed constable hurried towards the dog and tried to grab it, after a bit he succeeded, dragging the dog off. Neither reappeared.

'Stand back, let me see.'

Professor Drake was on his knees, bending down, using his hands, the rubber gloves stained brown. Softly the earth was being removed. The unmistakable sweetish smell of the breakdown of flesh into something that the earth and the creatures who live in it can use rose steadily to their nostrils, moving into the mouth and down the back of the throat. Life has many smells, death only one.

Feather fidgeted irritably. 'Why is he being so slow?'

'He always is slow, slow and careful.' Charmian kept her eyes focused on what the professor was doing. His large form blocked her view, until he moved away. He stood up, rubbing the soil from his hands.

'Take a look.'

The body had been placed on its back, the torn jeans, the blue and white trainers on the small feet, the striped shirt.

Slowly she took in what she was seeing.

'A boy,' she said. 'Not the girl but a boy.'

'So it is,' Feather nodded.

'You knew?'

'Thought so. The hand . . . I saw the hand.' The small hand was battered and torn. 'Looked to me like a boy's hand.'

'Yes, you're right. Sharp of you, I didn't see that.'

'I've been a boy myself,' said Feather with a wry smile. 'But luckier than this poor little tyke. What's he doing here when we were looking for a girl?'

And how many of them were there around, waiting to be found? Some never to be found.

The professor came up. 'Not what you expected, not what you wanted, I'm afraid.'

'I never want anything like this,' said Feather. Charmian said nothing, she had seen the window curtains move in Kate's room. 'So what can you say now?'

'Aged about eight, been dead some days, I can perfect that time scheme later. There's damage to the skull, he probably died from a blow to the back of the head. Or he may have fallen.'

'But he didn't bury himself so we have to accept that it's likely to be murder.'

'Likely but not absolutely sure yet . . . I'll be able to be more certain later.'

Feather sighed, he knew what lay ahead: he had a missing girl child, and now he had a dead boy. 'We shall have to establish an identity. The clothes may give some help. If he's a local child, then we shall probably get on to it all quickly, if not, if he doesn't come from round here and was just dumped, well . . .' He shrugged. 'I'm going to need help here.'

He moved to the side of the open grave – You had to call it that now, he thought – where photographs were being taken.

Even from this distance, he could see that the child's clothes were grubby and stained, not only by the earth. 'Has he been living rough?'

'I should say he hadn't washed for some days, but probably not living rough exactly. Under cover somewhere, I would guess.' The professor started putting his equipment back into his bag. 'Not exactly homeless, I'd say, but knocked about a bit. Or damaged himself. Who can say at this point . . . but at a first glance he had been eating, he's not emaciated.'

As they were talking Charmian, while still listening, knelt down to stare down into the shallow burial pit. She looked at the body, she didn't touch, just looked.

The shoes were of good quality, although not new, the jeans looked well made even if full of holes, but holes were fashionable still, weren't they? The shirt was well chosen, the colours matched the blue of the jeans, small blue flowers, oddly feminine.

The face was bloated, and bruised with death marks, but the features were neat, the hair was longish and curly.

At a first glance it would be hard to say if this was a boy or a girl, but the professor had done his check and knew the sex and Feather had looked at the hands.

She climbed back out. What had the missing Sarah been wearing? Had she bothered to ask?

The professor was moving towards his car, his assistant trailing beside him, which was her usual spot; Feather was giving instructions to his own team, walking as he did so. Charmian joined him.

It was going to be a lean, hard time for Feather, she thought, if she read all the signals right, and perhaps for her too. Her eyes moved to the window of the clinic, no sign of Kate, but she'd have to call and give her a censored version of what had gone on in Baby Drop land. Word would have gone round the hospital by now.

Feather came with her to her car. 'Called you out for nothing.'

'No, don't think that.' She sat in her driving seat, considering what to say. 'First, I don't think he's been there that long, my goddaughter who is a patient over there,' and she nodded towards the clinic, 'has a window overlooking the ground here, she saw movement one night, the night before last. It may have been when he was buried.'

'Thanks for saying. I would have been asking over there, of course, but it's a help to get a start.'

'Kate's not too well,' she said carefully. 'Nervous, but I think she saw what she saw.'

'I won't upset her.'

'The little creature down there, an enigma. Good-quality clothes, money was spent on him . . . her . . .'

'What do you mean?'

'Do you think she was a boy all along?' It was said in a halfway to serious voice. 'In spite of those dolls?'

Feather didn't know what to make of it, schools, doctors checked on that sort of thing, and, it was true, there could be strange anatomical developments, not everything was straightforward in these matters. Equally no one ever laughed at Charmian Daniels these days, not ever, in fact. 'People do strange things, cover up for years, I'm not saying you are wrong, but I'd be surprised.' Then he stopped himself. 'No, I'm wrong, I wouldn't be surprised. Anything is possible.'

'I agree. So it is.'

'But we could get into bad trouble, asking the wrong questions to the wrong people. Maybe the mother knows more than she's saying, maybe the child didn't go off in that way and she knows it, produced the story and the doll to pad it out.'

'And the child hadn't been at school for three days,' Charmian reminded him. 'If the mother is lying, then we don't know when and how she disappeared.'

'Got to take that into account, I agree, but go careful.'

'Don't worry, I won't do anything stupid, and I won't involve you.'

'Thank you, ma'am.'

'But what I'm going to do is just kick the idea around. Of course, if you get an identity for the boy that will be that.'

She left her car where it was and walked round to the Mother and Baby Clinic where she took the lift to Kate's room. The room was warm and comfortable, Kate propped up on pillows looked tranquil.

'Lovely to see you, Char'. I'm feeling pretty good this morning.' There was a vase of freesia by her bedside, a new book on her lap, and she had been reading a copy of *Vogue*, all good signs.

Charmian kissed her cheek, far too thin it was, and prepared to give her an edited version of events outside.

But there was no need, the nursing staff had got there before her.

'Confined to bed again,' said Kate gloomily. 'Sister said I'd been doing too much walking around. Ridiculous, I only went to the window to look out. Forbidden.'

Good idea, Charmian smiled with sympathy.

'And the annoying thing is that I'm quite sure that something interesting was going on out there, I could hear the noises: cars, voices, even shouting. I mean quiet shouting and that's even more interesting.'

Charmian nodded without saying anything. Yes, lying there, sick and tense, hearing sensitized by this long period of illness, she would pick up noises that were strange and unusual.

'I could even smell it,' Kate burst out.

Yes, that too, Charmian thought. Probably the diesel oil from the police cars.

'And you're keeping quiet,' said Kate crossly.

Attack being the best form of defence, Charmian said: 'I think you are looking better.'

'It's not me that counts.' Kate was still cross, she patted her middle. 'It's this creature in here. Nature's on this one's side, not mine.'

'Well, they are busy interfering with nature where you are,' Charmian reminded her. 'That's what medicine is all about, never mind what they say.' And all the better for it, she thought, nature left to herself was too brutal.

'So tell me what's going on, please.' Kate turned to wheedling. 'I know it's a mystery.'

'OK, yes it's a mystery.' Give her something to think about, to take her mind off herself, but sanitize it. 'You know about the missing child; without giving yourself nightmares, think about it. Treat it as a problem in a book, ask yourself why and how. There has to be a reason, probably a family reason.'

'My child will never be lost,' said Kate fiercely.

'Of course not, your child will be what you have been, extremely privileged.' Over-privileged, some say, but Charmian loved Kate. 'You're a clever girl, think about it, and if anything interesting comes of it, tell me.'

To her relief, the door opened to let in Rewley. 'And here's your husband, talk to him.' She kissed Kate, said goodbye to Rewley and said she would telephone him and took herself off.

She walked to her car where it was parked in Bowen Street. She was always glad to see her car again, unscathed, unvandalized, it was kind of home to her in which various possessions like a special rug and torch and bag of make up rested.

She got her keys out of the bag slung over her shoulder, she was still thinking about Kate, but looking across Baby Drop land and automatically assessing what was going on.

Too much. She could see the sturdy form of Professor Drake again and Dan Feather was back, they were talking.

She dropped the keys back in her bag and strode across the grass, the rain had stopped and the sun was coming out.

Feather looked up. 'Ah, glad to see you again. I was trying to get you.'

'What is it?'

He beckoned her across the ground around the grave, which was being searched by the police team. 'We have another body.'

Whispers from the Past

'The good girl knows how to behave, you tell her, Emmy.
No good girl has a baby out of wedlock.'
  'Gran, don't go on like that, she's only a baby herself.'
  'Never too young to learn.'

In bad years, infant mortality was about 74 per cent.
Among parish children and workhouse children it was
closer to 80 or 90 per cent.

Chapter Four

'But the small waxen form . . . had been composed afresh and washed and neatly dressed in some fragments of white linen: and on my handkerchief, which still covered the poor baby, a little bunch of fresh herbs had been laid.'

Bleak House

Charmian stood staring into the damp brown earth. She held a long moment of silence. There was something about what she saw that checked speech. 'What's this? A body, you said.'

Inspector Dan Feather let her continue to stare before he broke the silence. 'Not what you expected, eh? Shook me too, I can tell you. Not what I thought we would find.'

Charmian turned away. 'If you hadn't found the boy, then we should never have found this little creature.' She turned back for a closer look, her face sombre. 'I suppose it is a baby?'

'The professor says so.' Feather looked at Professor Drake, his face gave nothing away but he answered.

'I do say so.'

The small bones and tiny skull were brown and stained with the earth, but it was perfectly articulated, even the delicate finger bones were in place. A few scraps of material, once white but now darkened by the years in the soil, rested on the torso and around the head as if the infant had worn a bonnet. Or it might have been a shawl.

'How long has the body been here?'

Professor Drake shook his head. 'Can't say at the moment. Might be twenty years or two hundred. I'll try to get closer.'

Feather wanted something better than that. 'Which end of the margin do you go for? I do have a professional interest here. If it's twenty years then I have to do something about it. A hundred years, then we can leave it to the historians. So which is it?'

'At a guess nearer the older date.'

Feather drew in a sigh of relief. 'Good. Don't want to sound heartless, but I've got plenty on my plate already and if this little creature has been dead that long then everyone connected with her will be long dead.'

This one looked a female to him.

Charmian had gone back to studying the bones, she was looking at a filigree of dark brown something on the skull. 'I think the little creature wore a cap . . .' Her voice was soft.

'Might have been a shawl.'

'No, I think I can see the ghost of lace.'

How strange that the softness of cotton should have left a stain on the skull. There was no accounting for the way decay set it, leaving a shadow here, a ghost there.

Plenty of ghosts around.

'You know what they used to call this plot of land?'

'Fiddler's Fence, isn't it?' said Feather.

'No, in common parlance, in the nineteenth century and before' – because it must have been a custom going back through the years – 'it was called Baby Drop.'

'What was that?' asked Drake absently. 'Think I've heard of it.'

'It's where poor girls, married or not, usually not, I suppose, left their babies by the Foundling Hospital which stood where the Clinic now does. The babies were usually left on the hospital steps, but sometimes on the grass.'

'This one was buried,' said Feather.

'Yes, I suppose it was born dead or died soon afterwards. Infantile mortality was very high. A lot died.'

'Or were murdered.'

'That too,' said Charmian.

A shameful, secret birth, a suffocating death, a silent, secret burial.

'I suppose it is a baby and not a monkey.' Feather did not make it a question, he was pondering aloud.

'It's a baby, that's the sort of thing I'm trained to know, as you well know.' Then Drake relented. 'It does look slightly simian, I admit. That's due to immaturity, probably a neonate.'

'Stillborn?' said Charmian, seeking to establish something more. Perhaps the child had not been murdered but dead.

'I don't think even I will be able to tell you that. If it matters.' He gave Charmian one of his famous winks, which did not mean anything friendly but were more like the drawing back of lips over teeth on a Jack Russell, and meant: Keep out of this or I will savage you too.

Not an especially friendly man to anyone, he particularly disliked women in the police. A top woman police officer like Charmian aroused his deepest wrath.

He was irritable with Dan Feather too, as a matter of course, but also for private and personal reasons (must be personal, they said, he got so ratty, and Dan Feather pretended not to notice but did), which had long since been observed by all their colleagues, who had tried hard to find out the reason. The popular belief was that a woman was behind it. Charmian cried down the personal side, she thought that he just didn't like people too much. After all, he so often saw them at their worst. If you constantly looked death in the face, and death in some of its fanciest and least delicate forms, it was bound to alter how you felt about life and people.

Not much was known about the professor outside his police work, even in the university, where he had long held a Chair, he was something of an enigma, and an alarming one at that. Charmian knew he had a wife, a pretty, plump woman, because they had met once at a Windsor dinner party, but as soon as the professor saw how well the two women were getting on, he had taken his wife away.

Secrets there, perhaps?

'The remains look very fragile,' said Charmian.

A halt had been called to the work while the three of them stood there.

'Perhaps you ought to call the archaeologists in.'

She knew Dan Feather would resent this, and he did. 'Not that old for sure,' he said gruffly. 'But it'll all be handled with care, everything measured and photographed. We know what to do. But the first thing is to get the professor here to give a judgement as to death and approximate date and so on, and then we'll go on from there.' He gave Professor Drake a questioning look.

'I take my oath that the bones are not Bronze Age or Iron Age or Saxon or Norman . . .' He didn't go on through the centuries but stopped. 'Get on with getting it up' – he began to move away – 'and then I will have the bones in the lab and give them a look. After which, you shall know all I know. Right?'

'Right.' Feather nodded to his team.

'But I'm giving priority to the dead boy,' said Drake in a dry voice. 'Isn't that where we started?'

'Not altogether, I'm not forgetting that I started out by looking here for a little girl.' This time, Feather looked at Charmian.

'Well, it was my idea, I admit.'

'And I'm going to have to ask what gave you that idea?'

'I was talking to someone in the Clinic over there.' She nodded. 'That person had seen something. A person, movement at night.' She took a deep breath. 'I'll let you have the name.' Kate would have to face the questioning. 'A very sick young woman in bed in a room that overlooks this ground. You'll have to go carefully with her. Will you have to tell her about this infant burial?' And yet Kate could be tough, no one knew that better than Charmian. But about children, tiny infants, she was, at this moment, sensitized.

'I won't ask questions till she has someone with her. Her husband or nurse, or you.'

'Not me, better not me.'

'And I won't need to mention the baby, that burial took place years before she was born in all probability. Satisfied?'

Charmian nodded.

Charmian remained, fascinated by what she saw, unable to stop looking. It was not the first time by a long way that she had seen the dead unveiled, but she had never seen anything so small and fragile, so human and yet remote, exposed to her eyes before. It seemed an intrusion, she shouldn't be watching, the little creature should be left undisturbed in its sleep.

But still she watched.

The soil was brushed away from the bones and a pallet brought up to insert underneath so that the bones could be removed without disarticulation. They were like archaeologists, these men. Every so often, worked stopped for a photograph to be taken.

She didn't want to stay, there was work to be done, and she ought to be back in the office, but something held her there.

Three deep this case was now: it had started with a missing child, who remained missing, and now there was a dead, murdered boy, and hard by his burial place a much, much earlier death.

The sun had come out and the sky was clearing, with that clearing a wind had sprung up.

Something caught her eye in the earth, an edge of something that caught the light. One of the policemen saw as soon as she did and bent down to see what it was. He didn't touch it, but with a gloved finger cleaned the earth away. She saw an oval object, not much bigger than a man's thumbnail.

A small gold locket lay in the earth. As the earth fell away, there was mud on it but the locket looked untouched by the years. Gold does survive, she thought, perhaps when life on this planet has gone, gold will still be twinkling away among the ruins.

Feather came over to them. 'What's this?'

'Looks like a bit of jewellery, a locket,' said the man who had retrieved it; he was moving the locket gently towards a plastic bag.

'I'd like to see inside it. Does it open?'

'Might be a bit stiff. Jammed up with earth.'

'Sure.'

He handled it carefully, but there were unlikely to be fingerprints, and if there were, then wasn't the owner of the fingers likely to be dead these hundred years or more?

'Later, when you've finished examining it, I'd like to see it again.'

'Of course, ma'am.' Feather was always particularly

polite to her when he thought she was being interfering. She was interfering now.

'I wonder if it would open now? I'd like a look.'

'We'll try.' He was being polite again, as both parties recognized. But he wanted to look inside himself. Putting plastic gloves on his hands, he tried to open it, but he was clumsy and the little object slid between his fingers down to the ground. 'Damn,' then he looked apologetically at Charmian. 'Sorry.'

'I should have said the same myself.'

He picked it up but it slid away again. 'It's got a life of its own.' Then, as he touched it a third time, the locket opened quietly of its own accord. Feather held it in the palm of his hand for her to see.

Inside was an oval photograph, faded to sepia brown. Not the picture of a baby as might have been expected, but of a young girl with hair down her back, held back in a big bow. She was wearing a sailor dress with a big collar, that was all you could see, head and shoulders only here. So faint was the image that it was impossible to see much of the face, but there was a young, hopeful pose to the head that was touching.

Charmian's eyes met Feather's, and she saw that he was as moved as she was; she liked him for that.

'Not the child then.'

'No.' He considered. 'The mother?'

'Could be. Should help with the age of the skeleton. The dress of this girl is late last century or early this: Edwardian style, possibly. Sailor suits were the thing then for both sexes.'

Ever cautious, Dan Feather said: 'If it relates to the baby at all. It might simply have been lost. It wasn't round the child's neck as far as I could see.'

'But close, very close.' In fact, when they first saw it,

the locket had been some inches away, but Charmian was reluctant to give up the connection. 'It may have been moved slightly, an animal, some earth movement above, anything like that.'

'We haven't had an earthquake in Windsor recently,' said Feather. 'A big fire, yes, and some floods but no earthquake.'

'Inspector . . .' a voice hailed him from across the turf.

'Better go,' said Feather. 'Excuse me, ma'am. I'd better get back to the main game. This is just a side affair, probably never discover who this baby was.' And after all this time, does it matter? was what he meant. 'The main game is the dead boy and the missing girl. I'm not forgetting her. The search will go on here, thoroughly, just in case. But I reckon that activity your friend saw must be about the dead boy, burying him perhaps, but that doesn't seem likely since he'd been in the ground more than the one day. Not long but longer than that. Probably just checking up.'

'Probably,' agreed Charmian. 'Yes, that must have been it.'

She considered going in to see Kate again, but decided against it. Kate would start asking questions which she did not want to answer. So she went back to her office and answered letters, checked files on the computer, and read several faxes that had come in and which issued different orders from different government offices, some of which were mutually incompatible. As head of SRADIC, she had several jobs, one of which was secret.

At the end of the day, she drove home. No news from Feather, Rewley, or Professor Drake, but with dead bodies you couldn't hurry, and the professor, who was a slow worker, usually had a silent queue awaiting his attention. 'First come, first carved,' he had once joked with the mordant humour of his breed. But she thought that Dan Feather would put pressure on him to hurry, and if he didn't, then she would. She had her channels.

Public opinion might do it first. The news was already out in the town.

BODY OF BOY FOUND, said the *Windsor Clarion*.

She switched on her car radio and heard the local station asking: Is there a killer loose? A boy is found dead, a young girl is missing. Do we protect our children?

And the answer to that is, I don't know, thought Charmian, as she swung the car into Maid of Honour Row. Probably not in the right way. Little Sarah had been loved and protected but she had gone all the same.

Outside her house was a large car. A Rolls, long and gleaming. It was exceedingly beautiful but very large and took up too much parking space so that Charmian herself (as probably had several of her neighbours) had to drive past home and find another slot round the corner.

Who owned the car? It's Humphrey, he's come back and brought the Queen to visit. No, this car was silver, suave and elegant, and the Queen's cars were maroon, that difficult colour between brown and red.

This car was chauffeur driven, or at least he was sitting, hatless and shoulders hunched over the wheel, in the front where chauffeurs sit. A tall, slim, grey-haired woman was in the back; she opened the door and got out as Charmian approached.

Her hair was white, not grey, a beautiful white without a hint of yellow and no blue tint. A raincoat swung from her shoulders over a leaf-brown cashmere jersey and tweed skirt. No pearls, no rouge, no lipstick. She must be in mourning.

Oh God, Charmian thought, I know who she is.

The woman approached, held out her hand and looked Charmian in the face. 'Miss Daniels? I was waiting for you.'

'I thought you were.'

The hand was still extended, Charmian took it and received a cold, hard grip in return. She could feel the bones beneath the skin.

'I am Lady Grahamden. You are looking for my granddaughter, Sarah. May I come in?'

'Yes, yes, of course.' Charmian started to lead the way to the house, then looked back at the car. You didn't ask chauffeurs in, did you, unless you had a really big place with a servants' hall, then they had tea and hot food, but there was something about that back that troubled her.

Lady Grahamden saw her looking. 'Oh, we'll leave him there for the moment.'

That was that then. 'Right.'

The hall of her small house was mercifully tidy, although Muff the cat was sitting on the stairs looking baleful. Lady Grahamden came in, saw the entrance to the sitting-room and the door to the kitchen and chose the kitchen. This too was in order, Charmian was not an untidy person but she usually left the house in a hurry.

'What is it you want, Lady Grahamden?' It was quite a name to get your tongue round.

'I wanted to see you, to look you in the face.' She did just that, putting on a pair of pale horn spectacles which somehow graced her face. She stared silently through them, not owlishly but with a sharp blue gaze, then took them off. 'Yes, you are an honest woman.'

Charmian put her handbag and document case on the

kitchen table with a thump, she felt she could easily quarrel with Lady Grahamden. Muff, who associated kitchen noises with food, mysteriously appeared on the table too.

'I'm not the only person looking for Sarah, possibly I'm the least important. There is a whole police force at work.'

'A team is only as sharp as its leader.'

And you're too sharp by half, my lady. 'An investigation doesn't work like that,' she said politely. 'A picture is put together, built up. Bit by bit, everyone adds their bit.'

Lady Grahamden ignored this sally, only partly true in any case. 'I want you to stop the hunt. Stop looking for her. While there is publicity she won't come. When you stop, then she will.'

'What do you mean?'

'She has run away before and come back. Been somewhere and come home again. Biddy knows.'

'You mean she hides somewhere? That she has another home? Like a little cat?' Charmian was astonished at the information thrown out like this, as if it was a weapon, which it possibly was, but aimed at whom? She was sure that Feather knew nothing about it. 'I've not been told of this. Her mother did not say anything.'

'Biddy knows.'

'If Mrs Holt knew she should have told us. But if the girl has been missing before, why has she not been reported missing before?'

'You must ask her mother that.'

'I will, don't worry, and so will Inspector Feather.' And expect some good answers.

'I think Biddy knew she would come back on those other occasions.'

'And why not this time?'

Lady Grahamden was silent. 'I think it's because of the doll.'

'And what does the doll mean?'

'I don't know. I'm just telling you what I think.'

'Did you know of these other episodes?'

'Not at the time. I learnt later.'

'Who did know?'

'Her mother, of course. Ask Biddy, see what you get. She knows more than she admits.'

I believe you there, madam. 'Who else?'

'Her father.'

Charmian said: 'This takes some thinking about. I can't accept what you say without checking. No one could. And meanwhile, you do understand, don't you, that if you are wrong, the child may be at risk?'

Dead already, Feather judged, and he had experience.

'I understand that,' said Lady Grahamden quietly, sadly. 'There is always a risk in life, but let things go quiet, let the child rest.'

'Do you know what you are saying?'

No answer. But a tear came into the blue eyes. 'A loved child,' she murmured. 'A love child, but a loved one.'

A picture of the skeleton came into Charmian's mind, she saw that other dead love child.

'Where is the father?'

'Outside. In the car.'

Thought so. 'Why didn't he come in?'

'Oh, he's ashamed of me. All my family are ashamed of me. My mother and father were, all my husbands were, in the end. I'm too direct.'

'I think he didn't come in because you didn't ask him, Lady Grahamden.'

'Yes, you're direct too. I said you were an honest

woman. No, I didn't ask him because I didn't want him, but he can come now. And he is ashamed of me.'

Charmian went to the door, and beckoned to the driver. But he was already out of the car.

He came in to the house bringing air and movement with him, perhaps he always hurried. He focused on his mother, saying: 'Just heard it on the car radio: the body of a boy has been found in a bit of open ground.'

Lady Grahamden's high colour could not fade because it was artificial but she blinked. Not something she wanted to hear.

'I thought it might be Sarah when they started in on the announcement. But it's a boy.'

Then he looked at Charmian. 'Sorry, Miss Daniels. One way and another I am in a state of permanent anxiety.'

He was tall, with a shock of black hair, he had a charming voice, was charming altogether.

'Peter Loomis.' He held out his hand, his handshake was hard like his mother's, but warm where hers was cold.

Rewley was out, gathering information about this man. Was one of the things he would bring back that he was a man of enormous charm?

He did not look like a man who might have murdered his wife, but then Charmian knew from experience that killers came in all shapes and sizes and with all conditions of ugliness or beauty. Lady Grahamden returned doggedly to the subject she was interested in. 'It's very sad, but has nothing to do with Sarah.'

It was clear that she was about to embark upon her thesis again, but Charmian took charge of the conversation. 'You know why your mother came here? That she wants the search for Sarah to be given up.'

'Yes.' He nodded.

'Do you agree?'

'Not altogether. But she may have a point.'

'Clearly it's not what Mrs Holt thinks: she called the police in.'

'I haven't spoken to Biddy.'

Someone is going to. Charmian held up a restraining hand to Lady Grahamden who was trying to break in.

'Your mother says the child will come back if we stop searching. That's a hard story to believe.'

'You have to know the background.'

'I intend to.' Once again she held back Lady Graham-den who was trying to continue with her version. 'You tell me what you think.'

'Hold on, Mother,' said Loomis, in a tired voice. If he wasn't ashamed of his mother, he had sounded as if he had had enough of her. 'I don't know of my own knowledge as they say in the law courts, because I haven't been around, nor as close to my daughter as perhaps I should, but I have been told that she has gone off once or twice and then come back unscathed. Just little wanderings, children do that sort of thing, take leave for the day, I did it myself.'

'Family thing, is it?'

Loomis looked hurt. 'Children have their escapades, perhaps Sarah has. My mother thinks she's frightened now and she'll come back when things quieten down. Hiding, you know. Got a little secret hideaway. I'm not saying it's the case, but it could be.'

'It's been some time, too long surely.'

'Well, I don't know.'

'And you will know that Mrs Holt says she went off with a man. Was collected by him, that doesn't sound as if the child wandered off on her own.'

'I don't know about that. That's what Biddy says.'

'Are you saying she's lying?'

'I don't say anything. Speak to her . . . please.'

It was the second time he'd said this.

'Your mother says that Mrs Holt called the police because of the doll. Do you know about that?'

'I know about the dolls.'

'I've seen them. She had plenty.'

'We all gave them to her, it was what she wanted, she wanted one for every day of the year. She didn't quite get there.' He sounded sad.

Charmian was suddenly tired of the pair of them and wanted them to go. She had said nothing to them about the other buried child, the baby, nor was she going to, it needed a bit of privacy that baby before the world started talking about it.

Muff yawned, stood up, went to the refrigerator where she began to rattle the handle. She was good at dismissing people.

Peter Loomis read the signs. 'Come on, Mother. Let's go. You've said your piece.'

Charmian showed them to the door without a word. Lady Grahamden shook her hand. 'Goodbye, my dear. Here is my card, come and see me. I think we should understand each other.'

When she was in the car, sitting back inside the Rolls like a queen, Peter Loomis said, 'My mother isn't mad, you know. She just sees things differently.'

Charmian rested her hand on the car door. 'I didn't think she was mad, not at all, never.'

She went back into the house where a hungry Muff awaited her. Not mad, coldly logical and rational. But I just don't understand her reasons.

As they drove away, Lady Grahamden settled herself comfortably in the back of the car.

'I expect she'll go straight to the police.'

'Mother, she is the police.' And to himself: I thought you wanted them to be told.

'Yes, I know, I know, I meant the real police . . . Don't make that noise, dear . . . She'll tell them in the right sort of way. She struck me as a woman of great sensibility.'

Peter drove on in a state of savage anger.

I don't understand her reason, or understand her. What's she like underneath that manner?

There was one way to find out. She picked up the telephone. About this time, before dinner, you could usually find Lady Mary at home, dressing to go out. She might answer the phone or she might not, depending whether she was actually in the shower or roaming round naked after it. She did answer.

'Tell me about Lady Grahamden.'

'Oh, you've got to her, have you?'

'She's got to me.'

'Yes . . .' There was a thoughtful pause. 'Yes, it would be that way round. Let me just adjust the water or it will run cold before I get into the shower.'

'I thought I could hear it.'

'I like to spend a long while under it, boiling hot and then cooler. Relaxes me. Now about Emily . . . In the first place, don't pay any bills for her or let her admire any of your precious objects or lend them to her. You'll never see them again. She's like Queen Mary in that, wants every pretty toy she ever sees. *Noblesse oblige*, only it means obliging her.'

'Wouldn't think of it. But she wouldn't ask me.'

'She might do. She's got plenty of money, all that family has, but she prefers to use other people's. The house is lovely, built round a small grey courtyard with a little chapel hanging on to it. I believe it was a small nunnery before Henry VIII got his hands on it, so it's beautiful and genuine and madly cold and uncomfortable, not that she notices or cares. She comes from a long line of robber barons. Welch Marcher lords, Border chaps in Wales, take the hair off anyone. They had a place in Wales.' A 'place' in Lady Mary's idiom meant an estate with a great house upon it. 'Sold that, I believe it's a hotel now. She got most of the money. That said, she's a great lady. Is this any help?'

'Not a lot.'

'What is it you want?'

'Well, where does she stand in this business of the missing child, and what sort of lies would she tell?'

'No lies. Not always the truth either. As to where she stands, I can't say but she loved Sarah, I think they all did. Even I did, she was lovable.'

'Ever hear stories about her going on the wander?'

'No, never, she was a bit young for that, a good quiet little creature. But a bit fey.'

'The dolls, you mean?'

'Oh, you know about that? Yes, that partly,' said Lady Mary vaguely. 'Just something I felt about her ... I must go, darling, I've got to wash my hair as well as soak under the shower, and I must dry it and be out of the house in ten minutes and even then I am late.'

'Where are you going?' Charmian couldn't resist asking, Lady Mary went to such interesting and high-powered affairs that she was worth listening to, and she always knew which restaurant or club or bar was the one you actually went to as opposed to what the newspapers and journals thought was 'in'. Charmian didn't live that sort of life herself but she liked hearing about it. Moreover all information was useful and she rather thought that Peter Loomis had the look of a man who did live that sort of life.

'Rather boring really. A little party at Buck House and then the opera.'

'Nonsense, you love it.'

'Only in the Mews, the stables really, not exactly the State Apartments, but lovely people.'

Lady Mary laughed and disappeared in a cloud of laughter like the Cheshire Cat.

Lady Mary could lie with the best but never about her social activities. No need. She probably was going to the palace and no doubt the party was in a house in the Royal Mews and very nice. For a moment, Charmian felt envious: let all the party be bores and the opera poorly sung. Then she laughed and made herself some tea.

Better not try to ring Kate or Rewley. No news was good news at the moment.

There was a ring at the door, followed by a knock, and Muff sped from the table to the front. She knew who it was.

'Oh, it's you there.'

'Surprised?'

'No, not really. You come and go as if you had a magic carpet. Wish I had.'

'The traffic from the airport gets worse and worse.' That was the classic Humphrey non-answer, letting you know a bit but not too much. Automatic with him, she supposed, with all that Diplomatic and Intelligence training. Or had he just been born that way?

'Not wearing the ring?'

The ring was a kind of talisman with them, in the

frequent disagreements or downright quarrels the ring was not worn, thrown into a drawer.

'It's being altered to fit me.'

'Yes, Mama did have fat fingers.'

'I wish I'd known her.'

'Not sure you'd have liked her.'

'She could manage you.'

'That she could. Manage the county and that's why you wouldn't have liked her.'

'You mean I'm the same? That I'm like her.'

But he was too wary to fall into that trap. 'No, not a bit. No one's like you.'

He stood there, tall, a bit thinner in the face than he had been a few weeks ago, hair neatly combed but escaping with a few feathery strands at the sides, going grey in a neat way, a well-remembered, much-loved figure.

'Am I forgiven or are you still thinking it over?'

Charmian frowned. 'Nothing happened, you didn't touch me. Just as well, because if you had, I would probably have broken your arm. But you thought of it, and I didn't like that.'

'I didn't like it myself. We've been a tough lot sometimes, we Kents, and violent enough too, but never violent to . . .' He stopped as if he didn't want to follow that thought through.

'To your women, you were going to say, weren't you?'

'Now I've made you angry again.'

'You can be a damned patronizing bastard.'

There was a long silence.

'I hate it when you swear.'

'I do swear at work when I have to, and I can do worse. You're a romantic if you think I can't.'

A muscle in his face jerked and Charmian stepped

75

back, wondering what was coming. But he turned away, walked into the kitchen and sat down.

'Sorry. I seem to keep saying that, but sorry it is.'

Charmian sat down opposite. 'You don't need to, I can see I'm provoking too. Let's wipe this all out and start again. I do love you and if you promise not to beat me, then I promise not to break your bones.'

He laughed. 'I'll never beat you when you make me laugh.'

Not much of a joke, but Charmian found it good to laugh. 'Are you all right?'

'Oh more or less,' he said wearily. 'It's been a brute of a trip, hated bits of it, but not right to take it out on you.'

But it's what men always do, thought Charmian, and it's why I've steered clear of marriage until now.

'It's not been too good here.'

'No, I've heard about the Holt child being missing. I gather Mary Erskine got you into that.'

'I might have been dragged in, anyway.' She kept silent about the dead boy and the tiny skeleton, but noted that he had been in touch with Lady Mary of whom she was slightly jealous.

Across the room she could see her face reflected in the wall looking-glass, her hair was untidy and she could have done with a touch of lipstick, she looked across to Humphrey who was white and tired.

'War's over,' she said. 'A truce is declared, we can fight again another day.'

'And the day after that, if I know us,' said Humphrey with a slight groan. 'But yes, agreed. Battle honours will be awarded later.'

She cooked a light meal, they drank a little wine and went early to bed.

He was asleep before she had finished her shower. She looked down at his head on the pillow, his profile looked sharp and drawn.

'Something wrong there,' she said to Muff as she laid out the cat's usual night refections. 'And it just might be me.'

Chapter Five

The Old Curiosity Shop

In the morning, before she left home for the usual routine work in her office at SRADIC, Charmian telephoned Inspector Dan Feather.

Humphrey had left early, drinking a cup of coffee very quickly. 'I'm off to London. Join me there on Friday, and we will have a weekend there, theatre if you like.'

'Might do, try to,' she had said, doubtfully. 'Look after yourself. Are you all right?'

'Just a headache, nothing much.'

This was in her mind, a small question mark of worry, when she telephoned Feather. In a very few words, she told him the story that Lady Grahamden had retailed.

'Check it. I'd suggest you see Biddy Holt yourself, you might get the truth.'

'Right. You believed the old lady?'

God knows what Lady Grahamden would have made of being so called. 'I believed she believed herself.' Conviction had been Lady Grahamden's strong card. 'You ought to see her too.'

'Oh I will, but she'll have to wait her turn. There's a lot going on down here.'

'Busy?'

'You could say that. I can't see either woman this morning, I've got another case on hand and I must prepare a report for the legal eagles, but I'll set something up for this afternoon. I take it Lady G. might be difficult?'

'No, if she wants to talk at all, then you will find her astonishingly easy. I suppose she was interviewed earlier?'

'Only briefly, and not by me, she seemed not to have much to say.' He was turning over the pages of a report as he spoke. 'Yes, I see here that WDC Minors saw her and got very little. Slightly hostile, she thought.'

'Then she's changed her mind.'

'I suppose she's reliable,' he said doubtfully.

'I shouldn't think so for a minute, but she must be heard.' He muttered something that sounded like 'Yes, but I'll watch her.'

Then she asked him if there was anything to report on the body of the boy. 'What about the boy? Anything come through?'

'As yet, not. Too soon. We're not treating it as a part of the Sarah Holt case, so I am handing the inquiry over to Jim Dashland. But he'll keep in touch with me.'

'I'll let you know as soon as something comes in. Don't expect anything too soon, you know how it goes, might take time before we can establish who it is. If ever.'

He would do what he said, Feather kept his word as she knew. But not a man to nag, so she had to stay quiet and wait. She was philosophical, detection was, she knew, made up of a good deal of waiting for information to come through.

In the Incident Room set up in the big building on the London Road which backed on to the smaller building where her own offices were, there would be a small team at work, receiving and collating information. From what she knew of the cramped circumstances down there in the London Road, Sergeant Dashland would be tucked away in a small room close by with perhaps a team of two or three. She had worked in rooms like that herself in her early days, and knew exactly how inconvenient they could be.

And what about the tiny skeleton? Not even a room and small team for that little creature. Dead too long, more of a historical study than a murder investigation.

The boy was dead already, Sarah might not be, she had to get most attention.

She spent the morning working, her door open so that she could hear her assistants, Amos Elliot and Jane Gibson, in the other room as they came in and out. At intervals they spoke to each other, passing on details of the work they were doing, but they did not speak to Charmian.

It was late afternoon before the telephone rang and she heard Feather's voice. There was not that clear, certain note in his voice that usually marked him. He was a man who made up his mind and stuck to it, but now she could pick up doubt.

'Well, I saw them. Lady Grahamden first. She bucked a bit at being interviewed by me, said she'd answered all the questions that could be put, but of course I knew that wasn't true. I also picked up the feeling that she not only expected me but wanted me. Or someone like me. Maybe she'd rather have had the head of the Force.' There was a sardonic note in his voice.

'So?'

'She repeated more or less what she said to you; that the kid had a trick of running away and then coming back. She came across with it pretty quickly once she started which confirmed what I thought: she wanted me to know. So she should of course.'

'Did you believe her?'

'I dunno... Where did the kid go each time and where is she now? After all, she's not very old, she can't have a pile of money stashed away somewhere. Someone would have to be helping her.' Or guarding her, or protecting her, but he didn't say this aloud.

'The man she was supposed to have gone off with?'

'Could be. Anyway, dealing with the "supposed" bit, I went to see Mrs Holt. Relations between her and Lady G. are strained, I'd say.'

'I expect they are.'

'But close all the same. She didn't sound surprised at what her ladyship had come up with. But said she'd got it wrong. That child did wander a little once or twice but never far and never stayed away over night. I don't know which one to believe.'

'You can check. The school, neighbours, friends.' But, of course, he'd have thought of that simple act.

'I've got one of my best women on the job now, she's done a lot of work with children and knows the score. She can judge... I may say, she was very sceptical of both stories.' He hesitated, then went on: 'I can't make up my mind whether they are telling the same story but telling it differently, or whether it's the same truth seen through different eyes. Mrs Holt's in a bad way, you can see it in her face, and the house is a mess. I tried to leave a WPC with her but she wouldn't have it. Insisted she must be alone – I don't like that. I don't like anything about it.'

'You don't like them.' It was a statement, not a question. She had clear vision of Dan Feather, tall, sturdy, disapproving, and looking as if he didn't believe a word anyone said. He had probably made his feelings felt. 'I don't blame you, I can't get them right. What are they?'

'A loving, trusting family,' he said with some bitterness.

'There's something about it I don't believe,' said Charmian. 'And yet . . . there's a substratum of some sort, whether of truth or lies.' Like a rocky reef under water that you can feel without seeing. 'They hang together even if differently about what the child did, or what they say happened.'

'Yes, that's what's so horrible. The truth might be worse than the lies. What has been happening to that child?'

'Who is still missing.'

And who might be dead.

The thought stayed with her for the rest of the day. She was cheered by a visit from Rewley. 'I'm a messenger from Kate, she asks me to tell you that she feels a lot better, her temperature is down, and her spirits up. She'd like to see you when you have time and she thinks I ought to go back to work.'

'So you did take some off?'

'Only a day. Jane took over.'

'Was a day enough?'

'I think it was for Kate,' he said ruefully. 'She loved having me there all day but I stopped her thinking. That was what I was there for of course, but she seems to have the idea that if she takes her mind off the baby it will die.'

'Oh, so she's back to that again?' One of the more distressing aspects of Kate's illness had been the terrible sense of personal responsibility for the survival of the child which sometimes made her breathe very fast in case it was running short of oxygen. Reasoning with her did not control this. 'Not so much better then?'

'Physically, I think she is.' Rewley was dogged in his

optimism. His way of dealing with the situation had been to be as cheerful as possible, where Anny had stormed and raged. 'She's got Dolly Barstow with her and that always does her good.'

Sergeant Dolly Barstow, now rapidly ascending the promotion ladder, had been a colleague of his, they had worked on several cases with Charmian before their ways parted. He admired Dolly and had been a little in love with her before he met Kate. Charmian knew this but she also knew the young women were friends.

'Dolly's good for Kate. How is she? Haven't seen her for a while.' Charmian admired Dolly, who was hard-working and very clever.

'I saw her before I left. She's fine.' His face broke into the charming smile that made him so attractive. 'She's got a new bloke.'

'Oh?' Charmian raised a questioning eyebrow. The older she got the more she enjoyed a little gossip, shaming but true. And after all, people talked about her.

'She didn't say much,' said Rewley regretfully. 'No name given, I expect she's telling Kate all about it now.'

'I'll visit Kate myself this evening.' She fiddled with the pencils on her desk, wondering exactly why Rewley was here.

'Dolly didn't come empty handed.'

'Oh?'

'You know what Dolly's like . . . she picks things up, she's a kind of magnet for odd items of information. Sometimes they mean something and sometimes they don't.'

Charmian waited. It was true, Dolly was usually good value.

'She's picked up this story . . .' He looked directly at Charmian, so she knew he was taking it seriously. 'She says she's picked up some story of a little girl been seen in the street at Windsor.'

A little girl, running in the streets.

'Where?'

'Down Peascod Street and then outwards towards the Slough Road.'

'When?'

'Yesterday, and once before.'

'And seen by whom?'

'A woman Dolly Barstow met in a shop. She thinks the woman knew the child was Sarah although she didn't say so. She was telling everybody that would listen . . . One day the girl was dancing, the next day she was crying.'

Charmian drew some patterns in pencil on her blotter. 'Have some coffee while I think it over.' She nodded to the coffee machine.

He got up and helped himself. 'Can I pour you a cup?'

Charmian didn't answer, she was still occupied drawing a complicated series of circles.

'Kate is thinking of asking Dolly to be godmother to the infant.'

'I thought she might,' said Charmian absently. 'What you've just told me fits in with something the family are saying: that the child wandered. I don't know what to make of it. I'll have to tell Dan Feather.'

'Of course.' And then, because he had worked with her for some time, and was married to her god-daughter, and because he liked her, he said: 'How are things with you?'

'Pesky,' Charmian said, after a moment of thought, leaving Rewley to make what he could of that.

Which he did. Something in her own life is not right, and that only means one thing, her relationship with

Humphrey. I shan't tell Kate. He had mixed feelings about Humphrey whom he both admired and found alarming. There was a touch of remoteness that took some coming to terms with.

Feather said: 'Could it be her? Could it be Sarah?'

'The description fits, Dolly would make sure of that.'

'So she is still alive?'

'Could be.'

But doing what? Crying, laughing, dancing.

'This is secondhand. I'll have to see that woman for myself.'

'Of course.' But Charmian knew that Dolly would have got it right. Whatever that woman had seen, or had thought she had seen, Dolly would have checked and reported accurately. 'It fits in, in a nasty kind of way, with the stories we've been hearing.'

'Life is nasty.' Feather brooded. 'That I can testify to . . . I've got something else . . . Almost forgot to tell you, this stuff drove it out of my mind.'

'The dead boy?'

'You read my mind . . . Yes, the boy. He wasn't hard to identify, he was a runaway from a foster parent. His parents were killed . . . killed each other in a suicide pact. Had a shot at taking him with them but he survived. Not for long enough unluckily.'

'How long had he been on the loose?'

'The foster parents reported him missing twelve days ago . . . but it was from South London so he'd travelled. He had a bit of money on him and the social worker on his case had advised the foster parents to let him have a bit of freedom. He wasn't over what had happened to him, he was still disturbed. He thought he was homeless.'

'He was,' said Charmian. 'What was his name?'
'Joe.'

Joe, homeless, wandering, lost.

'There's a bit of good news . . . the locket. Now it's been cleaned up, the gold mark date can be read . . . it was gold, by the way. The date is 1906 and the mark is Birmingham. There are traces of the goldsmith's own mark but this is difficult to read. It helps date the baby's skeleton, beginning of the century, and the pathologists confirm this, so we aren't pursuing any inquiry there. That's one worry the less.'

Then he said: 'I'm sending you some photographs of the locket, and you can see the real thing if you come round.'

The packet of photographs was delivered just at the end of her working day when she was packing up to go home. She was alone, Jane and Amos had taken themselves off.

She spread the photographs, three in number, on the table before her. Greatly enlarged there was the front with a flourish of two entwined initials upon it, closed. Then the back, with a delicately chased pattern, and then the locket, open to show the photograph of the young woman, girl really, she was very young. Could she be the mother of the child?

The locket was solid, nice to look at, and good value for money. It could never have been expensive but it had survived the years in the soil in good shape.

She traced the outline with her finger, as if it would put her in touch with the baby.

I wonder if I could identify the child?

No, an impossibility. There was nothing but the locket and there were quite a few like it in the crowded display case of Mr Madge the jeweller's.

That evening, she dropped in on Mr Madge; he was pleased to see her and opened his shop.

She closed the door behind her whereupon it gave a pleasingly old-fashioned tinkle. She usually felt that she had stepped back a century when she visited the shop.

'The ring is not ready yet, I fear.'

'I thought I'd just ask on my way home.'

'I had one of your colleagues in here earlier.' Mr Madge produced a large soft chamois duster with which he started a slow, languorous polish on a small Victorian teapot shaped like a cannon ball. Charmian coveted it at once.

'That's a nice piece.'

'It is. It has my great-grandfather's mark on it. The old Queen.' This was Victoria in Windsor, no other queen quite counted. 'Her habitual wedding present to members of the court and her neighbours. Silver or silver gilt, depending on rank.'

Must ask Humphrey if he has one, Charmian thought, and whether it was silver or silver gilt.

'A few got solid gold,' said Mr Madge, 'but not many.'

'What was the call about?' But she guessed she knew: Sarah.

Mr Madge looked down at the teapot in which he could now see a distant distorted reflection, all nose, of his own face. The duster performed an extra flourish.

'To ask if I'd seen a child, a little girl wandering.'

'Had you?'

He shook his head. 'No.'

'I suppose you've heard all about it and know who the little girl is?'

'Yes, indeed. Naturally I have been interested and concerned. It's always a terrible sadness when a child is missing. Sometimes they just run, poor little souls.' He heaved a sigh. 'I used to try and help . . . ran a little club for those lost . . . I called them the lost, but I had to close it.' He shook his head. 'People get the wrong ideas of what you're trying to do.'

Charmian looked sympathetic. She had heard about the club, her business to learn that sort of thing. A long time ago and no harm meant was her judgement. Madge was an innocent in a rough world.

'I know the family. Long-time customers of this firm. My father and his father before him served them and we've always looked after the family silver. The jewellery goes to Garrards, but that one can understand.' Garrards also served the Queen and so deserved the respect of Mr Madge.

'So you know all about the family, then?'

Mr Madge put his head on one side as if he knew all about everything and everyone and had no intention of talking about it. 'One of our best families but they have known their tragedies.'

'Yes, indeed.' A neat way of putting it when scandal might be an apter word.

'Of course, they've always had money, that helps,' observed Mr Madge, revealing an unexpected strain of realism. 'More money than sense some of them,' he added, reinforcing this impression.

'It seems to be no secret whose child Sarah is.'

'I wouldn't say that.' Mr Madge put his head on one side again. 'Not common knowledge up and down Peascod Street. I know, of course, with my contacts with the family. Lady Grahamden brought the child in once or twice, they never made any bones about acknowledging the relationship. In fact, she was the only grandchild.'

He said was, Charmian noted, was the only grandchild, past tense. She didn't like that somehow, Mr

Madge knew the temperature of the local water better than most.

So the general feeling, in spite of these stories of the child being seen, was that she was dead.

'Of course, Mr Peter might start again. Pity he didn't marry when he had the chance . . .'

Some way of talking about a death by violence. 'He's got the chance still.'

'I meant with Mrs Holt, she's the one. But after the . . .' He hesitated.

'The trial?'

'Yes, after the trial, he turned in on himself. Well, you can understand that . . . he went abroad.'

The classic remedy of the English upper class when in trouble. No jury had found Peter Loomis guilty but his wife had died in his house and there had been a bruise on her head.

Murder or suicide? The jury had given Peter the benefit of the doubt. Society in general had not been so kind.

'She killed herself, poor lady. Somehow she did it to herself, unlikely as it seems,' said Mr Madge. 'She was Deveraux and that family have always been mad.' But he spoke without a lot of force.

Even he doesn't believe it, Charmian thought. Murky waters here.

His eyes were on her, he was waiting for her to speak. He knows I want something and it wasn't just the ring. Wonder what he really thinks about my marriage with Humphrey? Not the right class? Well, I could tell him something about Humphrey. Except he probably knows, knows all the family secrets, good and bad. Charmian reached into her briefcase where the photographs of the locket were. 'Have a look at these. Do they say anything to you?'

Mr Madge took them up. 'Wait a minute, let me change my spectacles . . . that's better. Is this connected with Sarah?'

'Not directly. I've just got a feeling about it.' Nothing had appeared in the press about the bones of the baby, but he might know. Mr Madge seemed to be tuned into the local ether.

He studied the photographs with care. 'I don't recognize the young woman.'

'No, I never thought you would. It's a blur anyway in the photograph and not much better when you see the real thing. Of course it was dirty.'

She shouldn't have said that, he gave a sharp look as he handed the photographs back. 'Been cleaned up, has it?'

'A bit.'

'Fingerprints?'

'No, no fingerprints.' Any fingerprints would be from hands long dead. Except it was itself a fingerprint of time.

'It's a nice little bit of jewellery. Not valuable, of course. I've got a tray of similar lockets over there.' He nodded towards the dark recesses of the shop where the top of a suit of armour, the headpiece, the helm sans ballon and beaver (living near the Castle you picked up information about armour, willy nilly), stood on the dusty table. From a shelf above the armour, an aspidistra dropped a sad long leaf, yellowing at the edge. But the bowl in which the plant sat looked like a decent piece of early Worcester. You never knew with Mr Madge's darker corners, the valuable jostled with the rubbish. He seemed to like them all, none ever seemed to be sold or to be dusted. Perhaps he liked the dust too.

He saw her gaze. 'The past does reach out and touch you, doesn't it? All the time. You can't get away from it.'

She didn't think he wanted to; she left him looking sad and thoughtful.

The telephone was ringing when she got into the house in Maid of Honour Row. For a moment she considered letting it ring so that the answerphone picked it up, but curiosity got the better of her. Probably curiosity was the reason why she became a detective: there were questions and she wanted them answered.

It was Rewley and this was his official voice, this was not to be a conversation about Kate.

'I've found the woman who claims to have seen the child, the little girl, dancing and then crying in the street.'

'That was quick.'

'Oh, I know a woman who knew a woman . . . it was a chain,' said Rewley vaguely. He always had mysterious sources of information. 'She's Ms Amy Mercer, and she works in a supermarket called Yourshop in Windsor. She works on a checkout desk overlooking a window so she gets a good view down the street and up the hill. She can see a lot. She says so and I've had a look myself and can confirm it.'

'Is she a good witness? Did you believe her?'

'She believes herself certainly, and that always carries a certain conviction. Yes, I suppose I did believe her, although that may not mean much. She described the girl; first laughing and dancing in the gutter, next day crying.'

'It was next day?'

'Yes, Thursday and Friday of this week.'

It was Sunday now: no rest days for either of them.

'She got the clothes right: cotton dress and little school jacket.'

But there was something in his voice.

'So what was wrong?'

'She used to work for Lady Grahamden. In the kitchen.'

'Ah. So not totally disinterested?'

'Well, you have to ask yourself . . . Might have some motive for inventing a story.'

Charmian considered. 'And she told a lot of people about the sighting?'

'She's that sort of woman.'

'And no one else saw anything.'

'If so, they're not saying. But someone might come forward.'

'I shall have to see this woman for myself.'

'Any day. Just go shopping.'

'I probably will. I need some cat food.' Muff was on the prowl already.

'Amabel Mercer, don't forget. And she calls herself Amy.'

The conversation ended there with no pleasantries. A missing girl, a newly dead boy, and a long-dead baby, a trio joined by the thread of time that had suddenly drawn a loop round them.

The telephone rang again, and it was Humphrey and this time, guessing who it was, she let the answerphone take the message.

Chapter Six

'Shall I ever forget the manner in which those
handsome proud eyes seemed to hold mine?'

Bleak House

Six days, one hundred and forty-four hours, how many
minutes, how many seconds? Too long for a child to
be missing.

Charmian did not like the way it was going. Time was
sometimes life itself, you could feel it ticking past. She
could today and not only her own life but perhaps
Sarah's also.

An unremarkable day otherwise with so many meetings and reports to read and to dictate that there was
no opportunity on that Monday to visit Yourshop. It
wasn't an establishment she had gone inside but she
had passed it once or twice and thought it looked cheap
and cheerful. A false reading probably, not so cheerful
and maybe not so cheap, because Rewley had supplied
the information (he always knew everything) that it
wasn't doing at all well.

She would visit when she could make time. There she
was, thinking about time again, it was on her mind. Or
her conscience. You had to use it well, her mother had
said, or it got back at you. Time with her now was
something she had to cut up into little slices and dole
out in portions, not always in the way she wanted but
in the way her life demanded.

Inspector Feather had informed her that a MIRIAM, a Multiple Incident Room, had been set up to deal with the two investigations: the dead boy and the missing girl. They might be linked.

No one was investigating the skeletal baby which was about to be given a small quiet burial. Since no one knew what faith, if any, the mother had professed, or whether the child had been baptized or not, the burial would take place in the large municipal cemetery on the London Road and would be conducted by the Vicar of St Alcuin's in the East.

She got her secretary to ask when the ceremony would take place. 'Early morning? Nine o'clock? All the vicar can manage?'

She went herself to the funeral, one of only two mourners, the other being Inspector Feather. As the simple ceremony went on, they were joined by an elderly woman in deep black whom Charmian, who had met the species before, recognized as a professional mourner.

Strange, how some people, usually women it had to be admitted, seemed to enjoy funerals. Perhaps they were doing the mourning in advance for themselves. This woman had kitted herself out with a loose black coat and a big hat. She sat several rows behind Charmian in the little chapel, then followed them out to the churchyard, where she watched as the little coffin was lowered into the grave.

Charmian shrugged her shoulders as Feather came up, and nodded towards the woman. 'Why do they come? And where do they come from?'

Feather nodded back. 'I've seen that one before. Or anyway the outfit. Perhaps they hire them out.'

'I'm going to have a word with her,' Charmian murmured to Feather. But when she turned round, the woman was gone.

The duality of life came home to her: she was worried about the girl, depressed at the dead boy, and interested and saddened about the little skeleton, now returned to the earth, but she would be going out to dinner at what would undoubtedly be an expensive restaurant and then on to the opera at Covent Garden.

The weekend approached with little or no news. There was one exception of a personal nature.

Before she went to London to meet Humphrey (of course, she was going) there was a letter on the doormat, a little chewed by dear Muff but readable, giving the inconvenient information that her house helper (which was how Mrs Chatham liked to be called) was going to marry someone she had met on the holiday and would not be coming back.

She met Humphrey who looked tired but said he was looking forward to the evening. The opera performed was Strauss's *Salomé*. Not perhaps the wisest opera, a tale of obsessive sexual passion, to see when relations with your partner are strained. As the last terrible words, *'Tuée cette femme'*, were uttered Charmian felt hollow inside.

Getting into the car, Humphrey seemed to feel the same. 'Sorry to subject you to that. I'd forgotten how savage it was.'

Charmian nodded. One way and another, there's been a lot of blood shed around me. And some of it has left a stain. —Only she didn't say this aloud. But it came out another way.

'I think I'll drive back to Windsor after all.'

'You won't stay overnight? I promise not to be a nuisance.' He looked at her. 'It's late and you're tired.'

'There's a case on the go that's worrying me.'

'The child?'

'Yes, the child.'

'Tomorrow's Sunday,' he reminded her. 'You could stay here and rest.'

'I want the day for thinking. And I think best at home.'

He let her go without arguing, but she thought he looked sad. Thin and tired.

I'll do something about that when I've got this case over, she thought as she went over Hammersmith fly-over and headed for the motorway.

As if to punish her, Sunday saw her laid low with a migraine so that she did no thinking but lay there in a thick, painful stupor.

In the middle of the night, she was violently sick, watched by an interested but unmoved cat. Then they both went back to bed.

That was the nadir, the bottom, when she woke up in the morning, she felt full of energy. The kitchen was bright with sunshine as she made coffee and toast and fed Muff.

On such a morning, she could believe that life, even her life, could knit itself together into a whole. All it needed was courage, she had a lot of courage.

She had finished her third cup of coffee and eaten two slices of toast and homemade marmalade (made by Birdie) when she heard the post drop through the door. She went through the narrow, white-panelled hall to get the letters before Muff could, so she was standing there holding them when the telephone rang.

'George.' It was Rewley, even before he spoke she knew who it was. Not because she had telepathy but because he had a way of rustling papers on his desk which she recognized. 'Anything wrong? How is Kate?'

'Offish,' he said. 'But that's not it. She wants to see you, I hope you can go.'

'Yes, of course, I'll try, I can't say when.' She was hastily trying to remember what her diary held. A committee, a visit from Chief Superintendent Custom about ethnic recruiting, not her responsibility but she was supposed to know everything, other appointments too probably.

And the current crop of cases, of course.

'Is there a special reason?'

'I don't know, I'm not sure, I think she wants to talk to you about something . . . Or she may just need company. I can't get in much. Especially today, I'm in court and who knows when I'll be through. It's a brute of a day,' he added gloomily.

'I'll do it,' she promised. 'I can't say exactly when, but I'll get there.'

She put her hand in her dressing-gown pocket and drew out her letters. Two bills, one circular, and an envelope addressed in pale blue blotched ink, as if it had been rained on.

Inside was a card.

Mary gave me your address. You asked for a photograph of Sarah, so here it is.

Did I ask for a photograph? Charmian felt inside the envelope for the photograph. The answer is perhaps I should have, but I didn't. But she wants me to have one.

A small face, wearing a large sunbonnet, stared up at her. A little peaky face, almost as if Sarah had been coming out of an illness. Perhaps one of those nameless little fevers that some children seem to pick up all the time.

The eyes did not look at her straight but stared obliquely over her shoulder.

Poor little scrap.

Charmian slid the photograph back into the envelope. 'I'll have to see you, lady,' she addressed Biddy Holt. One more task to fit into the day. She dressed while working out the details of the day ahead.

But she couldn't forget the little face and it reminded her, for no reason she could pin down, of the locket and the skeleton in Baby Drop land.

She tidied the house so that it was not too sordid to return to, and left some food out for Muff. Not that there was much food in the house, she would have to go shopping. Possibly to that new supermarket, where she could see the woman who had thought she had seen Sarah in the street? Suddenly, she remembered it was her turn to have Benjy, it was week and week about, this was her week, but with no Mrs Chatham it was difficult.

She knew whom to ask, her friends and neighbours the two white witches of Windsor.

Winifred Eagle and Birdie were anxious to help.

'I can suggest a nice young woman,' said Birdie, 'one of us, you know, very reliable. Not pretty but a good little face.'

'No, thank you.' She didn't want a white witch doing the dusting, you couldn't be sure what spells she might lay on with the polish. Charmian did not believe in witchcraft but some experiences of her neighbours had taught her that they and their peers knew a few tricks. 'And what about the dog? Can you have him?'

'Well, we could, darling, although we are going away, but he could come, he's such a good traveller, never bites anyone or not often, but he ought to be with you more, he'll forget he's your dog.'

'Oh, I don't think so.' Did any thoughts ever pass through Benjy's dreamy mind?

'And he did save your life once ... And may do so again.'

'And what does that mean?'

'Just a feeling I have. A picture of you comes into my mind, no details but it is dark.'

They played this game sometimes, hinting that they knew what her future was and that there was trouble to come. About once in three times, they were right. Which come to think of it, Charmian reassured herself, was about the score with one's own moods of foreboding.

'Now what about that nice little witchlet I can get you? Not quite trained yet, only one bare term at our college near Stonehenge, but very promising and a willing worker.'

You could never tell when Birdie was laughing at you or not. Surely she was now. 'I think not,' said Charmian. 'But thanks for trying.'

'You're no good in the house.' Birdie was tolerant but honest.

'I'll find someone.'

'Be careful with yourself,' said Birdie, and suddenly her voice was sharp and true: This is real, she was saying. I give you a warning. 'Don't be too nosy, you are nosy. Curiosity took you into your trade in my opinion.'

—Damn you, Birdie, Charmian thought, putting down the telephone and walking away.

As soon as she got to her office, she made an impulse telephone call to Dan Feather.

'Have you got a photograph of Sarah?'

'Yes, I have. Do you want a copy?'

'No. Her mother has just sent me one. Unasked.' She was sure of that now.

There was a pause. 'She must want you to have it.'

'I think so. I wonder why?'

'Generosity?' Feather's voice had a sardonic note.

'Perhaps.' In her experience you did not trust generosity, not even from a close relative, in a case which might involve death: there was always a motive, sometimes a hidden one.

Yourshop was the new supermarket which had recently (and not too successfully according to Rewley) established itself in Peascod Street. On the corner of the street a row of empty shops was being knocked down to be replaced by offices. These places were boarded up but Charmian's professional eye noticed automatically that a hole had been knocked in the boarding. Rats, she thought, human rats. By contrast, the supermarket was new and brash, perhaps too much so for the conservative shoppers of Windsor. Huge plate-glass windows fronted on the street. Behind these windows you could see a long row of checkout desks.

The store closed in mid-evening so that late shoppers could fill their food cabinets. Behind the checkouts the broad aisles were lined with expertly laid out displays of eatables, there was nothing original about it, the time-honoured formulas of where you put the fruit and vegetables and where you put the chilled meat and fish had been followed, but somehow it all seemed specially enticing. It was much more expensive than she had expected, the exterior, all bright colour and plastic, was misleading, but every item from biscuits to smoked salmon was of high quality. Windsor was a prosperous town and the quality market was being targeted, so it was surprising really that it wasn't flourishing. The recession probably, even food was being hit.

It was the first time Charmian had visited the store and she paused at the door for a look. It was true – the woman who claimed to have seen the child could have seen a lot from her perch on a checkout desk. There was one desk that commanded a splendid view up and down the street. Nosy, she could hear Birdie's voice in her ear.

At once she could see there was trouble. A uniformed constable was talking to a young woman who had her hands on a trolley which was stacked with goods. The young woman was crying. By the side of the pair was an assistant in a pale blue uniform. A man in a grey suit made up the quartet. Charmian stood at the entrance, watching as slowly the little group moved to the back of the shop.

The young woman stopped crying and looked tense.

At the checkout desks some of the girls were looking at the scene in between bending over the till for the next customer, but one or two were sitting stiff backed and carefully not seeing anything. None of them liked the scene being played out. Shoplifting was a crime, all right, but the kid was young and looked desperate. But perhaps she shouldn't have taken quite so much and how had she expected to get it out unchecked? That door at the back, stupid. Well known that door was.

The woman nearest to the door and not as young as the others, she who had the best view up and down the road and was Charmian's mark, was staring straight out into Peascod Street. Charmian could not be sure that she was seeing anything, her eyes had a blank look. She stayed that way until the man at the head of the line reminded her he was there. 'Come on, miss, haven't got all day.'

Her till proclaimed itself as being only for those with five or less purchases and since most shoppers bought considerably more than that, her line was short.

Charmian made her way round the store, carefully selecting her four items. Bread, cat food, salad, and a bottle of dry sherry.

She waited until there was no one else before going up to pay for her shopping. What was the woman's name? She dug in her memory, Feather had surely mentioned it. Amabel Mercer floated to the surface.

'Do you want a bag?'

'Yes, please.' Charmian accepted the plastic carrier bag with the name of the store splashed across it. 'Miss Mercer?' she said, putting her change in her purse.

She got a surprised look. 'I'm Amy Mercer.' Then the look became appraising. 'Are you a journalist?'

Not stupid, Charmian thought, she has connected me with her statement about the child. Perhaps she wants me to be a journalist and is looking for publicity.

'No, I am a police officer.'

'Oh?' The tone was cautious, even sceptical.

Charmian showed her police identity card. 'I'd like to talk to you.'

'I can't. I'm working.'

'But the store closes soon.' Charmian had timed her visit with care. 'Not late opening tonight. I'll be in the coffee shop across the road. Join me there. I'll wait.'

She didn't have long to wait. The coffee in her cup was still warm when she saw the slight figure crossing the road. Out of the blue and pink uniform which all the checkout girls wore, Amy Mercer displayed her own dress sense with jeans, a tweed jacket, and a cream shirt. She wore a round badge which said: I AM A BLOOD DONOR.

Charmian drew out the chair for her on the other side of the table between the two angles of the wall, thus effectively imprisoning Amy.

'Espresso or white?'

'White, please.' Amy moved her chair an infinitesimal fraction towards the door and escape, thus indicating to Charmian that she was a free woman. 'And sugar.'

Charmian pushed the bowl towards her.

Amy leaned forward to spoon some out. 'I got away early.'

'I don't want to get you into trouble with the store.'

'I don't care. I'm leaving anyway. Only a temporary job, the regular girl was ill and now she's coming back. Lot of redundancies there anyway. It's hard to get a job in Windsor.'

'I'd heard.'

'And I quite liked that spot, I liked looking out. That's how I saw the girl, that's what you wanted me to say, isn't it? I did see her.'

Charmian drank her coffee and took her time answering. 'You sat there looking, I expect.'

'Well, I did, till the supervisor came up and gave me a sharp look . . . we're checked there, you know. Have to pass so many articles a day through the scanner or we get a bad mark. . . . I always get bad marks, that's why they put me on that five articles only desk. Doesn't matter so much there . . . Yes, I sat looking, so would you have done, it was quite a sight, this kid dancing up and down the street, she was getting in people's way. You ought to ask around see who else saw her.'

'As far as I know no one else has come forward.'

Amy shrugged. 'People.'

'And you knew her?'

'Well, I thought I did. Why, that's Miss Sarah, I thought, what's she doing and what's her mother thinking of?'

'You knew her?'

'Course I did. Know the family.'

Charmian laid down the photograph that Biddy had sent her. 'Was this the girl?'

Amy studied it briefly. 'Yes, that's Sarah. Mind you, she's changed a bit since that was taken. Grown up more, not quite such a baby face . . . I've seen that photograph before. Who sent it to you?'

Charmian took the photograph back without answering.

'Not her ladyship, I'll be bound, not Mr Peter. Mrs Holt, I bet you.' She gave Charmian a sharp look. 'Since you don't answer, it has to be yes.'

And I'm still not answering. 'And you saw her again?' she said.

'You seem to know all about it already. Yes, I saw her again, the next day.'

'And she was crying?'

Amy silent, she stirred her mug of coffee. 'Yeah . . . I think you could say that. Looked like it. Not happy like the other day.'

'What did you do about it?'

'I didn't do anything. I thought, though.'

'But you knew she was missing.'

'I didn't know she was missing, wasn't in the papers. I haven't been in touch with Aunty.'

'Aunty?'

'She's Lady Grahamden's housekeeper. I worked there myself, I liked it, I like kitchen work, but there wasn't enough to do and Aunty and I didn't always see eye to eye.' She took a long drink of coffee. 'So what is it you want from me?'

Charmian stared out of the window. What do I want from this woman? I wanted to test her, to see if she rang true like a good piece of china. Was she one of those people who like notoriety and come forward with a made-up story . . . Did she really see the child? Yes, I think she did.

But there was something.

Amy caught the glance. 'You're not meant to like me,' she said. 'Just question me.'

Charmian ignored the thrust. 'Which days that week did you see Sarah?'

Amy frowned. 'Was it last week? Still seems like this week even if it is only Monday. That's the trouble, I can't be sure. One day is just like another when you work at a cash till.' She took another sip of coffee. 'But I'm working on it, trying to remember, pick up just that little extra detail that will say to me, well it was Friday after all. That's what you want me to do, isn't it?'

'It would be a help.'

'But at least it shows she was still alive. Whenever I saw her, that is. Let's say it was early last week.'

'We don't know that she's dead.'

'Likely though, isn't it?'

Nearly three weeks now, she had been gone.

Dancing, then crying, what a picture it summoned up. 'Why was she dancing? Why was she crying? Where was she going and where had she come from?'

'Problem, isn't it?' Amy shook her head. 'Sometimes when children go missing, they seem to creep into holes and hideaways like little animals.'

'Yes.' Charmian remembered an earlier case in a Windsor school and the hideaway that a frightened child had found. Yes, children did find a hole to hide in, not necessarily a good hole or the best hole, but one in which they felt safe. Lost, frightened children. Was that what Sarah had been? If so, she had learnt something about her which hadn't come out. 'You seem to know.'

'Ran away once myself.'

'Where did you go?'

'Oh, here and there. I hid under the arches down by the riverside once, not for long, there were rats.' Amy was carefully vague, she didn't say which riverside and which arches although it must be Windsor, and must be those near the old railway station. 'And came back. Coming back, that's the trick.'

Charmian probed. 'I suppose the old railway arches could still be used that way. Of course, the police will have looked.'

'Always new places,' said Amy, as if it was of no interest to her, not of interest to anyone but she might as well say it.

There seemed no return from this remark, so Charmian made none.

'What will you do when this job ends?'

'Look for another one. I like housework best, that's what I am really; a kitchen worker.'

'You could go back to Lady Grahamden.'

'Yeah.' Amy shifted her eyes. 'Not easy. Quarrelled.'

Charmian picked up the menu, tore a scrap from it, and scribbled her telephone number on it. 'I need help in the house. Ring me if you feel like it.' She put some money on the table and left.

Amy watched her go, then picked up the piece of paper and stowed it carefully away in her pocket. Then she returned to watching Peascod Street, it was always an interesting thoroughfare to a girl with an open mind.

Charmian knew that Amy was watching her as she walked away, she had developed a sense about that sort of thing.

She longed to take a shower to wash the day off her

body, but first things first. Dan Feather had a right to know what she was up to, Rewley too of course, but Feather had the best claim. It was his case she was walking into. He couldn't say anything, of course, but he could certainly think it. On the other hand, sometimes he gave the muted impression of being glad of her help, as if he admitted that she saw further into the dark wood than he did.

'I've had a talk with the woman who claimed to have seen a child, the child, in Peascod Street.'

'Oh you found her?' His tone was neutral. 'I've had a word with her myself.'

'It wasn't hard to find her. I think she wanted to be found.'

'What did you make of her?'

Charmian was careful: 'I thought she spoke up well.'

'I didn't think much of it myself. Not that tale of dancing and crying, too . . . fictional.'

'I felt there was a kind of veracity there, but I wasn't sure what.'

—That's a help, she could almost hear Feather muttering under his breath.

'How it fits in with the mother's story of Sarah going off cheerfully with a man is not clear, but I suppose it could. The man has a home and Sarah has been in it. With intervals of running up and down Peascod Street once happy and dancing and once in tears. I suppose that could happen.'

'I'm considering it,' said Feather. 'She made a statement to a woman detective I sent down.'

'I thought she'd told the story before.'

'Oh, I think so, don't you?' he said drily.

'Made it up as she went along, you mean?'

'Could be. I think she likes to tell a tale.'

'She knows the family well,' said Charmian carefully.

'So not totally disinterested? Is that what you're saying?'

'Might have some motive ... protecting them in some way.'

'Why would she do that?'

'Your guess,' said Charmian, giving a shrug. 'Or she might be telling the truth ... And there's something else. She hinted that the girl might have a hiding place in the town. I wonder if she knows? I suppose you looked?'

'We did.' Feather's tone was ever dryer: he didn't like being taught his own business. 'All the usual places were searched. Thoroughly.'

'But there are always new ones. For instance, at the bottom of Peascod Street where a row of shops are boarded up ... I noticed just now.'

Feather kept his temper. 'If they have not been searched, then I can promise that they will be. But I would guess they have been done.'

Somewhat reluctantly, but conceding that he had better tell her, he said: 'Got the post-mortem on the boy Joe. He'd been smothered. From the stomach contents, it seemed as though he had been given a strong drink, whisky, which probably fuddled him. So probably we ought to be looking for some dosser with a taste for boys.'

'Had he been sexually assaulted?'

'No, and that's odd. Might have expected it. Not beaten up, nor raped, just killed. But perhaps the killer got his kicks out of killing, you never know.'

Poor Joe.

'There was dust in his hair and on his clothes so where he was killed was probably somewhere derelict. He hadn't eaten much for some days, but he had been given a meal just before he died.' There was an odd note in Feather's voice.

'Given?'

'Yes, it's the only worrying thing. I say given because it wasn't something he was likely to have bought for himself, although he might have stolen it. Smoked salmon apparently.'

'Yes, it doesn't fit in with the rest of the picture, not with the derelict house and the dosser.'

'I said it was worrying.'

It felt later than it was on that damp autumn evening. But it was time to see Kate.

She was sitting by the window of her room with a book on her lap, wearing a warm dressing-gown with a shawl round her shoulders, she said she always felt cold, even when her temperature was up. The curtains were drawn but she had pulled one aside as if she had been trying to look out.

Charmian kissed her. 'I've brought you some magazines.'

'Thank you and thank you for coming.'

'Don't you get many visitors?'

'As many as I want. I don't want everyone, they say the wrong thing, I know it can't be helped and it's me that's being tricky. Dolly Barstow came in.' Kate smiled. 'She didn't try to cheer me, she just said "Yes, it is hell," and then she talked about her latest case.'

'Ah.'

'Oh, it's all right, not the missing child and the dead boy and skeleton of the baby. About which you didn't tell me. You see, even you aren't honest.'

'You seem to know it all.'

'Of course I do, the woman who brings in the food told me about it and got me some newspapers. She doesn't treat me as if I was a child.'

'Sorry.'

'I told you I saw a figure out there in the dark. That was real, not imagination.'

'I know. And I believed you. And I acted on it. That was how the police came to investigate.'

Kate was quiet for a minute. 'Oh, I didn't know that. But then you went all silent and never talked about it and the nurses kept me away from the window.'

'We were wrong,' said Charmian humbly. 'You're not a child.'

'No. Only Dolly seems to know that.'

Mentally, Charmian saluted Dolly Barstow's tact and diplomacy in getting the tone right while saying nothing.

Kate hadn't finished. 'Isn't it odd that the other body, the new one, was on top of the very old little one?'

Her words summoned up the picture of the small bones with a surprising and shocking vividness. Charmian knew that the girl must be seeing a vivid picture herself. 'Not on top,' she said gently. 'Not exactly that. Near but not quite.'

'But the bones would not have been discovered if the police hadn't been digging, and they would not have been digging if I had not told you of what I had seen.'

'No, probably not.'

'So it was my doing, in a way?'

'There was a search everywhere for the missing child,' said Charmian in a neutral 'let's not worry about it' tone, which probably irritated Kate. 'Would you rather the bones had not been disturbed?'

'In a way. But I think they had a right to have been found and then given a proper burial.'

'That has been done,' said Charmian.

'I know. You went?'

'I did.'

'I knew you would, you're good. I value that, God-mother.' She held out her hand and gripped Charmian's.

'Not sure I deserve it, love, but thank you.'

Kate settled back in her chair. 'I feel better now . . . There is something else . . . I could tell you something else that I have seen.'

'Go on.'

'I saw this in daylight. A yellow car used to park in that side road and someone would sit in it and they would be looking out. I could see the face turned this way.'

'Man or woman?'

Kate hesitated. 'A woman, I think.' And before Charmian could ask, she said: 'And no, I haven't seen it since. I have looked. I have hopped out of bed and looked, after all I was not tied up. I don't know if it's important, but it's something you didn't know.'

Kate smiled, and in the face of that smile, how could Charmian tell her that so often these fascinating details, that look so promising, turn out to be no help at all in the end. Either they meant nothing, or they could not be understood.

'There is always something you don't know,' said Charmian.

A case is not a static thing, it is growing all round you all the time you work on it, even as you investigate it, uncover this and that, new mysteries are forming themselves, it is people made and people do not stay still.

Biddy Holt opened her door to a peremptory ring.

'Oh.' She was surprised, not too pleased. 'I was expecting someone else.'

'I suppose I may come in?' But Emily Grahamden was

already in the house, sweeping past Biddy, in her ancient but beautiful fur cloak. 'Who were you expecting?'

'I thought someone from the police might come. There's a woman – I liked her. Not like the rest.'

A look of sympathy came into Lady Grahamden's eyes. She sighed. 'I suppose they're in and out all the time? Yes, with us too. It's how they work. I remember it of old.'

Second time round for her, Biddy thought, remembering the murder of Peter's wife. For me, too, for that matter.

'Does that mean there is news?' Emily Grahamden was looking round the room. A mess. But you could hardly blame Biddy. 'You mustn't let them get you down. The thing is to stand up, be strong . . . Heavens, you're doing your Christmas cards.'

'It's something to do.'

'I haven't even decided if I'll be here at Christmas.'

'Oh, come on, Emily.' Biddy sounded weary and exhausted. 'You'll be here.'

Emily Grahamden cleared away the mess on a chair and sat down. 'You're on your own too much, Biddy. I'm just sorry Peter can't come. He's got a terrible chill.'

'Peter can never stand much.'

'He stands what he has to,' said his mother, tartly. 'What about your husband? I should think he might come back and give some support in the circumstances.'

'I haven't seen him for over a year. He's living in Spain now, and he has got a new girlfriend, she might have something to say. He did telephone when he heard and said, "You're having a bad time, Biddy, let me know what I can do." Then he rang off. That's about his limit.'

'This policewoman, why do you expect her? Did she say she was coming?'

'I sent a picture of Sarah. Inspector Feather has one, I wanted her to have one.'

'Was that necessary?'

'I thought so.' Biddy's face was determined. 'I'd like them all over the town. On the Castle walls, put up in the Great Park. It's what Sarah deserves.'

'All right. I understand. Why do you think I came today? To give you support. I loved Sarah too.'

'Love, love, love,' said Biddy fiercely. 'No past tense.'

Emily reached out and took her hand. Her own hand was loaded with diamond hoops, with a great emerald in an old-fashioned setting on her little finger which she never took off even to bathe or garden as far as Biddy knew.

They were holding hands when the bell rang.

'Don't go, leave it.'

'No, I must.' Biddy stood up.

But she had left the door unlocked and Charmian opened it, wondering if there was anything wrong.

She saw both women, one sitting, one standing. They both stared at her with the same unwelcoming look.

Clear, almost arrogant, and dismissive.

Chapter Seven

'Covering a multitude of sins.'

Bleak House

'I'm sorry,' said Charmian. 'I didn't mean to burst in, but no one seemed to hear the bell and the door was unlocked.'

Biddy collected herself and came forward. 'My fault, the bell doesn't always ring in here.'

Two lies in one moment, Charmian reckoned, because I didn't ring the bell, just walked in when I saw the door was open, as any detective would, you don't ignore an open door when on the job, and she didn't hear what didn't ring because she was so deeply into whatever they were talking about. An ongoing scene here.

Biddy continued to look distracted. 'I thought you'd come, or might do. About the·photograph . . .' Suddenly she became the hostess, not entirely naturally, but like an unwary lady caught at a garden party. 'Do you know Lady Grahamden?'

'We've met.' Lady Grahamden stretched out a hand. She was wearing a plain linen skirt with a silk shirt, but Charmian got the impression of a flowing gown and the stiffness of rich silk and the flirt of a furred sleeve. Behind her stood generations of ladies of great estate: Victorian *grande dame*, Regency aristocrat, Tudor patrician, right back to the medieval women who ruled their husbands' manors while their lord was away on the Crusade, handing out justice, hanging, imprisoning, and banishing with a firm hand. Dispensers of the law, every one, even if sometimes the law was of their own making.

'You've come about Sarah.' It was a statement, not a question. 'If there was real news, then there would be a lot of you. I've had experience in these matters, you see.'

So she had.

'I've heard about the boy you've found. It can't have anything to do with Sarah.' This too was a statement, but there was a kind of question behind it.

Charmian decided not to answer so this left a hole in the dialogue which Lady Grahamden filled in. 'We used to call it the Baby Drop ground when I was young. Very young.'

'I had heard.'

'You know what it meant? It was the place where the poor young creatures used to put their babies, in the hope that they'd be taken into the hospital. Sometimes it was worse than that and the child would be stillborn or smothered. No one had heard of cot deaths then.'

'Is that name in common use?'

'No, only among old Berkshire families who have a sort of folk memory. Or Army families, the place was near the old barracks. I know it, I was born near here, and my mother's old nurse, who stayed on with us, was a Windsor girl, in fact her daughter still works for me.'

Biddy had moved away to a side table where she was pouring a drink. she'd already had several by the tight, white look around her mouth.

'I'll have a gin too,' said Lady Grahamden, not turning her head to look at Biddy, 'but not so strong as that one. You'll have one, Miss Daniels?'

'Just tonic, please.'

'And of course, I know Humphrey.'

'I believe he has mentioned you,' said Charmian carefully.

Lady Grahamden laughed. 'I won't ask what he said. But I will tell you what he said about you: he said you were as clever as a wagon load of monkeys . . . when you wanted to be.'

It had the authentic ring of Humphrey in a rather sharp mood, they must have had a disagreement.

'Are you going to be clever about us?'

'Yes, Lady Grahamden. If I can be. For the sake of Sarah.'

And that other child, the boy, and that one who was but buried bones.

'Good . . . Come and sit down, Biddy.' She put out a protective but firm arm and drew Biddy down beside her. 'You don't look too comfortable yourself, Miss Daniels.'

Charmian moved around on the padded chair, the cushion beneath her shifted. 'I think I'm sitting on . . .' She looked. 'A nest of dolls.'

Underneath the cushion were four little plastic dolls, they were naked, with price labels still round the neck.

'Oh, they are Sarah's reserve dolls . . . She kept a few extra in case anything happened to the others.' Biddy hurried across. 'I didn't know they were there.'

'You don't keep the house in much order, Biddy.' Lady Grahamden took a drink of her gin and tonic. 'You wouldn't notice they were there.'

Charmian said quickly: 'I wanted to talk to you about a story I have been told by Amy Mercer. You know her? She claims she saw Sarah in Windsor. Recently too.'

Biddy gave a little cry.

'Oh that girl, she's such a liar,' said Lady Grahamden.

'No,' protested Biddy.

'Is she?' asked Charmian, interested.

'Well, an hysteric who tells tales.'

'What sort of tale?'

'Oh, about seeing things, people who can't really be there.'

'Ghosts, you mean?'

'Well, images, phantoms . . . If you can believe in such things.'

'She said that she once saw an old man sitting by the kitchen fire, no one else saw him, and when she looked again he wasn't there, it hardly constitutes hysteria,' said Biddy wearily, as if they had been through this before. 'It was a trick of the light or something, it's very murky and shadowy in that kitchen of yours, anyone might imagine something.'

Lady Grahamden raised a sceptical eyebrow. 'You can't rely on someone like that.'

Not a reliable witness, she was saying. Between them they had destroyed the story as evidence.

'You don't believe her?'

'How can I? It's unlikely. Even Biddy doesn't and she wants to.'

Charmian turned to Biddy: 'You'd heard this story?'

'Inspector Feather told me. He said he felt he must do so, but he managed to let me know how little it probably meant and how little weight he placed on it.'

Like the yellow car, Charmian thought, a something and a nothing.

'You didn't believe but you sent me the photograph. Why was that?'

Biddy looked away. 'For love,' she said, eyes staring out of the window. 'For love.'

Charmian finished her tonic, which was flat and luke-warm. Perhaps it had been a mistake to come.

Biddy suddenly came to life. 'Something I have to tell you . . . Of course, I was wrong in thinking I had seen the man who took Sarah away. I was confused, things muddled in my mind. Now that I am clearer, I see I did not know him and had never seen him before.'

Charmian nodded.

'It was his clothes, you see. He was nicely dressed: jeans and blue shirt and a tweed jacket . . . but it's what you see in an advertisement in a magazine or in a shop window, that sort of gear. I think that must have been what I was really remembering.'

So now he's not a real person, Charmian thought. More detail about his clothes but now he's a male model from a shop display.

Biddy reached to the table behind. 'Look, you see, here . . .' She was leafing through pages. 'I think this is what I was remembering and I got confused.'

Charmian took a look. Yes, a young male model wear-ing jeans and tweed jacket, the shirt was cream and not blue, but that didn't matter, a girl was entitled to make a few mistakes. A good-looking face.

'Did he look like that?'

'Oh, I don't think so, do you? I've got it all wrong.'

'What about his voice?'

'Oh, very ordinary. I couldn't say he had an accent. An educated voice . . . I think,' she added doubtfully.

'Make up your mind,' said Lady Grahamden.

'It was.' Biddy looked as though she might burst into tears. 'Not very educated but quite.'

Charmian put down her empty glass. One step for-ward and two back; as Biddy offered more detail, so she seemed to tell less.

'I'll pass this all on to Inspector Feather. Unless you've told him already?'

Biddy shook her head. 'No, it just came out now. I hadn't quite realized before. Things seem to disappear in your mind, don't they? Like a dream, you know how that fades so quickly. You think you will remember for ever, and when you turn round it's gone.'

What a witness, Charmian thought, the more she says, the less she tells, God help us if we have to depend on her in court.

'Just think of anything you can that will help us in the search for Sarah. If no one is around to tell, then write it down. Keep a pad of paper and pencil handy and just get it down. Put it all there, never mind if you think afterwards it wasn't all so, not how it happened, even made-up things can be helpful to the police. A lie can tell a lot.'

Biddy stared at her with a set face, and Charmian realized she had gone just that one step too far. I did it deliberately, she told herself, she irritates me beyond belief this woman, I don't like her, or is it that I don't trust her?

Did Lady Grahamden give a short, sharp exclamation? She couldn't be sure.

'I'm going to scream,' Biddy said.

Charmian stood up, but Lady Grahamden remained where she was. 'Slap her on the face. Once on each cheek,' she said calmly. 'That'll stop her.' And since Charmian showed no sign of doing this, and Biddy had started, she rose herself and delivered two stinging slaps on the face.

Biddy went quiet and started to cry, not noisily but with quiet despair.

'I've had practice,' said Lady Grahamden. 'Not the first

face I've slapped. 'I don't think you'll get any more out of Biddy just now, she has these turns.' Her voice was tolerant. 'She can't help it and I don't blame her. I feel the same myself but we didn't scream much in my time, just gritted our teeth and got on with it. I don't know, perhaps a scream makes more sense.'

'I'll let you know if there is any news of Sarah.'

Lady Grahamden nodded, her face without hope as if she knew that good news there could not be.

'Give my love to Humphrey, I hope he's all right. I hear he's been seeing that brain man at the Royal Oxford.'

How can she know that when I don't, thought Charmian. She stumbled a few vague words, as she left, not knowing what to say. Damn Humphrey, what have you kept quiet, and why?

Outside there was now a car parked behind her own along the grass verge.

As she approached, she saw Peter Loomis. He smiled at her. 'I've come to collect my mother.' He held out his hand. 'Miss Daniels . . . Good to see you.'

Nice manners, she thought, as might be expected, but better not to trust to them. She could see his attractions, but he looked thinner, greyer, the skin stretched tight over his elegant bones.

Deep-set blue eyes.

Empty.

It often happened to those who had been through what he had. When it was over there was nothing left inside.

Charmian looked aside for a second, it was too painful. So that was what they looked like, those who had been to the brink and come back.

'She doesn't drive?' she said, for something to say.

'Oh yes, of course, sometimes.' He smiled. 'She can do anything, my mother, when she chooses, even drive this beast of a car.'

Of course, even the Queen can drive, one has seen pictures of her doing so, but she only does it when she chooses. Lady Grahamden was the same.

'No news, I suppose?'

'Nothing hard.'

'How's Biddy?'

'Not good.'

'Can't expect it. I don't go in, I set her off. Can't blame her. She looks at me and sees Sarah.' Charmian nodded, and got a sad little nod in return. 'One or other of us got something wrong.'

Peter Loomis went into the house, where his mother seized him in both her arms, kissed him.

'You were talking to her, I saw you from the window, we can't let her go on, we must shut her up.' She tried to whisper in his ear. 'We must stop her drinking.' But Biddy heard.

Peter put his mother gently aside, removing her hands firmly but with love. 'Hello, Biddy,' he said awkwardly.

'I'm afraid she suspects Biddy.'

'I know she does,' said Biddy. 'I can see it in her eyes, she thinks I killed her or massacred her or abused her or something.' The gin was making her voice unsteady.

Peter took her in his arms. 'Come on now, Biddy, steady on. I know how you feel, I've been there, you know.' He stroked her hair, rough and uncombed. 'Come back with us.' He felt a shudder run through her. 'Well, go to my London flat.'

'No, I must stay here. Just in case Sarah comes walking in. I feel as if she might.' Biddy looked round the room. 'Perhaps she's here now.' She dragged away from him and raised her voice: 'Sarah, Sarah? Are you there?'

'Oh dear, oh dear,' said Lady Grahamden. 'This is going to be bad.' Although it had always been bad and always would be. 'Stop her, for Heaven's sake.'

Peter put his hand gently over Biddy's mouth.

Charmian sat in her car for a moment, she felt sick inside. She pushed all thoughts about Humphrey into the back of her mind where she guessed they would fester and eventually burst forth while she concentrated on Biddy. What was the matter with that woman that made her so uneasy?

Meanwhile, all around her the case was growing like a great vegetable mass. Like a giant fungus, say, or one of those huge rhubarb plants that bring the skin up in blisters where they touch. She sensed this, could feel movement without realizing that she was helping the growing.

Chapter Eight

'The Law is an Ass.'

Oliver Twist, by Charles Dickens

She could be worrying about Humphrey – she had the feeling that they had parted as if they would never see each other again . . . she ought to be worrying about Sarah, but suddenly, as she made herself some supper, coffee and an omelette, she found she was once again brought to think about that long-dead infant whose bones she had seen given respectful burial.

A telephone call came through from Dan Feather. He had various routine matters he wanted to pass to her, but he ended with what she suspected was his real motive for the call.

'Just something to tell you: about the bones. There's no investigation there, as you know, but we did photograph the bones, I'll let you have them if you like.'

'I would like to see them, please.' She was always polite to Feather, he had patches of thin skin and she wanted good relations. 'Can you send them round?'

'Tonight if you like, drop them in myself . . . And one of the pathologists had a look at the bones, more from curiosity than anything else. He hasn't exactly put in a report but he has added a comment to the photographs . . . the child, a female, poor baby, had an extra finger on each hand. Just thought you'd be interested.'

'Anne Boleyn had an extra finger on one hand, I believe. Not lucky perhaps.'

'Are you thinking what I'm thinking?' Feather said: 'No idea how the child died, probably natural causes my scientist said. But he also said the extra finger might have something to do with it . . . easy to neglect a child that wasn't quite like the others. Especially if it was born out of wedlock and the mother was poor, might be just the factor that swung the balance.'

'Yes, it did cross my mind. Poor little soul.'

'Might not have had much of a life if she'd lived,' said Feather. 'Be dead now, anyway. Long since.'

'I wish I knew more about her.'

'I'll see you get the photographs. I'll just shove them through the door.'

'I'll be grateful. Nothing about the boy?'

'No more just now,' said Feather in a heavy voice, as if he found the thought troubling. 'We're really pushing out the boat there. He was smothered and someone knows who killed him. The forensics are doing what they can, but that takes time. I'll be putting out a statement for the press later, and if you've got anything to add or suggest, ma'am, I'll be grateful.'

'I don't know . . . Ask whoever is examining the body to see if the feet look as if he had been walking a great deal . . . He was wearing trainers, wasn't he?'

'Yes.' There was a touch of excitement in Feather's voice. 'And they were not what he had been wearing when he left the Home . . . Nor did they fit him . . . You may have something there. Thank you. Feet it is.'

'And Sarah? Any news since we last spoke?'

'I would have told you at once. Trying hard there too. As you are. Has Rewley brought anything in?

Charmian shook her head. 'No.'

'How's his wife?'

'Up and down.' And this was true, some days good, some days not. The doctors were beginning to hint that there was a psychological element there, but were too wise to say so to Kate, who would strenuously have resisted it.

'It's not true lightning doesn't strike twice, is it?'

'Never thought it was.'

'There's that family in trouble again, and I'm not as surprised as I might have been . . . I was on the Loomis case. Only on the edge, nothing important, just checking statements, but I had a chance to see him. Didn't like him then, don't like him now. We thought we had him, but his counsel was too much for us. He should have gone down.'

'You think he was guilty?'

'I do.' Feather was clear. 'Certainly do. We all thought there was more behind it than we picked up.'

'What sort of thing?'

Feather had no real answer. 'It was just a feeling. He and his wife had quarrelled and she was a shrew if ever there was one. But no one thought that was why he killed her.'

'Not even the jury.'

'Especially not the jury,' said Feather sourly. 'Motive or lack of it was what got him off. That and charm, he had such nice manners, even in the box. And I remember thinking when the verdict came in: "But this won't be the end of it." I don't know what I was expecting but I felt it . . .' He had got drunk that night, drunk for him, which was not so very drunk. 'But we ought to have got him.'

'We don't always get it right,' said Charmian. She had never heard that Feather was the sort to get emotionally

125

involved, but he had on this one. Something about Peter Loomis' acquittal had rubbed a sore spot which was still unhealed.

'—Charm the birds off a tree,' she heard him mutter. Well, perhaps, but what had fluttered down had been vultures. She had a nasty feeling that some of them were professional vultures.

With Dan Feather as First Vulture.

It had been an interesting if slightly depressing conversation, which seemed to merit some more coffee.

I am thinking about Humphrey, she told herself, stirring forbidden cream into her coffee. There's a hole where he ought to be, but if he doesn't tell me anything, what can I do about it? No letter, no message on the answerphone, silence. It was always painful when others knew more than you did about something close to your heart, and that seemed to happen all the time with Humphrey.

It might be his fault, or more likely, all hers. She was used to bearing a burden of guilt in her relationships with men and she had to admit they were usually justified.

Feather rang the bell, twice, loudly. 'I shouldn't stay.' He handed her a folder. 'There are the photographs. Nasty business it must have been. I suppose the baby was dead when it was buried, you've got to hope so.'

Charmian took the packet, resisting the temptation to open it straight away. 'I wonder no one saw the burial at the time.'

'That piece of land was much rougher and with more trees then . . . I've checked.'

So he too was interested.

'Where did you do that?'

'Town records in the museum; they have photographs. Not of that site as such, but of the old barracks which are across the way and you can see the ground between the barracks and the old workhouse. It was a workhouse by that time. Perhaps someone did see and looked away . . . Like to think it couldn't happen now.'

'You and I know it could,' said Charmian, thinking of the dead boy, Joe.

'Not for the same reasons though, not because society is bloody-minded.'

A bit of feeling there again, Charmian felt. She seemed to recall some story about his daughter having a baby.

'Oh no, could never be like that now,' she said quickly, and saw his eyes lighten.

'There's the boy, too. Different century but the way he was living was like something out of Dickens or Mayhew's *London Poor.*'

'Yes, wandering and lost.'

'And there's this.' He produced a small packet. 'It's the locket. You seemed so interested, I thought you might like a look. I'll have it back when you've done. We aren't making a case, there isn't one, so there's no reason why you shouldn't have it.'

'I won't keep it.' She held the packet in her hand, it was heavier than she had expected. 'What will happen to it?'

He shrugged. 'I suppose it might go in the police museum sometime. Or even the Local History one in the Guildhall.'

'One other thing . . . Meant to tell you, there's going to be a TV slot about Sarah. Local and national news. I asked the mother, she said she couldn't do it, so I am.'

'You think the girl is dead, don't you?'

'Hard to assess on what evidence we have now. Not sure, sometimes I go one way, sometimes another, but most of the time I think if she was alive we would have found her by now. Or had ransom demands or some such. But nothing. Not even the usual run of false sightings, although they may come later. Just silence.'

'What about the supermarket cashier, what she saw?'

'That did give me pause for thought when I first heard about it, but you know what you thought yourself, you were doubtful, I saw her, spoke to her, but like you I did not know what to make of the woman. She's not an ordinary liar, or the type that phones in false reports for a joke or for the hell of it.'

'We're calling in all known pederasts and child abusers, just in case. This applies to both the dead boy and Sarah.'

The district had its usual share; Charmian let her mind run over a few names, not all men; Ed Marlow, Dennis Barrter, MD, and more's the pity. Mrs Eleanor Lean and Mr Lean, not a married couple but mother and son, James Flitter, dustman. Or he had been when she last heard, no doubt he had moved on. And a new name on the file, Teddy (Totty) Barnes. Or Bridge, was it? She had a good memory but it slipped sometimes. 'I keep an eye on that list. But they've all been pretty quiet lately.'

'You can't tell, they're worth a look, and sometimes it gives us a start, they know more than we do very often and will let something drop, we could get lucky.'

He sat down and had a cup of coffee with her, absently stroking Muff's head as he did so. He had come in saying he mustn't stay but here he still was. In spite of the fact that he said his girlfriend was waiting for him, he seemed quite willing to carry on talking. He was a tall, thick-set man with deep brown eyes.

'The electricity failed in the Incident Room,' he said. 'We're using the old Records Room, and the wiring there needs replacing. Set us back, but we got through it.'

She knew that room. It was one with all the Incident Rooms she had ever worked in: too small for all the men, women, and apparatus crowded into it. Smoke-laden air, although not so many smokers as once there would have been (SMOKING CAN DAMAGE YOUR HEALTH on every wall), and either over hot or too cold. Incident Rooms never got the temperature quite right and no piece of furniture ever seemed comfortable for the human body, yet in spite of the noise and occasional confusion, they were peaceful places in their way, because everyone in it was working to one known end. She had never thought that her presence in such a room kept the language restrained (nor did it), but her present rank did.

'We could do with a new building.'

'It's promised.'

'We all know what that means. This year, next year, some time, never. When there's the money and there never is.' He heaved himself up. Years ago he had been wounded in the leg by a man long since out of prison and playing football and his thigh still troubled him. He covered it well but you could tell. 'Thank you for the coffee. I'd better get home; we've had my girlfriend's daughter staying with us with her kid, and she's off soon.' He didn't say more, but Charmian gathered that family life had its stresses at the moment.

At the door, he gave her a smile, stood back so Muff could depart in her usual stately way (to come back through the kitchen window almost at once), and wished her luck.

Luck with what? Charmian asked herself as she closed the door. With life in general or something in particular?

She thought she remembered a gleam of something like sympathy in Lady Grahamden's eyes. So what was all the sympathy for?

Her professional life was always under attack one way and another. As a high-ranking woman police officer, and one running her own show in SRADIC, which gave her powers beyond the average (powers which she was well known to have negotiated herself and insisted upon), she could easily be sniped at. Dan Feather was always polite, she had thought of him as a supporter but he would probably know of anything in the way of trouble brewing up for her there. Yet Lady Grahamden knew nothing of her working life and cared less.

There was one sphere, however, in which both might take an interest: her private life and relationships. And rumours did run around.

She had an uneasy feeling that she had a part in a play but no one had told her the words. It wasn't going to be a comedy.

In case it was Kate who was the focus for this unexpressed sympathy, she made herself telephone Rewley at home. It had been a rule with her lately that she would not bother with questions to him or Anny (Kate's mother and her closest friend), except when Anny, aggressive as ever, attacked her – which was quite often).

She hesitated about telephoning: she had her share of emotional stupidity and didn't always get it right where her affections were involved. But who did?

She rang Rewley's home number. Kate and her husband had made a very happy home in a modern flat, which Kate was rich enough to decorate in her own style (not to everyone's taste, but now it was her own home she had become more orthodox and peaceful, her kitchen being plain white, unlike the deep red one she had insisted on creating for Charmian); expensive French cottons in apricot and pink hung in the sitting-room with a carpet made to Kate's own design. Charmian could imagine the telephone ringing. Presently, Rewley would lean over the arm of the pale leather sofa and pick up the receiver.

The telephone was ringing out in that empty way it has when no one is going to answer it. She let it ring once more, then put it down and walked away. This was where a cigarette would have been useful but she had long since given up that indulgence.

She made herself some more coffee although she felt twitchy enough already, and would certainly be much worse after another cup or two, so she ate a biscuit which was meant to be calming.

Muff jumped up on the table to suggest that she too was under strain and needed food.

'You always do,' said Charmian, as she opened her refrigerator which, in spite of her trip to the supermarket, was almost empty. She closed the door sadly and gave Muff some biscuits, cats' specials.

There was no doubt about it: empty cupboards did make you feel less a woman, whereas a full refrigerator made a woman feel good. It must go right back to primitive man when a hunk of mastodon hanging in the cave made a woman feel safe.

However, she had many years of feeling unsexed, since in her early days in the force at Deerham Hills, her fellow officers had had many ways of diminishing a woman, ranging from the simply idle to the openly prurient. She had known how to kick all those critics back, and now, of course, as head of SRADIC, she was treated with respect. Maybe not liking but always with respect. She was someone now who knew too much.

She decided to give Rewley another ring. Perhaps he was at the hospital? She knew he went in as often as he could, always if he was worried about Kate, which was most of the time.

A polite voice informed her that she could not talk to Mrs Rewley, who was asleep.

Was her husband there? He was not. How was Mrs Rewley? Very comfortable, and the doctors were pleased with her, perhaps she would call again in the morning?

A bland, polite response, but soothing in its way: Kate was asleep, and Rewley was not there, so he was not sitting by her bedside in a state of anxiety. He might even be out enjoying himself with friends. Or silently drinking alone somewhere. No, that was not Rewley's style.

She put the worry over Kate aside, she could pick it up again tomorrow.

The packet that Feather had given her was on the side table where he had put it down: she picked it up and let it rest on the palm of her hand while she considered his motives in giving it to her. He was never an easy man to read; his large, well-covered face had learnt long ago to disguise his feelings. She wondered how his family managed this opacity, but one meeting with the tiny Mrs Feather, who had shaken her hand in a vice-like grip and told her she was called Fluff, had convinced her that Feather was nicely managed at home, fed on good puddings and thick steak. A snapshot she had once seen of him as a youngster, newly in the force and a champion runner, had shown him to be long and thin. Times passed. He now had a new partner and she thought he might be losing weight: so the new lady was creating a new man.

He seemed willing to humour her interest in the long dead child, bringing little details about the skeleton as he learned them.

She opened the packet which had been stuck together with zeal, but eventually she had the paper apart. The locket had been cleaned, when she held the gold oval, it was heavier and more solid than she had expected. A good piece of eighteen-carat gold, and no piece of Victorian pinchbeck.

This added to the feeling she already had that the child was not the child of poverty. Unwisely conceived, unhappily delivered into the world, but not poor.

The locket seemed to get heavier. The past gripped you sometimes, stretched a hand and took hold.

She wasn't the first to handle this object since its rescue from the earth, it had been photographed, been cleaned, and then parcelled up, but she felt in touch.

The catch opened easily and there it was once again, the faded sepia photograph of a very young woman. On the back of the locket was engraved some initials, so curved and entwined that they were hard to make out.

An E or B with a C or a D? And curling in and out a W or an M. She couldn't be sure, the engraving was so worn.

Going back to a childhood trick, she went to her desk to find a piece of thin paper and soft pencil. A crayon would be better, nursery memories of red and green and deep blue crayons stirred, but she had none, the pencil would do. Then she pressed the paper over the back of the locket, and passed the lead over it, back and forth, not too hard, but hard enough to make an image.

It began to look more like an M and a C entwined.

She was staring at it when she heard a car draw up outside. Maid of Honour Row was a quiet street where most of her neighbours went to bed early.

When she looked out of the window, she knew the car, dark blue, newish, powerful. Humphrey's car. She waited for a moment, then ran down the stairs and opened the door. A cold damp breath of wind blew in, making her shiver.

'You're cold,' he said, putting his arms round her, and pushing her through the door.

'I'm glad to see you.' She was hugging him back. 'Didn't think I would be somehow.'

'I always meant to come.' He sounded surprised. But grateful too, he had not always got such a warm welcome from Charmian.

'I've been worrying about you.' Also about bones, a dead child, a lost child, but underneath always about you.

'This isn't the place to kiss you, which I mean to do, let's go upstairs.'

Charmian drew back. 'No, wait a minute. This is where you say: "But there's nothing to worry about." '

'Let's go up.'

'Is there anything?' she persisted.

'Shall we talk about it later?'

'That means yes ... I've been sitting in the kitchen, drinking coffee. Let's go there.'

'Working?'

'You could call it that. Thinking, anyway.'

The kitchen was warm and quiet. The coffee pot still hot and fragrant, Muff asleep on the chair. She opened one eye, gave a purr, and went back to sleep. Her tail lashed once or twice.

'I don't know about coffee. I could do with a drink.'

'Whisky or brandy?'

'Brandy, I think. You've been smoking?'

Dan Feather had not smoked but the smell of cigarettes hung about him permanently, and he left a faint legacy of it behind.

'Not me, no. But Dan Feather called. He didn't smoke here but he had been, it's those terrible little cigar things he goes in for.'

Humphrey sat down at the table. 'That was the work, I suppose. Anything new?'

'Not about Sarah, nor the boy. He brought me something . . . I called on Biddy again, and I've met Lady Grahamden and Peter.'

'What did you think of them?'

Charmian tried to assemble her thoughts. 'What did I think? Still sorting it out. Odd, is the first word.'

'They are odd. She's a throwback, this isn't her century. When he was younger I used to think Peter was as near mad as made no difference. Do anything. But he's toned down a lot lately.'

'I think he's very unhappy at the moment, all three. I don't know if they were lying or acting. I'll get the brandy.' She was shocked at his appearance. A kind of whiteness under the normal healthy tan, he looked exhausted sitting there, arms on the table. He made as if to rise. 'You stay there, I'll get it.'

When she came back with the brandy, he was studying the pencilling she had made.

'What's this?'

'I was trying to make out the initials on the back of this locket.' She was pouring out the brandy. 'It was found near the baby's bones. Belonged to her, I guess. Was a girl, by the way. I just had the idea that I might somehow find out a bit about her. A long shot.'

Humphrey gave her an enquiring look but he said nothing.

With the first draught of brandy, the colour was coming back into his cheeks. He looked better. 'You've done a good job. These engraved initials are always hard to make out. The flourish was what they wanted.' He took the locket in his hand. 'It's heavy, good stuff.'

'I know, that struck. I could see it must have cost something.'

'Why don't you take it into John Madge, he might help.'

'Yes, he would try. I have already spoken to him about it, showed him a photograph.'

'You surprise me sometimes, do you know that? This is an historical investigation, not a bit of detection.'

'Same thing, I suppose, in a way.'

'Why do I get the feeling that means something more to you?'

'I'm interested,' she said, unwilling to admit that she couldn't let go. The bones rattled in her mind all the time, setting up a dance that called her in.

Muff purred, the room was warm, the coffee smelt good. She poured them both a cup.

'So, now tell me, what's it all about? What is it you are going to tell me?'

Dan Feather had been sympathetic and Lady Graham-den had hinted about whatever it was.

'I wondered if it was my fault . . . perhaps you were having second thoughts about our marriage . . . I know I'm not easy.'

'No, not you, never you.' He reached out to hold her hand.

'I know you've been having a lot of headaches.'

He held on to her hand as if it was a comfort. 'I began to think it was a bit more than a headache or so . . . My eyes were playing up. Not all the time, but sometimes.'

She waited, longing for him to go on but dreading what seemed to be coming.

'I saw my own GP, he sent me to a brain man . . . I had a scan. That was today. He thinks there may be something there that will need an operation . . . I shan't know for a couple of days.'

'I knew there was something. I wish you'd told me.' Several people seemed to have made guesses, right or wrong, she had not.

'It wasn't so much telling, but I couldn't talk about it.'

'We don't talk enough, you and I,' she said sadly. 'We bury a lot.' And now there might not be much time for talking.

'I don't want to die and leave you.'

Charmian held on to his hand. 'Don't worry about me. You stay alive for your own sake.'

'Thanks.' He could manage to laugh. 'I'll be doing that too.'

She wanted to say: 'I'm not going to believe in it. It's not going to happen, I won't let it,' but she knew she couldn't. Some facts are so big, stone hard and monumental, that you have to see them, you can't walk round them or over them or under them. Better to stare at them, spit at them, kick at them if you have to.

'When will you know?'

'Next few days. My GP will ring me.'

—So that's how they did it? Read out the death sentence by proxy. 'Let's have some more brandy.' Alcohol was not lifting her mood, the stone misery was heavy in her stomach like a kind of emotional indigestion, but she poured with a generous hand.

'Have you eaten?' she asked suddenly.

'Not for some time.'

She was brisk at once, this was what she could do.

'I'll make an omelette. It's what I had myself. Cheese do? Won't take a minute.'

He knew her omelettes, they could be thick and heavy or thin and runny. Not good to laugh, though, she was prickly about her cooking. Too many lovers, she had said, expect you to be a good cook as well as everything else. In any case, he liked her style.

'I don't think I've told you why I love you.'

'The usual reasons.' Her voice was light. 'That's what I thought, but I suppose I could ask.'

'Because you can be so hideously practical,' he said.

She whisked away, saying nothing, being hideously practical. Not knowing how to be anything else at that moment. Possibly she never had known and this was her weakness.

She was beating the eggs with vicious concentration as if she was whipping all those people she disliked most at that moment: the killer of Joe, whoever had abducted Sarah, the long ago woman who had buried her baby, dead or alive. Not to mention all those people from Biddy Holt to Dan Feather who might have lied to her.

'A lot of the things we haven't said, ought to be said. But I don't know if I'm ready for them yet.'

'Let's leave them then.' Whisk on, Charmian, this might get painful.

'Leave the eggs.' He came up and took both her hands. 'Come and sit down. I want you to know that I love you. But you haven't always made it easy for me to show it. You run away. And that has made me angry.'

'I've felt that,' said Charmian. 'You are good at showing anger. I haven't liked that. Nor the hint of violence.'

'I would never hurt you.'

'That's always said, isn't it?'

They were tearing away the bandages and underneath there was raw flesh.

'I don't want to go on with this,' said Charmian quickly. 'Not now, it's not the right time.'

'There you go again.'

She stood up, dislodging Muff from the chair next to her by the force of her action. 'You cook the eggs.'

At this point, the telephone rang. She seized it with relief. 'Rewley? You must have telepathy. I was trying to get you.' Her voice was uneven.

'Are you all right? You're talking in gasps.'

'No, I'm fine, nothing at all.' She could see Humphrey looking at her with a frown on his face. 'Is it Kate?'

'No, nothing to do with Kate, as far as I know she's asleep. No, they have a pederast in the Interview Room, he came in and confessed to having held and kidnapped the boy and also Sarah. He's talking like a canary.'

'Who is it? A new man? Or one of the old lot?'

'Totty Bow, that's the man. I got the name, not sure I know him, but I swear it meant something to the other two.'

Totty Bow. So it was Bow, not Bridge or Barnes.

'Did they tell you all this?' She knew how closely they hung on to information, each team for itself and sometimes each man.

'No, I just happened to be down there. I went to see Kate earlier, and she really is fine, by the way, less uncomfortable, and Dolly Barstow came so I knew she'd have company. I'd been working late to catch up . . . I was sitting in the car, and I saw Jephson and Farmer, I knew they were part of the team and I could see something had happened . . . So I was sitting there, watching. I read their lips . . . I thought you'd want to know.'

'I do, I do. Thank you.'

Charmian turned back to Humphrey who was watching her gravely. He couldn't lip read and he didn't practise telepathy but he knew his Charmian.

'It's bad, isn't it? Don't worry about me, do what you have to do.'

She pushed her hair back from the forehead. She had been cold and now she felt too hot.

'I can't take all this in . . . I'm going down there.'

He didn't ask where, he had probably worked out most of the dialogue with Rewley.

'Will you be here when I get back?'

'Do you want me to be?

She hesitated. 'Yes.'

Chapter Nine

'The dog whose name's called, eats. The dogs whose names an't, keep quiet.'

The Old Curiosity Shop

Dan Feather was there ahead of her, he was just walking into the building as she arrived. So he hadn't gone home.

Had she really thought he intended to? Feather had sounded honest, but that was his skill.

He hadn't noticed her car, so she sat back in the dark, letting him get ahead. Time to confront him later. Not too much later, she decided, as she didn't want to miss anything important. She watched Feather's back disappear; he was walking slowly as if tiredness came even to his indestructible form. He was known, in a fairly friendly way, as the Iron Man. The name went back to his youth when he had lifted the wheels of a motor car off a child, and also to several later episodes when his treatment of sex attackers had been adamantine, and only what was called ironically 'the Feather Fan Club' had kept him out of trouble. Charmian was not a member of that fan club, women were not admitted, but a number of high-ranking officers were. Charmian herself liked investigation carried out with a subtler touch but no one had ever faulted Feather. He had the reputation of knowing where all the bodies were buried, but by now Charmian knew where a few were stowed herself and had helped put some away.

She was beginning to wonder if the Sarah Holt case with the Loomis–Grahamden connection was going to be such a burial, and if Feather had started the process by calling on her.

But that would be politics calling the cards in and although Lady Grahamden looked capable of anything that suited her, she couldn't see the case for it here.

She leaned back in the car. Count to twenty, then go in.

She had got to fifteen when Rewley tapped on the window. 'I was watching you, wondering what you were going to do.'

'Go in. Join the party.'

'Did you see Dan Feather?'

'I was watching him. He's a wily beggar, told me he was going home. If he went there at all, then he didn't stay long.'

'I think he came from his office, got a telephone call, and walked across to the Incident Room.'

The Incident Room had its own small interviewing room which had been much in use.

'He won't have had his supper,' said Rewley, 'and he's a tall man turning fat who likes a square meal, so he's probably not too happy.'

A wily, hungry Dan Feather didn't bear thinking about. No mean protagonist at the best of times, on an empty stomach his mood might be alarming. But she could be formidable herself and she too was superpowered tonight, charged with energy derived from anxiety.

'What about you?' she asked Rewley.

'I'm going home.'

'Yes, you've done your bit.' She was undoing her seat belt, and fastening the lock on the brake. Even though this was a police car park, theft was not unknown.

'I hate having to walk on eggshells, don't you?' said Rewley.

'Not so you'd notice and certainly not at this moment. I shall trample as suits me best.' She looked down at her neat black shoes, she could do damage.

An alarming lady, thought Rewley, who was fond of her as Kate's godmother but respectful of her as his boss.

'I'm wondering if Dan Feather brought me in that certain locket to keep me occupied on that matter, and out of his way. He's devious enough. Thank goodness for you, Rewley, you're my magic trick.'

'They know what I do, you know. That I'm your look-out man, that I watch out, observe and read.'

'Didn't know tonight.'

'No, not tonight,' he agreed. But it wouldn't last for ever, he thought. People would go on guard, or take to wearing face masks. 'I'm off.' He was useful to Charmian Daniels, he knew that much, and he owed his rapid promotion to her, but also knew that he was good and would get it anyway and that in some respects her patronage might have harmed him, since she was not universally loved. But he worked for her because she was almost always on the side of right ... I'm not a mind reader or great on intuition, in spite of what some think, I operate on logic and application. What she operates on I don't know but it must be high-octane fuel. Sometimes she seems to fly.

He watched her walk firmly towards the Incident Room, where all lights were on. At the entrance, she turned and waved. She wouldn't be welcome in that room, as she well knew.

Daniels into the lion's den. And he waved back.

Dan Feather had his back to Charmian talking to another officer as she walked into the room, but he felt her eyes on him and swung round. 'Hello, there.' It was a jovial sound to cover up surprise. Possibly displeasure too, she thought.

She gave Feather a friendly smile. 'You must be hungry . . . no dinner.'

He hardly hesitated for a second. 'I grabbed a few sandwiches.'

Ham or beef with a large dose of mustard pickle, he was not a cheese or egg and salad man. She knew those sandwiches in the canteen.

He seemed to have brought a supply of them in with him, she could see a large plateful and several mugs of tea on a central table.

'Not guilty,' he said, seeing her look. 'They were here before me.'

'For the prisoner?'

'Hardly. And we aren't calling him that yet, just talking to him . . . I don't think he can eat. He's scared silly.'

'Where is he?'

He nodded towards a door. 'In there. We have an interview room rigged up for him.'

He did not ask her how she knew and when she had learnt of the detained man, but he could probably guess.

So she answered the question he hadn't asked. 'Bush telegraph.'

He grinned. 'Always works well for you, ma'am.'

'Who's questioning him?'

'Archibald and Simes? You know them?' Charmian nodded, she knew the detective inspector and the sergeant, although she had never worked with them, they belonged to what she called the 'macho team'. 'But you don't have to question – he's pouring it out like . . !' He hesitated, decided that none of the usual profanities would do and left it hanging. 'He's being encouraged to talk about both Joe and Sarah just in case, Archibald and Simes are on the Sarah Holt case. But there are lookers on from both teams.'

As she followed Feather into the interview room, she realized the truth of what Rewley had said; he was not entirely happy. Something about this set-up discomforted him.

The room was brightly lit and stuffy, and crowded, it smelt of tired hot men. Both Archibald and Simes swung round to look at her, looked at each other, took an inward vote, and stood up. Simes had extra-long arms which gave him a simian look but he had a kind face (not necessarily a true indication of what he was) whereas Archibald was tall, thin, and hostile. He frowned and drew in his lips. That was how he looked, but there again, it might not reflect his soul.

Charmian took a deep, controlling breath; she must move carefully. She was a guest, no one had asked her in, and although, because of her rank, she could not easily be moved out, still she could be given the frozen treatment. She had had this treatment several times in the past and had learnt how to survive it.

Or even, as she intended in this case, to circumvent it.

She kept a grave face, made a small movement that almost amounted to a bow and intimated that she was there to observe only.

In practical terms this meant that she sat on a chair and planted her feet firmly on the ground while she looked at the man being questioned.

Totty Bow, a small, pale young man, was sitting across the room from her in an upright chair that allowed of no relaxation. If he had been talking, pouring it all out, as Feather had said, he had gone silent now. The recording machine had been turned off, perhaps he needed that. Although everything about him was clean, surprisingly clean, pale blue jeans, a white shirt, he still managed to look stained.

Dirt really does work from the inside out, Charmian acknowledged. He had small neat white ready-to-bite-you-with teeth, and watery pale-blue eyes. She wondered why his eyes were watering so young – he was in his late teens – and wondered if Archibald or Simes had hit him.

Feather drew up a chair beside Charmian, gave some secret signal to Archibald which started him off.

'Let's start again, Totty, shall we?'

Totty opened his childlike, horrid mouth, showing his milk teeth, and started to talk.

'It was all an accident, see, not meant, nothing on purpose.' He dabbed at his eyes with the back of his hand so that Charmian got a good view of his long grubby fingers with bitten nails.

'Not your fault, you saying?' It was Archibald speaking. 'But you would, wouldn't you?'

Totty made a noise which was something between a groan and wail.

'Worries you, does it, that you've killed her?'

'I didn't say she was dead.'

'She is, though, isn't she? And the boy. Was he there?' Silence.

'You've admitted you knew him.'

'Saw him, just saw him.'

'Where? Let's have place and time, shall we? Where did you see him?'

Silence again.

Archibald tried again. Let's go back to the girl. You killed her?'

'Not on purpose, I never said on purpose, it was just one of those bad things.'

146

'That happen to you, Totty? Come on, be more specific, let's have the details.'

'I've said, told you once. I've confessed.' He seemed pleased with the word because he said it again: 'Confessed.'

Charmian looked at him twisting and twirling on his chair. His mouth was saying one thing and his body was saying another: I am uneasy with what I am telling you.

I know you, Totty, Charmian thought. Where have I met you before? She thought about this as she listened. Totty had a sweet baby voice which seemed natural to him and which she could swear she had never heard before so they had not had a talking acquaintance. Just his face, and the way his body leaned forward from the waist.

She thought about the neighbourhoods where she might have met him. London, she ruled out, because she hadn't been there for long, and Deerham Hills where she had once worked because he was too young.

Nearer in time and space was Merrywick, an expensive village on the edge of Windsor but with its quota of weirdos. One or two cases had taken her there.

Not to forget Cheasey, that sprawling industrial suburb beyond Eton, with its large, indigenous criminal population of long standing (all Anglo-Saxon family names) superimposed on a small, hard-working honest population which was always declining in size both physically and numerically – it must be something in the genes. The bottom of the heap were the Cheasey dwarfs, lovely little men (the women were huge) whom none would own to. If you had no record and had not married into a criminous family, you never admitted to living in Cheasey, you said Slough or Hounslow or Eton Wick.

'Let's go right to the beginning. Begin with Sarah. You knew Sarah?'

'Didn't know her name, knew her.'

'And you got to know her how?'

'In the kids' playcentre in Prinny's Park?'

'That is the playground in Prince Consort's Park.'

'I said.'

'Say it again.' Then with a hint of menace and a sideways look at Charmian. 'Please.'

The Prinny's Park playcentre was a carefully superintended playground with swings and slides and roundabouts. Totty claimed that he had worked there and that was how Sarah knew him, she had been in it often.

'Oh come on, Totty, don't tell me you worked there, you're the sort of person they work to keep out . . . I can check, remember.'

'Well, I did work there one day . . . when I was at my best.'

'Not looking too sleazy, you mean? Couldn't they smell what you were?'

Apparently they could, the one day, unpaid and unacknowledged appeared to be it, he was warned off. Anyway, that was what could be read behind the statement: 'Told me they could manage.'

After that he had seen her several times when he had been sitting in the park near to the playground. 'I talked to her and she talked back. She was a nice kid.'

'She wasn't on her own?'

'No, with a woman . . . I guess it was her mother.'

'Did the mother see you?'

Totty was silent. —Not if I could help it, could be read in his face. 'Might have done,' he said.

'And after that?'

Well one day last week he had seen her just wandering around on the loose, on her own.

148

He had not meant to kill her, she was a nice kid, but she fell and banged her head.

'Where was this exactly? We'll need to know, Totty, got to go down there and take a look.'

'Under the railway arch . . .'

The two observers across the room from Charmian stirred and looked interested. Archibald responded to the silent thought.

'Was anyone else there?'

Silence. You could almost see Totty working out what it was best to say. Should he say he was on his own, or should he claim that there were others there too?

If he had a problem deciding then it meant there were others.

Suddenly an even nastier picture than the one already presented was building up. A group of men and maybe Joe there as well. Sarah had been killed and then Joe.

Or had Joe helped? And then been killed because he was dangerous?

'Do you know this boy?' A photograph of Joe was handed across from the other pair of detectives, one of whom Charmian knew by sight: Bill Fletcher, a CID sergeant of some repute. Totty decided silence was safer, his baby lips shut.

They left him alone for a little while, took a break in the outer Incident Room which had gone quiet, it now being after midnight. One telephone line was open and manned, and a couple of detectives sat hunched over their desks, pulling papers around, but otherwise the room was empty.

The room still stank of cigarettes, so Charmian went outside to lean against the door and look up at the sky. The rain had stopped, the air was cold and chill, she could see the stars.

No one invited her to go back in, possibly there was a hope she would melt away, but when she heard movement inside the room, she followed the group back inside to where Totty sat.

Dan Feather drew a chair forward for her.

'Thank you.'

No answer, just a polite nod from a face increasingly in need of a shave. He seemed to want to deflate her, but he need not have bothered, she felt empty.

There had been, she decided, a kind of confab between the men while she was outside, she could see it in their eyes. Whether it was aimed at keeping her out or counting her in, she could not decide.

They seemed to have settled on a change of voice: Feather took up the questioning.

'Tell us more about Sarah, how you got to know her.'

'Didn't really know her, just saw her and liked her. Then I thought she was lost and I would help her.'

The thought of Totty being a help to a lost child made the blood run cold. Feather clearly felt the same, she saw his lips tighten but went on trying to get more detail out of Totty.

He did not admit that he had known where she lived, and he did not admit to being the man who had collected her. He was shifty here, no, he had seen her lately. Asked again about Sarah's mother, he had said yes, her mother might know his face, he couldn't say.

'You're not saying much now, are you, Totty? You're not giving us much. Where is she? What did you do with her?'

'I've said.' Totty dabbed his left eye, he had confessed once and more could not be asked of him. 'It's gone a blur.'

'You saying you've forgotten what you did with her?'

'Totty's forgotten.' He was deliberately, knowingly

regressing into childhood. It made Charmian want to hit him, she was alarmed at the active fury that arose inside her. He put his head on one side. 'River? Totty likes the river.'

'But that would be difficult for you on your own. Who helped you, Totty? You didn't do it all on your own, now admit it.'

His neat little feet in their soft grey suede boots crossed and recrossed as he did not answer.

Outside, the distant church clock of St Alcuin chimed the hour.

'It's a mismatch. Bits of it seem real, most don't.'

'Is he the sort that confesses to everything?' Simes asked the air.

'Wouldn't put him down as that.' Feather frowned. 'Wish I could. But he's feeding us lies, I'm sure of that much.'

'But not all lies,' said Anstruther quickly. In a back-handed way he was Totty Bow's patron, it was to him Totty had first confessed, he had an interest in maintaining his guilt. 'He knew the girl. We showed him a gallery of different photographs and he picked her out at once. Oh, he knew her.'

'But has he killed her?' This was Feather. 'You can't work him out, can you? Where's the body? He doesn't seem to know, might be in the river ... We need more background on him. I mean, what is he?'

Charmian spoke, almost for the first time. 'I don't know exactly what he is now, but I know who he was.'

Feather looked at her.

'He was Tommy Brosser. Kept the same initials, you see. He was only twelve at the time, so he won't be on the records anywhere, too young.'

'So what did he do?'

'Bestiality it was that time, but he may have progressed onward and upward since then. On present evidence, I'd say he had. Not a high IQ, but I never knew whether that was an act.'

'Where'd he come from?'

'Need you ask? Cheasey'.

'Did you see his face?'

'Yes,' said Feather shortly. 'He's a liar.'

Charmian nodded. 'And did you see his shoes?'

'New, spitting new. And not cheap.'

So Feather had seen what she had seen. 'He's in the money. And he isn't frightened. He's confessed to killing her, but he says it was an accident. He doesn't seem to know where her body is, it's all a blur. He doesn't think much is going to happen to him.'

'So what will you do?'

'Hang on to him for the time being . . . And look for the body.'

Feather sounded matter of fact and calm as if he knew he was doing the right thing. Sarah Holt might be dead, her body might be in the river or it might be elsewhere.

A doubtful meal had been offered him but he had eaten of it and was satisfied.

Totty had sounded as if he too was satisfied. An appetite filled here as well?

Charmian mouthed a few quiet words: Do some dogs eat and fall quiet?

She let herself into the quiet dark house in Maid of Honour Row. Muff wound herself round her ankles and she bent to stroke the soft fur.

'Humphrey? You still here?' He was of course, he had to be, there was his car in the street.

No one answered.

He was lying on the bed, asleep.

She drew the cover over him with a gentle touch. In the middle of the night she put her arms round him and held him. He had come home to her for comfort and support and assurance and she knew she could offer it.

Whispers from the Past

'She's a girl, you have to talk to her, let her know how to behave, tell her how dangerous it is to be a woman if she doesn't tread careful, keep the rules.'

'Nan, times have changed.'

'They never change for girls, more fool you if you think they do.'

Jane Cooper was very sick during her confinement, poor and naked.

Hanged.

Sarah Allen had been forced to leave her work when she became pregnant. She suffocated her infant in the workhouse.

Hanged also.

Chapter Ten

'I did what I could to make the baby's rest the prettier and gentler; laid it on a shelf and covered it with my own handkerchief.'

Bleak House

In the night, she whispered: 'I think, I really do think, that Feather's been got at in some way. I can say this now aloud, to you, because you are dead asleep and not listening. I also think that Totty Bow is a bloody liar and has been paid to tell lies, but maybe bits of the truth are there too.' She leaned closer to Humphrey. 'Unluckily, which bits are far from clear. Is the girl dead or alive? Is she in the river or not?'

Having unburdened herself, she tucked herself round him, and went to sleep.

No one sleeps late with an independent-minded vigorous young cat in the house and although Muff was not as young as she had been when she had joined up with Charmian, she showed no sign of ageing yet.

Her voice was usually raised in the house so Charmian was not surprised to hear a long wail close to her ear. But she was surprised that it came with a chink of china and a strong smell of coffee. She rolled over towards the smell and opened her eyes.

A tray of coffee and toast was on the table beside her. So was Muff, whose paw was reaching out towards the butter.

'Hop it, Muff.' Humphrey lifted the cat down, then sat on the edge of the bed. 'Took me some time assembling that tray of breakfast, love, so eat it up before it gets cold.'

The coffee was strong and hot. 'You look better this morning.'

'I had a good night's rest. Which was more than you had.'

'I was late.' Charmian buttered some toast and took a bite. Food did help to clear the mind. 'The man that was brought in, lad really, confessed to killing Sarah Holt, but I think he told more lies than truth.'

'You always get the false confessor, don't you? Aren't there plenty of them around?'

'They're not all like Totty, he's an unusual kind of horror. Dante would have found a special little hell for him.'

Death and Dante were strong in her mind at that moment. Toast wasn't helping to wipe out hell this morning.

'I did hear some of the things you were muttering at me.' Humphrey, who was fully dressed and had clearly been awake and around for some time, poured some coffee for himself. 'Something about a chap called Feather.'

'Dan Feather. I like him, used to like him, but I felt a kind of double talk last night. I wonder if anyone's leaning on him and if so why?' She sipped the coffee. 'He has local loyalties, they may operate. Or am I just tired, suspicious, and paranoiac?'

'Well, it has happened.' And sometimes her anger had lashed out over him. 'But it's a nasty business. It always is with children.'

'I think it's going to get nastier.' She threw back the

blankets. 'I suppose I'd better get up and start the day. Things get better if you face them. As a rule . . . We've both got things to face.'

'I think I've faced mine. With your help.'

'Thank you for saying that.' She grabbed her dressing-gown and went to the looking-glass. Her hair needed attention, she would have to go to see her hairdresser. 'I must have been pulling this in the night.'

He picked up the tray. 'You could have been. You had a nightmare last night. I was worried about you.'

'I did?' She turned away from the glass to stare at him. 'What did I do?'

'Talked a bit. I couldn't make all of it out.'

'What was I saying?' If there was a thing she hated, it was being out of control, and a nightmare was a prime example.

He hesitated. 'Seemed to be about smothering a child. You said it several times. I thought you were crying and tried to comfort you but you pushed me away.'

'I'm sorry.'

'I didn't take it personally. It wasn't me you were pushing away, someone else entirely.'

'I don't remember any of it.' But this was not quite true. Odd bits of memory were pushing through like dry twigs through mud. Death certainly figured, someone's death, perhaps an infant. 'I have been thinking about child murder and infanticide lately, had it pushed at me, so I suppose I can't be surprised if I dream.'

'Bones and babies and dead boys and missing little girls, you've had the lot. No wonder you talked about hanging.'

'Did I? I don't like the idea of capital punishment any more.'

'Not even for people like Totty?'

'Oh, him . . . I don't know. Castration, maybe.' But she had an idea that in her dream it was she herself who had hanged. No, surely not. It was symbols, anyway. 'Totty's the sort of little weasel that will get away with it some-how, and he knows it. But I'm not happy with his con-fession and I'm not happy with the way Feather is taking it. He doesn't believe him, but I have the feeling that he just might settle for Totty as the perpetrator.'

'The child may turn up.'

'Think so?'

There was a moment of silence while she finished dressing. Jeans and sweater, this was no day for dressing smartly. Sackcloth and ashes felt the thing.

'I don't like the family's line. No truth there, either. But families do cover up in matters of this sort, there's always something to hide.'

'Want me to talk to Loomis? I could do. I used to know him pretty well. He might say more to me.'

'Yes, thank you. Good idea.'

'I'll telephone.'

'Now that you're going, I don't want to lose you. I want to hang on to you.'

'You can do that. You've cured me, I think.'

'I wish.'

'I'm going to believe it.' Yesterday he had needed help from her, today it was her turn. In the mysterious way that happens in close relationships, power, energy, strength, whatever it was, had seeped from one to the other. He had been weak and was now strong. 'Go and see Mr Madge, talk about the locket, you'll never iden-tify the baby but you can talk about the locket. It's heavy gold.'

She was obsessed by that little bag of dry bones to which they had given due burial, last night he had not known what advice to give, this morning all was clear: she was used to thinking about problems in a concrete way and it might help her to do so now. 'Madge can't tell you the name of the child but he can date the object and then you consult parish registers and birth registers.'

'I doubt the birth of that child was ever registered.'

'You never know. You might get some clue to a family name, then you can guess. Isn't that what you do all the time?'

'I ought to shoot you for saying that,' but she was laughing, he had achieved that much at any rate.

Their dispositions were soon made. He was off to London and then possibly to Rome, he would telephone from wherever. He was purposely vague. She would finish dressing and go off to work.

She consulted her diary where, as only to be expected, there was the usual hodge-podge of engagements and duties, some of which she would enjoy doing and others which she would rather ignore. In the first category came the promise to attend, nay, to open, a charity bazaar in Merrywick, a promise extracted from her by her friend Winifred Eagle. Once she got there, if she got there (and she'd better, or Winifred or Birdie Peacock would issue a mandatory spell of bad luck), she would enjoy it. So much for that in the evening. In the second less happy group of engagements, she must chair a committee on juvenile crime in the district. This was the third meeting of the committee, whose members manifested lower spirits with each session, since they felt hopeless and helpless. There had been one hilarious moment however when they had interviewed a trio of lads who had volunteered to talk to them, they had arrived on foot, kempt, clean, and recently purified, given their spiel on the newly discovered happiness of virtue, and left in three cars stolen from the committee car park, Charmian's being one. It was laugh or cry, and they had decided to laugh. The cars had turned up later that day not far away, neatly parked side by side, and of course, by that time, wheel-clamped. The joke was on them.

There were also various inquiries she had initiated where she must read the reports. But her first responsibility was to Rewley.

'I thought you'd want to know about last night.'

'Certainly would. Especially as Dan Feather walked right past me this morning without a word. To be honest, I don't think he saw me, but he has his moods, you know. He doesn't like living in a city, not even Windsor, he's a countryman pure and simple, but he's had his ambitions.'

'He wasn't talking to himself as he walked past?'

Rewley laughed. 'No, and if he had been he wouldn't have let me read him, he's on to me there, he puts his hand up. I was on his team for a while just after I got out of the uniformed branch and into plain clothes; he regarded me as an aberration of nature, I think, and he got rid of me as soon as he could.'

'He may be in a bad mood because his girlfriend is going off to Canada with her daughter. Whether for ever or just for a holiday no one seems to know. Opinion is he doesn't know himself.'

Not like Rewley to gossip so he must have thought it worth her while to know. Which it was, of course; if Feather was in a difficult position she would have to walk with even greater care than usual.

'He's a friend of Clive Barney.' Rewley's voice was carefully vague. 'Walked their beat together.'

Ah, now he was saying something. And something she didn't want to hear. Clive Barney had been in charge of the investigation of the murders in Bridewell, a charming village where Charmian had, in a passing way, owned a house. And also in a passing way, there had been a relationship between her and Barney. It had been very private and neither of them had talked about it, but, as was to be expected, other people had noticed and done the talking for them. When Charmian had drawn away, Clive Barney had been hurt. He was too reserved and proud a man to say much, but if there was pain, then Dan Feather would have seen it.

Clive had taken it well when she had made it clear that was it, thus far and no further, he had nodded, said it was probably the right thing, but a pity because he liked her a lot, and would she like another drink? (They were in the bar in a smart country hotel in a village between Oxford and Windsor where they had met and gone on meeting.) But she had heard that he had taken a spell of leave just after (but anyone might do so, after all), and then later she had heard a rumour (that might not be true) that he was considering a transfer.

None of us like to think of our mistakes, the times we have not behaved well, and Charmian was no exception. She realized that every thought about Barney was set around with brackets and that was what he was in her life: a man in brackets, not part of the main stream. This was not something to be proud of for either party but she had been able to bury the thought while apparently he had not.

Barney wasn't the sort to have said much to Dan Feather, but the signal Charmian was getting from Rewley was that he had said something, enough.

'I think Feather may be keeping something back from you.'

'I'm sure he is, I'd expect it.'

'If you'd ask he'd tell, but he's hoping you won't ask.'

'So, you know what it is?'

'Well, they can't resist joking around that team, not Feather himself so much but the others . . .'

The Feather Fan Club, she thought.

'Simes is the worst. He was kidding around this morning saying that Feather had a new witness who had seen the girl around with a man.'

'Is that so funny?'

'It was to Simes because from the description it sounded like the child's father, Peter Loomis.'

'Who is this witness?'

'Don't know that, or whether it's a trustworthy source, but he must think so, he's no fool,' said Rewley with regret, 'but the report came in last night so Feather knew even as he was questioning Totty Bow. It would be a treat for him to get Loomis, he's always disliked him.'

'He didn't work on the case, did he? It was the Met.'

'No, but Feather has a grudge against Loomis, it goes way back.'

'Don't tell me Feather and Loomis were at school together and have hated each other ever since?'

'No, Loomis is probably Summerfields and Eton and Feather, who knows? But there is a connection. Something to do with a close relative who worked for the family and was treated badly. I believe it was a cousin who was a gardener for them and was dismissed for pulling up the wrong plants.'

Personal relationships shouldn't influence an investigation, but they so often did. 'So Feather had decided even last night that Totty Bow had nothing to do with the girl and was lying?'

'No, not entirely, he's hoping to tie Totty in somewhere, because he doesn't like him either.'

'Neither do I. Thank you for telling me. I may hear from him myself.'

She thought she heard Rewley laugh.

She gave Muff breakfast and did a modest amount of tidying the house; there was enough disorder and dirt and blood in her working life to make her want tidiness at home.

All the time she was debating: Who was this witness? Was it Amy Mercer again? No, Feather wouldn't take that tale twice from the same woman.

She rang Kate, had a brief conversation during which she learnt from Kate that her mother, Anny, was coming back to Windsor.

'She's ordered what she insists on calling a layette from the White House. I didn't think babies wore layettes now. Especially hand-embroidered with initials . . . You need a coronet or two to justify that sort of thing. I don't know what my darling will say.'

Charmian grinned to herself. Which is why Anny is doing it, Anny and Rewley had never seen eye to eye.

'Never mind, I'm on your side.'

'Thanks, Char. How did your mother treat you?'

'Does,' corrected Charmian, 'she's still alive, but I had a very alarming old grandmother.'

Kate sounded full of life and happy. Vibrant, energetic, thank goodness. 'I'll be in to see you,' Charmian promised.

The clock in the kitchen tinkled out the hour. If she hurried she would not be too late for her first appointment of the day. As she was slipping her papers into her briefcase the telephone rang. She let the answerphone deal with it, listening for a moment, and when she heard Dan Feather's voice, she picked up the receiver.

'I am here, just slow getting to the phone.' Not true and he probably knew it. 'What were you saying?'

'Something new came in, and I thought you ought to know.'

'Oh yes?' She couldn't resist a hint of satisfaction in her voice. 'Another woman spectator sport? She saw the girl with her father? Is that it?'

'Oh, you've heard that, have you?'

'It did get to me.'

'I thought it might do.' He sounded amused. 'You used the word sport, I think that story was just a bit of sport on the part of one or two chaps. A joke.'

'You mean they made it up? A lie?' Her tone was bleak. She didn't relish being made a joke.

'Just fooling around . . . they didn't know they could be overheard.'

'Oh, I understand.' And she did: the story had been fed to Rewley for him to pass on to her. They both hated being laughed at. Damn you, Feather, she thought. I'll get back at you. Anger being a wasted emotion unless you did something about it. But she controlled her fury. 'So what is the real story?'

Feather reined in his amusement, he had scored his goal and could rest on that for a moment, but business was business, he became serious: 'Not a story this time, more a viewing. A picture.'

'Go on.'

'As you know, we've been calling in all the security videos made by various outfits in the town: shops, banks, building societies. Most of them are inside views but several focus on the streets.'

Charmian understood: this was a royal town with a castle, a barracks, and a daily Army parade through the streets as the guard changed. Security was tight and watchfulness the word.

'The story that the girl had been seen in Peascod Street made the search important, even if we didn't believe it.'

'You didn't believe it?'

'Jury is still out. What about you?'

Charmian didn't answer. 'Go on about the video. What have you got?' Obviously there was something.

'In one shot there is a kid that looks like Joe, he's moving down the street.'

'So?' Nothing too surprising here, Joe had been in and around the town. What would be helpful would be if he was clearly with someone. Say Totty. Totty Bow in the shot would be a marvel to receive.

'In the next frame, when he had moved a bit, there is the back of a girl child who might just be Sarah Holt.'

'I'd like to see it.'

'You shall . . . whenever it suits.' Having scored his joke, he was being obliging. 'We'll be showing the mother.'

'Of course you will.' She was thinking that she would like to see how Biddy reacted. 'When? I'll come along.'

'Not fixed yet. I'll leave a message for you.'

'Thank you. I'll be in and out.'

'Did you see my TV appeal? Went out on the morning news. Be repeated this lunch time and later. On national and local networks. I'm hopeful of a reaction. We usually drag in the calls even if you have to weed them out. So I'll see you.'

End of conversation, she agreed she would wait for the message, just for the moment, she was on the end of his hook.

But he didn't let her go just then.

'Well what did you make of my TV appeal? On the Breakfast Show. I thought it went well, the producer said it caught a big audience.'

'I'm sorry, I didn't see it. I'll watch later.' He sounded pleased with himself.

'On again on the main news, all channels.'

Yes, definitely he liked being a media personality. She was learning more about Dan Feather every day. Also more about herself, because she felt a small pang, just a little tweak, of envy.

She was on the point of leaving the house when the doorbell rang. Once, twice, loudly.

On the doorstep was Amy Mercer carrying a bag with what looked like an apron in it and wearing a big smile.

'I've come to work. Clean your house. As arranged.' She was in , still smiling, before Charmian could speak. 'Don't say you don't want me. But I can see you do.' She was taking a brisk look around the hall and into the kitchen. 'In need of a good clean up, I'd say. I don't think your last lady did you justice.'

Charmian hesitated, she was about to leave: she knew nothing about the woman beyond her own observation, but she thought she was honest. She decided to trust her, they could talk money later.

She followed her new helper into the kitchen. 'Right, well go ahead, you'll find cleaning things in that cupboard, and the broom and brushes in with them.'

Amy started bustling around with a pleased look, she was a pretty woman except for a small scar across her cheek, but she covered this well with make up.

'What about pay?'

'The usual, by the hour. We can settle that later.'

'I have to go now.' Charmian once again made a move to leave, there seemed no end to this morning already.

At the door, she decided that trust worked both ways.

'Would it distress you very much if you learned that Sarah was dead?'

'But I saw her. Twice, I said so.'

'I know, but if you were wrong, and the child was dead. Could you face that? Death?'

Amy blinked. 'I guess it's like full-frontal nudity, you have to take it head on when it comes your way.'

Charmian drove down Maid of Honour Row, turned right in Prince Consort Place, and then into Royal Road. There was very little traffic, she was too late for those hastening towards trains and offices and too early for the shoppers and ladies going to the hairdressers.

She was reminded of her own need for the services of her good friend Beryl Andrea Barker, hairdresser and retired (or so Charmian trusted) criminal. She considered making an appointment for today, Baby was good about fitting her in, which was understandable since not only had they known each other for many years, been professionally acquainted on different sides of the law, but somehow they had ended up friends. Charmian found Baby a good source of informed gossip. Baby also had a shrewd eye for a lie when she heard one, sorting out truth and falsehood with the skill of one who had heard them all.

And there were a lot of lies floating round this case.

Charmian was approaching the corner of Royal Road where it runs into Castlereagh Street and thence on towards her office, when her car telephone rang. The road was quiet here without a line of parked cars so she steered into the side.

'Ah, got you.' Feather sounded jovial. 'Been ringing around, this was my last try. It's about viewing the video in company with the mother, that's what you wanted?'

'It was on offer, wasn't it?'

'She won't come except in a group, father and grand-mother to be included. To get one, you've got to have the lot. Any objection?'

'There might have been advantages in letting them view separately. Should be interesting, though. Have to watch them.' Faces often revealed more, much more, than speech. She wondered if they wouldn't let Biddy come on her own, she thought she had picked up family tensions. 'Think she'll bring the dolls as well?'

Feather ignored her black joke. 'I've had to be accom-modating about time: four o'clock this afternoon. Any good to you? I might be able to negotiate a slightly later time.'

'I'll take four o'clock.' It was interesting that he used the word negotiate. 'I can do it.'

'And we're going on looking for a body. Just in case. We keep trying.'

They always kept trying. As she drove away, she thought of some of the people she had worked with in the past, who had kept trying: Inspector Fred Elman, Superintendent Father, Clive Barney (she mustn't keep thinking about him), all now promoted, retired or moved away.

She drove on, stopped at intervals by traffic lights and pedestrians crossing. A few yards ahead was the shop of Mr Madge, Jeweller to the Queen. The Queen was Queen Victoria but the first queen whom the family had served had been Charlotte, wife to George III whose portrait hung in the shop. Mr Madge, who was at the shop window setting one brilliant diamond ring into position with the air of one arranging a crown or at the very least a coronet, saw her and waved his hand.

There was a kind of royal command in the wave,

which she found herself obeying. In front of the shop was an old-fashioned cobbled stretch of road on which motorists avoided parking because it looked so old and holy somehow, and also because they instinctively knew that it would damage their suspension and tyres. Charmian bumped her way across to stop outside the shop.

The exterior had always charmed her, with its gentle crooked roof and the sloping walls with their air of having settled into the earth before the rest of the town was built, and the shop window with its narrow panes made her think of the Old Curiosity Shop, although it has to be said that if there were curiosities in Mr Madge's emporium they would have been mighty expensive ones since he did not deal in trifles.

'Any news?' he asked at once. 'I saw the television interview. Bound to get results, I thought.'

'Bit early for any result on that.'

'True, true.' He had moved back to the old-fashioned counter on which a few choice objects were displayed. 'They usually do though, don't they? People ring in, trying to help.'

He keeps too much valuable stuff around, Charmian thought almost angrily, as she had done often in the past. Everyone knows he does, why isn't he robbed? And yet he never was.

'It's not all the real news,' she said. 'People invent scenes, sometimes even think they saw what they didn't. But yes, we do get lucky. I hope we do this time.'

'It's sad to think of an old family like that dying out, isn't it?'

Charmian didn't think it mattered very much, but did not say so.

'There was a brother, you know, little Anthony.'

'Little?'

'He died young, a mere baby, he's buried in the family vault. They have their own chapel, used to have a chaplain once but that's long gone.'

'So I should imagine.'

'Ah, you're not sympathetic. You can't be.'

'I am, I like the idea of old landed families, but perhaps it isn't an idea for today. You seem to know a lot about them.'

Mr Madge had taken up a soft yellow duster with which he was polishing an antique silver rose bowl, and he continued with this gentle pursuit, performed in a careful, loving manner while he talked.

The shop was dusky and quiet, crowded as ever. One or two new objects seemed to have arrived to join the throng. Charmian didn't remember seeing that parure of opals set in silver and displayed on a bed of black velvet. And was that carnival mask of gold and emerald with glitter as of diamonds round the eyes, for sale or decoration? He must have a small fortune tied here.

As well as the portrait of Queen Charlotte, Mr Madge had added some photographs of his own, his father, his grandfather, and faded sepia pictures from an even more distant past. You trace the resemblance from generation to generation and it was there in William Madge himself: tall, delicately boned hands and face with a firm strong mouth and nose.

The air of the shop was scented by a great bowl of potpourri set on a side table of fine old walnut, undoubtedly valuable. The china dish itself looked like Meissen and probably was.

What a place, Charmian thought, looking at Mr Madge as he mused on, full of his memories.

'I was always there as a child. My father, and his father before him and great-grandpa before that, used to go there once a week to wind the clocks, and I often went with them and had tea in the kitchen. I did the clocks myself for a long time, I don't go now, of course, those days are over. I don't know who attends to the clocks now. Mr Peter perhaps. More likely her ladyship. She knows all about the house and everything in it.'

He put down the silver he was polishing: 'Come and see what I've got,' he said in a secretive way. 'In here.' He led her into a back room which was even darker and more crowded than the shop. Here he switched on a lamp, opened a morocco-leather box to reveal the solid glitter of a large diadem. It had a high curving baroque front, set with emeralds and diamonds. It also had a kind of battered, elderly look as if it needed a helping hand.

'I'm repairing it, a big job.' He spoke with satisfaction. 'Splendid thing, isn't it? Part of the old Russian crown jewels.'

'Wherever did it come from?'

Mr Madge put his finger to his nose. 'Ah, you may ask . . . We all know which member of the royal family had a taste for picking up valuable articles at bargain price . . . No names, you know. Well, it's in the blood, and I won't say who the buyer is but you can make a guess. Came from Russia very very recently. Where it's been all these years, I couldn't say, but it's here now to stay.' Something amused in his voice, told her that, in spite of his genuine love and admiration in all their ranks for the descendants of George III and his Queen, he also had the cynical scepticism enjoyed by all true courtiers. They knew the emperor had no clothes, nor did they care, it was their joke too.

'Very handsome, isn't it? Not quite what you and I would want to wear, conducive to a bad headache, crowns are, you know.' No doubting his quiet amusement now. 'And badly in need of a clean. My bill will be a pretty one, I assure you.'

In this quiet dark room where the scent of dried roses and lavender floated in from the outer shop, Charmian felt bold enough to dig in her purse to bring out the gold locket.

'I showed you a photograph of this before. Can you look at it and see what you can tell me about it?'

Mr Madge held the locket under the lamp. 'Ah now,' he examined it closely, glass loup wedged firmly into his eye. 'Now that is one of ours. We sold that to whoever it was. I know the mark, we always put our own special mark.'

He let Charmian see a tiny curlicue.

'That'll be my father's mark ... No, I correct myself, I believe it is Grandpa's.'

'There's a difference?'

'Oh yes, my mark is straighter, more angular, I haven't the freedom of line that my father used. He had better control of wrist and fingers, lovely slender entwined line he could produce. Grandpa was a thorough Victorian and his work reproduces that, he managed a very florid, well – embellished circle. Yes, this one is his.'

'I believe you. I don't suppose . . .' No, it couldn't be done after all these years. 'You can't trace who bought it?' And if he could, then it might be a present, handed on.

'I can look in my books. I have the shop records going back to Josiah Madge in 1847. Not easy to read owing to mice and damp but I have the stuff.'

'It would interest me.'

'May I keep it while I search?'

She thought about it, but he would be a careful custodian. 'Yes, for a bit.'

'I'll lock it away . . . but examining it slowly may give me some pointers . . . I don't know, but it may . . .' He hesitated, then asked the question he had been longing to put: 'Is it connected with Sarah?'

Charmian hesitated, wondering what to say. 'No, not exactly, but one thing has led to another.' Connected more closely with a little bag of bones.

He led her to the door with his usual politeness, but there he paused to point out a picture hanging on the wall by the door. 'This is the Big House.'

Charmian moved closer, it was placed high but she could see it. Not a photograph but a charcoal sketch, obviously by an amateur but with charm.

'You did it?' she said, turning to him.

'Twelve years old, I was. I had some talent then, but it melted away.'

The house was low and old, dark stone covered here and there with ivy. On either side a range of buildings, one side having a clock, and the other a bell tower, stables perhaps. In the distance a small churchlike structure, which must be the chapel.

'You admire the house?' It seemed evident to her.

'Respect. Some houses command respect.'

Crouching there with the hills on either side, the side wings stretched like paws, it was like an animal.

If ever a house could growl, this one could.

Mr Madge delivered his judgement, with satisfaction it seemed to her: 'A house like no other.'

Chapter Eleven

' "Lady Dedlock, my dear Lady, my good Lady, my
kind Lady. You must have a heart to feel for me,
you must have a heart to forgive me. I was in this
family before you were born." '

Bleak House

Inside the house that was like no other, Peter Loomis
was talking to his mother in her own sitting-room, still
called the boudoir by her and the one old servant who
had been with her all her life and had been born in the
household itself. Things like that wouldn't go on much
longer, as they both knew and as everyone told them,
but the two of them kept up the old ways. Emily Grahamden was m'lady and her servant was 'My Lady's
own maid'. It didn't mean servility since they were equally rude to each other, also equally kind on occasion,
but it suited them.

It was mid-afternoon on that dark November day so
that the lamps were already lit over Chantrey House,
her ladyship liking a lot of light. In this, her own particular room, the light was diffused and gentle. One silver
lamp-stand in the shape of a naked lady who held an
opalescent lampshade aloft was matched by a tall floor
lamp with a pleated silk shade. A small pyramid of
burning oil, scented by sandalwood, smoked
underneath.

The boudoir had been decorated by Emily's mother

in a high early nineteen-twenties style, sleek and angular with a fine display of French black-enamelled furniture made in 1926, set out with Lalique glass, all remotely reflected in a large Venetian mirror. In this looking-glass, Emily was doing her face. She had been out, had only just got back, and would have described her face, if asked, as ravaged. She felt ravaged inside, life was pinching her hard, but she had survived before and would do so now.

'Are you going to be much longer, Mama?' Peter was so familiar with the room that he hardly saw it, but once or twice recently he had thought that the ambience of the room created by his grandmother, a friend of Noël Coward and an ex-Gaiety girl, had influenced his life, making him smoke too much, drink too much, and be unhappy in love. You can't blame a room for your life, but he would dearly like to have done. He took a straw-coloured cigarette from a gold and platinum case, which had been Grandma's wedding gift to her husband.

'As long as I like, dear,' she said calmly. 'When you are my age it takes longer to put yourself together.' She went to the door and called loudly: 'Mousie, Mousie, bring me my fur coat.'

A distant voice called back: 'Get it yourself, m'lady.'

'Oh come on, Mousie. Who pays your wages?'

'Who earns it, three times over? All right, all right, I'm coming.'

Peter said: 'You let her get away with too much.'

'She has a lot to do.'

'I don't know why you got rid of Amy.'

'I did not get rid of Amy, as you put it, she left. She didn't get on with Mousie.' Who had hit Amy with the back of her hand on which a ring had torn her cheek. Amy had departed at once.

'Oh, I know Mousie is the one who counts.' Peter had wondered what the quarrel was about but it almost certainly had something to do with his mother. Secrets, he thought, damn them both. But he had his own sad secrets.

'Loyalty is to be treasured,' said his mother. 'I didn't trust Amy.'

'She was a nice woman. And brave. I've never forgotten how she rescued my terrier from the bulldog.'

'People will sometimes do things for animals that they won't do for humans. I think that wrong.'

There was a sharp note in her voice which her son registered.

'I love Sarah. I want you to know that.' His hands were shaking as he took out another cigarette. He hadn't finished the first.

Emily Grahamden put away her bright red lipstick.

'Smoking again, I see. Thought you'd given it up.'

'I'm upset.'

'Which is precisely why I'm letting Mousie alone: she's upset, I'm upset, we're all upset. It's very upsetting having to see this video.' She went to the door to shout once more: 'I'm still waiting. If you want to come too, bring your own coat.'

Peter said: 'I don't think she should come.'

'Certainly she should, she's as good a witness as we are. Biddy's the one I wish we could leave behind. Unfortunately we cannot. Shall we try?'

'What a monster you are.'

The door was flung open as Mousie marched in, carrying a long dark mink coat and wearing her own thick tweed, buttoned to the neck. 'Here you are, my lady.' She held out the coat so her employer could insert her arms. 'You're putting on weight. I'm coming.'

Mrs Moucher was the only full-time servant now employed by Lady Grahamden, since Amy had been given notice. Or departed, whichever version you followed. Mousie was the nickname Emily had given her as a child and now she knew no other name; she had started as a kitchen maid and now controlled the household under her Ladyship's domineering eye. Daily staff came and went.

They were much of a height and Emily Grahamden knew, although she was not going to make a point of it, that the grey tweed was a coat of her own from Lachasse that she had by no means made up her mind to cease wearing.

Peter stood up. 'Come on, then, let's get going. Biddy will be waiting.'

'I don't know why she can't drive herself.'

'Because I'm driving her. And it looks better if we all go as a family. God knows we're a rum enough family, anyway.'

Mousie said: 'I put this coat on, m'lady, because I thought you'd want me to look nice, and my old red coat is really past it, besides not being the suitable colour for such a sad occasion.'

'It's not a funeral, Mousie,' said Peter Loomis. 'Just a viewing of a video with a lot of policemen watching our faces.'

'No one suspects you of anything, Mr Peter.'

'Don't they just? I've been there before, don't forget. That large policeman who isn't nearly as nice as he pretends let me know they link Sarah's disappearance with a boy whose body was found. You've heard about that? I dare say he thinks I did the boy in.'

'No one forgets what you've been through, Mr Peter,' said Mousie with dignity.

'I don't think we need fear the police,' said Lady Grahamden. 'Anyway, not the fat one. I'm not so sure about the woman.'

'He's not fat, Mother. Just large.'

The three walked out into the dusk to where the big old Rolls stood in the drive.

'We are taking that, are we?' asked Peter. 'Why not my car?'

'A Rolls always commands respect,' said his mother.

'Which of us is going to drive?'

Mousie volunteered. 'I will if you like.' She had her own battered car.

'No, certainly not. A Rolls is a man's car to drive.' She looked at her son.

'I always intended to drive.' He was drawing on his gloves. 'Why don't you get a chauffeur again.'

'I can't afford it.'

'You always afford what you want, Mama.'

'I can drive her ladyship as well as anyone,' said Mousie. 'She can always ask me.'

The three of them walked out on to the gravelled drive which curved in front of the house. The big car was already there waiting for them. Peter locked the house, checking that the alarms were switched on, and glancing across to the old stables where Mrs Moucher lived.

'How's Moucher?' he asked, reminded of her husband's existence. His was a secret absentee presence as he was a merchant seaman.

'Away at sea.'

He was always away at sea, Peter had long surmised that Mrs Moucher could only tolerate a husband who was away a good deal. Perhaps it worked that way for Moucher too. He might prefer the North Sea or even the Arctic Ocean to home with his Mousie.

'Any particular sea?'

'The Caribbean. It's a cruise.'

He helped the two women into the back of the car before taking the wheel. He sat for a moment, his hands cold and tense and yet sweating. He dreaded what lay ahead.

The video and seeing Biddy and seeing Biddy watching the video. He knew this was going to be painful for her. 'I've let you down, Biddy, and been cruel to you and there's every chance I'll do it again.'

She brought it out in him, with that soft, passive way of hers. The child, Sarah, had something of the same manner in her too, God help her.

He shuddered, he couldn't help it.

'Get on with it, Peter,' came from behind. No shuddering there, just grim and utter determination to face what must be faced and see it through.

He got on with it.

It was a short fifteen-minute drive to Biddy's house, the Vinery, through dark lanes, with the smell of cattle on the air, and there was Biddy, waiting for them at the door of her house, quiet but tense, waiting as ever for the blow, which was always hanging over her, to fall. It fell daily, she survived it to wait for the next one. She was buttoned wrongly into her coat, and her hair was untidy. He looked at her with love and sadness.

He stopped the car and waited, not getting out. Biddy stood where she was.

'I don't want to come.'

'Help her, Peter.' Lady Grahamden opened the door. 'Sit in the back with us.'

'Come along, Biddy. You must come. We are going along to watch a video to see if Sarah has been captured by some pervert. That seems to be what the police are suggesting.'

'There was no need to say that, Peter.'

'On the contrary, there is every need. We might as well know what we are facing.'

Helped by Peter, or pushed along by him, because it felt like being pushed, Biddy got into the car where she disposed her body, legs and arms to be no trouble to anyone, carefully not touching Lady Grahamden. Whether Sarah was dead or not, she knew she herself was, and had been for some time now.

Peter drove off, hoping that Biddy was not too drunk, she had certainly been at the bottle, for which he did not blame her, but it gave him the uneasy feeling that she knew more about the disappearance of his daughter (because Sarah was his daughter, however he had acted) than she was saying.

'I didn't kill my wife,' he said inside himself, 'but no one's ever going to believe me, especially now.'

And really, sometimes, he hardly believed himself.

He parked the car, squeezing the Rolls in between two police cars and into a slot marked *For the Use of the Chief Constable*. He took some pleasure in doing this, knew there would be trouble and didn't care. The dark Rolls had a regal look, perhaps they would think it was the Queen.

He led his trio of ladies towards the room indicated to them, then stood back to let them walk in first. Always the gentleman.

The room was over-full with the police team and the technicians setting up the video. He saw Charmian Daniels in one corner. She would not be one of his believers. He wondered what Biddy had told Lady Mary Erskine and what Lady Mary had told Charmian. Nothing good.

He remembered Lady Mary's voice as she cornered him at the Castle party, soft but cold and clear as she could be when angry. No angel herself, her own record not unspotted, as he would like to have pointed out: 'I don't believe you killed your wife, and you know I don't believe it, but you damaged Biddy, perhaps for ever. She will never settle to her marriage with James while you are around. And it's James she loves, get that? Not you.'

There are darker truths here than you know, Lady Mary.

He caught Charmian's eye. Just as well you can't read my thoughts.

But to a certain extent, Charmian could. No lip reader like Rewley or extra-sensorily aided, like her friends the white witches, Charmian was a good guesser.

She saw a man who was angry, uneasy, and uncomfortable. He won't be any good to us. I suppose he will look at the video but I doubt if he will see it.

She knew from Lady Mary that he was as successful a merchant banker in the City as a man can be who has good connections but has stood his trial for murder, and was as popular there as a man can be with the same reservation as before.

It wasn't her show, Dan Feather was managing it, so she sat back while he got Lady Grahamden and Mrs Moucher and Biddy Holt into their seats. No one took any notice of her, which was how she wanted it, she sat back, ready to observe.

'There's no hurry, we can take our time and run the film backwards if we want, and freeze it as we want for you to get a good look . . . The image varies, of course, some shots are better than others . . . But where we are lucky is that it's in colour. Most outside videos are black and white. This one isn't.' He was being jovial.

The room went quiet as the video was played. Charmian watched the screen but also watched the watchers.

There was Peascod Street on a late autumn afternoon with street lights coming on, shoppers came into view, then disappeared. A cyclist walked his bike. A dog shot across the screen and disappeared. Two women were caught full face. A figure, a young man, walking forward, he seemed to be approaching someone.

Totty, his back, his face as he turned.

Then a boy somehow sliding into view.

Feather said: 'Freeze it there.' He let the image sink in. Mrs Moucher said nothing, nor did Peter Loomis. Charmian thought that Biddy had closed her eyes. Only Lady Grahamden reacted.

'Anyone there you recognize?'

Silence.

'Now there's a face . . . the young man, does he mean anything to you?'

Lady Grahamden and Mrs Moucher looked, then turned to each other. A shrug seemed to pass between them. 'No.' Lady Grahamden answered for them both.

'Mrs Holt?'

Biddy hardly looked at the screen before shaking her head.

'Mr Loomis? What about you?'

'Never seen him.'

Not one of them admitted to knowing him. Dan Feather was not too discouraged since he would have been surprised if they had. Totty did not move in their social circles.

Then he asked to look at the boy.

Lady Grahamden surveyed the face. 'Not a good picture, is it?' Nor was it, the boy had turned aside and was seen in profile.

'Who is it?'

Feather took it slowly: 'We think a boy called Joe, surname hard to establish.' In his short career it appeared that Joe had had several names.

Lady Grahamden studied the frame. 'Dead?'

'Dead.' Feather nodded his head and let his hands move together in vague benediction. 'Dead, m'lady.'

There was a moment of silence. Then he said, and now he was asking the question to which he really wanted an answer, 'Look to the right of the boy. Do you see a girl? A young girl. We think she might be Sarah.'

'But she has her back to us.'

'Try . . . Mrs Holt, does this say anything to you?'

Biddy hardly took a look. 'That is not Sarah.'

'Are you sure? Please give her a good look . . . What about the clothes?'

'Those are not Sarah's clothes.'

Feather turned to Lady Grahamden. She shook her head. 'No.'

'Mrs Moucher?'

'Too thin and tall,' she said succinctly. 'As to clothes, can't say.'

'Mr Loomis?'

Peter stared at the screen. 'I've got an idea that I've seen the boy, but probably not . . . as for the other child, no, not Sarah.'

Charmian asked Dan Feather to move the film on. The boy and Totty were still there, the boy looking in a shop window, but the girl seemed to have disappeared. A car moved down the road.

Charmian stared at the car which was strong yellow. She was recalling something about a yellow car. Hadn't

Kate said something about seeing a yellow car from her window? A car in Flanders Road, overlooking the graves of Joe and the baby?

She thought about it as she moved to speak to Biddy. 'I'm sorry about this, it must have been a strain for you.'

Biddy nodded without speaking. She had said so little the whole time and never seemed to take in what was going on in any sensible way. But she was there. She had come and she managed a half smile for Charmian.

'Come on, Biddy,' said Peter. He put his arm round her. 'Come on, Mother, Mousie. Sorry, Inspector, not been much use to you, I'm afraid.'

'Oh well,' said Feather as they left. 'I never expected a lot but I had to try. I've still got to get Amy Mercer to have a look. Didn't want to call her in the same time as the family. You've had your word with her, haven't you? Thanks for coming yourself.'

'I was interested.' Was this the time to tell Feather that Amy had joined her household, even if on a temporary basis?

'Get anything out of it?'

'They loved the child,' Charmian said thoughtfully. 'Sure of that.'

'Quiet about it, though. Didn't see a tear, did you?'

'Some people just cry inside.' She knew about that way of life, she thought.

'Anything else?'

'The car. I have a witness who saw a yellow car parked in Flanders Road within the period when the boy was buried.'

'Yellow cars aren't so common,' said Feather thoughtfully. 'We'll follow it up. See if the scientific lads can bring more details on the video. Car number would be handy.'

'Wouldn't it?' said Charmian, with amusement.

'Might not mean anything.'

'No.'

But he was resolute. 'I've got others to ask: the headmistress of the kid's school, the mothers of other children at the school, Amy Mercer. Oh yes, haven't forgotten her, don't think it. She might have something to say. After all, she's given tongue already. She might not be the best witness on the scene, but she's worth having in. Sometimes it's the least likely person who comes up with just what helps.'

'Oh, I agree. You think it's one of them, don't you?'

'I think they're nursing a little secret amongst them, and I bet you do too. The mother's story is rubbish.'

'You think it's the father.' It was a statement, more than a question.

'No, I'm reserving judgement. My team favour him. On a scale of one to ten he scores five. That's because they don't like him. If they could get a motive or a bit of evidence against him, his score would go right off the board. But that's just how they feel.'

'I'm worried about the mother, I agree, her story can't be true. Whether we believe Amy Mercer or not. If she's telling the truth, it alters the picture.'

'Oh, I suppose someone around the town saw the child and thought she was a desirable little object and got hold of her somehow. And we might never find that person.'

'Is that what you really think?'

He shrugged. 'It happens and you know it. We have our monsters like everywhere else. Got nice faces and good houses and smart cars, some of these monsters.'

'I hope he's found then.' It had to be a he, it usually was, and sometimes, horribly, more than one.

'Come into my room and have a cup of coffee. Or a smoke, if you do smoke. I daren't myself, give in to one and I'd want a hundred. I was an eighty-a-day man.'

His room in the adjacent building was small but tidy, no surprise to Charmian who had already got him marked down as a tidy man. She sat down, accepted coffee, and waited. He was up to something.

Feather was making up his mind to be generous, she'd get to know anyway. 'Got some forensic evidence that links Joe and the girl. Several blonde hairs that match with some of hers as taken from a hairbrush in her home, some scraps of cotton and wool that might have come from her clothes. Colour and fabrics are right. And there's something else . . .'

He paused while Charmian waited.

Then he burst out, irritated. 'In his pocket, the head of one of those damned dolls.'

So Joe and Sarah were linked after all, no doubt there. And Totty Bow? Was he a killer, or just an innocent lad who was passing by?

'What about Totty?' she asked.

'I dunno,' said Feather, now justifiably irritated. 'I'd like to get him.'

It was hard to imagine that Totty was the prime mover and killer, someone else, bolder and more wicked, was in there too. Was it possible that Dan Feather guessed or even knew this? And wasn't saying anything? She looked at him and wondered. He was keeping the lid on something.

'Good luck with Amy Mercer,' said Charmian as she left. 'She was in my house this morning. Cleaning. I seem to be employing her.'

*

188

When she got home, Amy had long since gone. The house was shining. Charmian felt that she was lucky, and Muff too for she had been fed and was now asleep in her basket.

A slight untidiness was Amy's only fault, she had left out the vacuum cleaner and had gone away leaving a duster and a tin of polish on the stairs.

Chapter Twelve

' "I can't go and live in no nicer place," replied Jo. "They wouldn't have nothing to say to me if I was to go to a nice innocent lodging. Who'd go and let a nice innocent lodging to such a one as me?" '

Bleak House

No Humphrey, no telephone message. No Muff, not even a mouse stirring in the house or a bird fluttering in the chimney. The house in Maid of Honour Row was clean, polished, and empty.

Charmian felt empty too. Only one thing to do when you are in this mood: go out and eat something disgustingly rich and full of calories. Afterwards you could repent.

She showered, hoping all the while that the water splashed round her to hear the telephone or to hear a cat miouw. Nothing, so she threw aside her working-day clothes which were usually dark and unobtrusive because it was, after all, a man's world in which she operated, and although the men in it liked a dolly bird look with long flashing legs and bright skirts as well, if not more, than most men, they did not expect it where they worked. Sex had better be neutral there. Charmian paid lip service to this prejudice: her clothes were dark and if you didn't recognize a Jean Muir jacket or a Jasper Conran skirt, then she had the last laugh. She put on a pair of expensive jeans from Milan which were looser than fashion decreed but she could not bear to squeeze herself into them like a teenager. You had to know when to stop. She brushed her hair and cleaned her face but reapplied some lipstick and maybe it was a touch brighter than she wore during the day: these Italian jeans demanded some uplift. That seemed to be it. Then she went back at the last minute to apply a healthy spray of French scent, Shalimar, so with a cotton bra from Marks and Spencer (the best), and English shoes, and American lipstick (the best too), she was international.

She took with her under her arm a file of photographs and reports which she planned to read over dinner. Then she took herself off to the nearby Italian restaurant.

But first, she put out cat biscuits for Muff and a bowl of milk, and then with one last look at the silent telephone, she was off.

She was eating melon and Parma ham while she read the forensic report on Joe. She intended to eat pasta with a good deal of cheese, salad, and a rich pudding, and consume a carafe of wine. Tomorrow, if necessary, she would go hungry.

On the table before her she had the details of what had been found on Joe's body and on his clothes. A single hair and some microscopic threads of fabric that might have come from Sarah's clothes had been taken from his jacket, and from his pocket the head of a doll and several sweet and chocolate papers.

A handwritten note attached to one sheet informed her that the textile traces would be compared with the uniform pinafore that all children of the school that Sarah had attended wore. A match looked likely.

Well, that could be done, let them get on with it. She

was certain it would prove positive. Those two children had met, dead or alive.

She forked up a well-filled envelope of ravioli, it tasted good. She turned to another page: there were several pages and various columns of figures, this was all about the stone fragments and dust that had already been noted on Joe's clothes.

Not brick dust, it seemed, so nothing to do with any sojourn under the brick railway arches. These arches had been inspected and scraped for specimens, compared with what was on Joe, struck to his clothes, in his hair and on his skin, and there was no match.

The technicians were obviously being very busy. Let them go on with it. Dan Feather needed all the help he could get.

He had Joe, who was dead, who had been in contact with Sarah, but he still had no idea where the child was nor who had abducted her, if that was what had really happened, or where she had been taken.

Charmian sat there eating and thinking: they were looking for a hideaway that was grey and stony and probably damp. Not a very agreeable place to live in, not nice at all, poor Joe. And where was it?

Her mind toured Windsor and its environs. Well, there was one place.

Try the Castle. In that great structure there must be many secret recesses, called cellars or dungeons, where a boy could hide. Or be hidden. It would not be easy to get in, of course, but it might be managed. She doubted it, yet it could not be ignored.

She got up and went to the telephone which rested on a shelf in an alcove in a corner near the kitchens. Waiters came and went while she dialled. They knew her, she often ate here and very often used the telephone.

First she dialled her answering machine at home to hear if any call had come in from Humphrey. Nothing, no message.

Then she called Feather at his home. She was surprised to find he was there and that he answered the telephone himself so promptly.

'Just an idea,' she said. 'Try the Castle.'

He understood what she meant. 'I had thought of that myself, but I can't believe it.'

'It's not a question of believing.'

'Right, I know that, it's a question of doing. I'll see what I can do. It won't be easy, you know what they're like in there. In the first place they won't accept any living creature could have got in and hidden, and secondly they won't let us in to look . . . although I have wondered sometimes if we wouldn't find a few mislaid tourists wandering round trying to get out.' He had allowed himself a joke.

Charmian went back to her wine and her slice of chocolate cake thinking about Feather, who had a question mark over him: he was a great team player who belonged to several clubs and fraternities in the town to whom he would give loyalty. Supposing one of the members, say a revered, wealthy, and established figure in the association and in the town, could be suspected in connection with the death of Joe and the loss of Sarah . . . ? She wouldn't call Sarah's absence more than loss at the moment, she couldn't bear to consign the child to her grave.

Supposing all this, would Feather admit it?

In the end, yes.

But he might keep quiet for as long as he could, investigating himself but not passing the word around. Damn you, Feather, she thought, that is exactly what you would do, and it is why I am not trusting you here.

It worked both ways, as she knew. He didn't trust her either, of course, but her role as head of SRADIC, with her own investigatory powers, made her powerful. He could not ignore her.

Out of her file, she pulled the photograph of Sarah; several copies of this had now been made to hand out to the investigating team, it had also been used on the TV presentation.

She studied the child's face, hoping for a stimulus to thought, but nothing came. Strange child, with her army of little dolls, one for every day of the year and all alike. Perhaps a lot of children would develop an obsession like it if they were not constrained by the rules of parents and school. Or possibly it came from the mother.

So what did Sarah's doll collection say about Biddy? It was hard to know what Biddy was like normally; now she was a pretty but dishevelled slightly drunken hysterical woman who had lost her child.

But I might be like that in her position, thought Charmian. Only I believe I would be roaringly angry as well and I see no anger in Biddy, just a kind of acceptance, and I find that worrying. Did she blame the father? He had been checked by the police; he had been staying with friends who testified for him.

Biddy had fallen in love with a man who was married, and who had been charged with murdering his wife, she had had his child, made what looked like a marriage of convenience with Simon Holt, who appeared to have left her. Not a lucky lady.

But she had always had money and was out of the same social drawer as Peter Loomis, you could tell that by the way she spoke, by the way she dressed, and even by the way she got drunk. She knew the ways of her social set and in her own manner she conformed to them.

It might be worth talking to Lady Mary Erskine about Biddy, that lady had been very quiet lately.

You drew me in, Mary, asked me to see her, trusted in Biddy then, now perhaps you do not. I'm thinking about that. What's happened that you know and I do not?

She considered telephoning Lady Mary this instant, but a fat man with a Filofax in his hand was wedged by the phone talking away fiercely. He edged closer to the instrument and mouthed into it. He wasn't moving away in a hurry. Just for an instant, she had Rewley's gift: 'Darly, darling,' the man said. Love talk then, and going slightly wrong?

She took out her diary, looked at the next day's events, and chose one gap in which she would speak to Lady Mary Erskine.

The watchful waiter smiled at her, pretty lady but hard to read, and poured her some more wine from the carafe.

As Charmian drank her wine, she noticed a couple of young women dining together in a table across the room. They were laughing together, one wearing a soft silk shirt and the other girl, whose face she could see and vaguely recognized, was wearing a thick tweed suit and looked hot in it.

I know that back, thought Charmian, I think I even know the silk shirt, I know the hair cut and the set of the shoulders. Then the wearer turned round and gave a smile and a wave. Dolly Barstow.

Dolly got up and walked across. 'Come and join us?' She looked at the table. 'Bring your wine and have coffee with us. We've just got to the coffee stage.'

Charmian picked up her glass and motioned to the waiter; he carried her chocolate cake over for her. 'I didn't see you till just now.'

'I saw you come in, but I didn't know if you'd want company.' Dolly glanced at the scatter of papers on the table. 'I could see you were working.'

Charmian pushed everything back into the file. 'Not getting anywhere. A lull seems indicated.' She followed Dolly to the table where the other woman smiled up at her.

'You know Alice? Alice Braddon.'

'I know we've met, but I can't remember where?'

Alice had a cheerful, round face. 'No reason why you should . . . I came up to you after one of your talks and asked a question.'

'Dr Alice Braddon,' said Dolly. 'Alice and I were students together. I was the plodding one and she was the clever one.'

'Not that way round at all,' said Alice.

'I can't believe Dolly was ever a plodder.' Dolly was as sharp as a needle but kind with it, a rare combination in Charmian's experience. She valued Dolly accordingly. She studied Dr Braddon: she took in the alert brown eyes, the strong hands, and made her guess. Not a Doctor of Philosophy, she decided, too young for a Doctor of Literature for such were usually old and grey after a lifetime labouring in the arts, probably not a Doctor of Theology; she opted for medicine. 'Do you specialize?'

'General practice, but I do several clinics in pediatrics.'

Yes, that was right, thought Charmian. Alice would be a reassuring and comforting presence to child and mother.

'Alice has just had a paper accepted by the *BMJ* so we're celebrating. She's also divorcing her husband, so we're celebrating that too.'

'Only thing to do,' said Alice brightly.

Charmian drank some wine and watched while the waiter brought the coffee. Sign of the times, when she'd been their age it was the wedding you celebrated, not the divorce. She might have said something to this effect had Dolly not given her a sharp look. So Alice minded, was probably unhappy, not really being bright and gay about it all and Dolly was helping her.

'What's the article about?' she asked, seeking the safe comment.

Alice produced a copy of the *British Medical Journal* and put it on the table. 'Not in this issue, some months ahead, but it's called "Some Congenital Diseases in Children".'

'And it's brilliant,' said Dolly firmly.

Charmian finished her wine, and picked up her coffee cup. Might be why there was the divorce, some husbands couldn't stand brilliant wives. No, I must not think like that, she told herself firmly, it's sour and sexist. However, she thought she knew what she was talking about, having spent all her working life in a world where brilliant women were rare and not specially welcomed.

Still, she thought with some savage ill humour, it could be said that not many of her male colleagues were brilliant either.

She drank her coffee, which was strong and bitter. I am in a rotten mood, I must stop being like this. She smiled to herself. And I have known men who were honest and solid and I do know a few who deserved to be called brilliant. But, after all, what is that word brilliant? A much overworked term that ought to be forgotten.

'Why the smile?' asked Dolly.

'I was just thinking that I had worked with some good men . . . don't ask why.'

'I think I can see the train of thought,' said Dolly drily. She had seen some prejudice, although she had not suffered from it herself: she was canny and knew where to put her feet. But Charmian, older, bolder, and less careful, had felt conflict and been hurt by it.

'I'm not shouting about it.'

I'm standing on her shoulders, Dolly remembered. She's fought some of the battles from which I benefit. And she'd had it rough; Dolly herself had never had to kill anyone in pursuit of her duties, Charmian had, and come close to being killed herself. There was one or two lines round her friend's eyes that came from those battles.

Alice saw the look that the two other women exchanged and saw amused trust in it. Women did let you down less than men, she summed it up, but then perhaps you committed less to them.

'Alice and I did think of celebrating with champagne,' said Dolly, picking up something of her friend's mood. 'But we decided that would make us too high, so we settled for a good Italian red because we wanted to feel cheerful, but solid somehow too.'

'And is there anything that you are celebrating?'

'I don't know if celebrating is quite the word, but I do feel happier about one thing. I went to see Kate just before coming out tonight and she is so much better.'

'I'll drink to that.'

Alice obviously knew all about Kate. 'I think she's over the worst, but people do fluctuate, you know. Emotion does come into it.'

'I think we may have made it worse for Kate in the way we all hang about her.'

'She's obviously much loved.'

'She is,' said her godmother. 'Good about Kate and thanks for telling me. There's been a bit too much going on in my life at the moment and I don't know if I've been concentrating on Kate in the right kind of way.'

'The missing child? Kate did get hooked on Sarah, it was bad luck that the body of the boy was found where it was. She made it something to do with her.'

'She saw something,' said Charmian. 'She saw a person there. I don't think she saw the boy being buried, no one seems to have seen that particular episode, but I believe she saw the killer looking at the grave. I didn't tell her of that idea, but I didn't have to ... It was in her mind without me prompting her. There is something else I'd like to ask her but I don't know if I can. I feel I've dragged her into enough as it is.'

'You didn't do any dragging. It just happened. What is it you wanted to ask?'

'About a car she saw, about its colour.'

'I can answer that for you: she saw a yellow car. She told me, she's been talking quite a lot about it. I'd say it was on her mind. The car was yellow, a dirty yellow.'

'So not a new car?' The car in the video was yellow, old, and dirty.

'And she thinks there was a woman driving it.'

'I'm surprised she could see all that ... it wasn't close.'

'Perhaps it's imagination.'

'I don't want to think that, it might be useful.'

'Tell me,' she said to Alice. 'If you have a scan or they take a bit out of you to test and the result is bad, it's malignant or whatever, do they whisk you in and operate straightaway?'

Alice looked surprised. 'No, not as quick as that. Not

unless you are already under anaesthetic, that can happen sometimes, to certain cases. No, you get time to arrange things.'

Oh good, so Humphrey hadn't been dragged into the maw of some operating chamber without her knowing. He was out there somewhere, perhaps not even ill at all, and he would be in touch.

Alice looked discreet (if slightly surprised at this last question), so Charmian decided it was safe to talk cases in front of her. Besides, she wanted Dolly's opinion.

'It looks as though the boy whose body was found, Joe, had been in contact with Sarah Holt, although we don't know where she is or had been, but forensics found traces of her, hair, possibly clothes, a bit of one of her dolls.'

'It doesn't actually prove they were together . . . he may just have rubbed against traces she left behind.'

'True enough . . . it's a link though. And it seems that the boy had been living or imprisoned in somewhere that left grey dust, stony traces on his skin and clothes . . . From where? I wondered about the Castle.' She gave Dolly the report to read then sat looking at her.

The waiter waved the wine bottle over their glasses. 'No, I won't have any more. I have to drive.'

'No.' Dolly raised her head from her reading. 'No, not the Castle. I know there are good Victorian precedents for children, chimney sweeps and so on, hiding away in the Castle, but that was then, this is now. Besides, one child might get in, but two? No.'

There was a calm lucidity about Dolly's words that carried conviction.

'Yes, you're right. It was just an idea.'

'Try a church or a chapel.'

Or even a grave. But no, that could not be, Joe had

been buried in the earth, near to the remains of the long dead baby, and had known no other grave.

The papers from her folders spilled out on the table between them. 'Is that Sarah?' Dolly picked up the photograph. 'I don't remember seeing it.'

'Yes, her mother provided that for me.'

'I heard the TV interview went well but no feedback so far.'

They nodded at each other. 'Takes time.'

Alice had picked up the picture of Sarah. She was examining it with what Charmian recognized as a professional look; she was noticing certain things, checking other points, frowning. Then she put the photograph down, and drank some more wine. A splash of red fell upon the white tablecloth.

'So?' questioned Charmian. 'You had an assessing look, as if you'd made a judgement.'

'Not quite that. But I was thinking . . .' She paused. 'I was thinking that just from that look, you know, she was very close to being a Very Odd Child.'

It was Charmian's time to frown. 'What do you mean?'

'It's just a phrase we use . . . some children do have a look, eyes, features, it can be intangible but real, which sometimes reflects physical or mental abnormality. You learn to see it and read it. Then you try to find what lies behind it.'

'And you see that here? In the child's face?' Charmian picked up the photograph and looked at it. Sarah looked back at her, a sad, peaky little face whose eyes did not look at her squarely.

'Well, I can't be sure from a photograph, of course. I'd know more if I had actually seen the child face to face. But even then it is not always easy. You just get a sensation.'

Those gentle dark eyes would study a face and pass judgement. Kindly done but with the ruthlessness of the professional, which applied to her, Charmian, too. It was called 'doing your job'.

Charmian took the photograph back and stowed it away. 'We may never know now. What's the outlook for these odd children?' If Sarah had been one, poor child.

Alice shrugged. 'Many different causes, some worse than others, but in general the prognosis is not good.'

That means really bad, Charmian thought. She wondered what were the right questions, if any, she should ask, and settled for silence.

Alice got up. 'Just go and powder my nose.' She was taller and thinner than she had looked sitting down, not older but younger and more vulnerable. She stalked off, a kind of defiance in her walk. She didn't look at the waiters who parted on either side of her as she went.

Charmian said: 'Does she frighten you, your friend?'

Dolly laughed. 'She's a love. Don't let her frighten you. Not about the child, she was snapping out a comment, just looking . . . we've had a bit to drink, the two of us, it may not be a fair judgement.'

'I don't know what to make of it, whether it has any importance in the case or not.'

'You could ask the parents . . .'

Not a prospect I relish, thought Charmian. Saying: 'Is your missing child defective in any way?' Supposing they don't know, supposing it's not the case? 'Probably not a good idea just at the moment. I'll wait.'

Alice was making her way back to the table, she really was remarkably pretty as well as all else.

'Thanks for cheering her up.'

'Did I?' Charmian was surprised. Alice seemed thoroughly in charge of her life and everything about her, infants, patients, and adult women detectives, not the sort of person Charmian could cheer up, even though she had guessed the girl was in need of it.

'She's not as jolly as she acts. She loved that husband, the louse.'

'Oh, really? Well.'

'And don't say we all make mistakes.'

'I wasn't going to, I was going to say that if you have to make a mistake it's as well to make it when you are young, and she is young.'

'Anything personal there?'

Charmian was silent. She was beginning to wonder if she had had too much wine. Perhaps all three of them had.

'Did you know,' she said, 'that the skeleton of a baby was found close to where Joe was buried? Not too far away. Been there for decades, nothing to do with Joe.'

'I did know.'

'I've been trying to get an identity for the little creature. It seemed so sad it should be nameless.'

'I bet it seemed safer at the time,' said Dolly, 'after all, the mother must have wanted to get rid of it.'

'Oh sure, a time-honoured practice. It was called Baby Drop, that bit of land, but the babies were usually dropped alive outside the Workhouse or Infirmary or whatever it was. That sort of thing doesn't happen now, or not often, they either get aborted or the parents hang on to them. Some things have got better. I had thought that if I found out the initials on a locket that seemed associated with the child, I could go through the church registers . . . of course, it wouldn't have been christened but I might have made a guess at the family name of the mother . . . families hung together then, stayed in one place more. I don't think I'll get far, though.'

'This is a bit fanciful for you, Charmian,' said Dolly.

'I know, not the way I usually go on, practical Charmian that's me, but I feel' – she did not want to use the word that she really believed in – haunted – 'I feel deeply interested in that child.' An understatement if there ever was one.

'You'll work through it,' said Alice, she sat down again, drank no more, which was probably wise of her, but finished her coffee. A trill came from her pocket. 'Damn, I'm on call . . . I'd better go to the phone and find out what's wanted. Excuse me.'

'Time for me to go,' said Charmian standing up. After all, it hadn't been such a bad evening, she'd enjoyed it, Dolly was always good company and Alice had given her something to think about, taking her mind off her worries about Humphrey, worries that might be nothing at all. 'I'll go and see Kate tomorrow.'

'I wish you would, I know she seems so well but that baby might come soon.'

Both of them waited to see if Alice would say anything, but she shook her head. 'Don't look at me, I only deal with the finished product, I don't deliver it.'

'I'll go first thing.' Charmian looked at Dolly, wondering how much Dolly had had to drink. 'Are you all right to drive?'

'Oh, I'll get a cab,' said Dolly cheerfully. 'Alice didn't have much really, she's careful, she knew she might be called in.'

Alice came back as Charmian was leaving. 'Glad to have met you again. Can I give you a lift? Dolly, I have to go back, a small crisis.' She sounded cheerful and alive, as if the small crisis which needed her help more than made up for any ex-husband.

*

Driving home slowly and carefully, Charmian passed the small block of flats where Mary Erskine now lived, having sold the family house at some great profit. Although Mary always called herself poor, as she was indeed by the standards of some of her friends, she had a good head for money. Of all Charmian's friends, she was the most worldly wise. Dolly Barstow was cleverer, and street sharp, as a police officer had to become, but Lady Mary was more sophisticated. She was also, as Charmian had discovered once or twice to her cost, of all her friends the most guileful and sweetly deceptive. Lady Mary, who knew herself without illusion, said it came from following her grandmother's precepts about behaving like an English gentlewoman.

Charmian stopped the car, looked up at the windows on the third floor where the light in Lady Mary's sitting-room shone out. It might mean she was home, it could also mean she was entertaining, but it was worth trying.

The porter, who knew Charmian, let her into the marbled entrance hall and said he would ring up to Lady Mary. He came away from the telephone with a smile and a nod. 'She says to go up.' He opened the lift doors to stand watching as Charmian sped upwards.

Third floor, two red front doors, one slightly open. She pushed it wider apart, feeling something sticky on her fingers.

'Come in, I opened the door for you, I'm in the kitchen.'

Lady Mary was wearing a big blue butcher's apron and had her hands in a mixing bowl. There was flour on her cheeks and on her hair.

'What are you doing?'

'Making a cake. A sponge.'

Charmian looked in the bowl. 'Is that how you do

it?' There was a pale mixture inside which Lady Mary was manhandling.

'It says to beat it, I'm beating it.'

She seemed to have a small but heavy instrument in her hand. 'What are you using?'

'It's a kind of little mallet.'

'Mary, I think that's what cooks use to beat steak with to make it tender, I don't think it's meant to beat a sponge up with.' A badly bruised cake, it was going to be. 'A wooden spoon or even your hands would be better.'

'I've got it all over my hands and my face,' said Lady Mary as a piece of batter hit her eye.

'Why are you doing it? You never cook.'

'I can cook. I went to Atholl Crescent but I mostly cut it and I must have missed cakes. As for why, I'm going to marry a poor soldier and we won't have a cook.' She paused. 'I think I'll have a rest, my wrist aches.' She looked at her hands, decided they needed a wash, and put them under the tap. It was hot and she gave a small scream. 'Lovely to see you but is this just a social visit or do you want something?'

'I saw your light on as I was driving past, reminded me I hadn't seen you lately. I thought I'd call.'

'Oh, come on, that's not like you.'

'Shall I go away?'

'Coffee? I'm going to have some.'

'Yes, please,' said Charmian, thinking that she must be close to caffeine poisoning.

'So what is it?'

'I guess you know, really.'

Mary walked to the window. 'It's started to rain, did you know?'

'You sent me to see Biddy Holt, engaged my sympathy, but now you've gone quiet. What's happened?'

Mary still looked out of the window, she didn't want to talk.

'Come on.'

'You're too sharp . . . All right. When I asked you to see Biddy I was totally on her side, but now I don't think she was telling the truth. Or all of it.'

'Why did you believe her the first time?'

'Well, wouldn't you? You wouldn't think anything but that the child's mother was being honest. It was on the telephone . . . I didn't see her face to face. I know Biddy pretty well, when she's drunk and when she's sober, she is drinking a bit at the moment. But when I saw her and we talked about what had happened, I could tell there was something not quite right.'

'What was it? Did you get an answer?'

'No. I said: "Biddy, are you telling me what really happened the day Sarah was missing?" She swore she was, but I didn't believe her.'

'You could have forced her.'

Mary raised an eyebrow. 'You force her. All I got was tears and tears, floods of them.'

'I will, I'll be round there asking questions.'

Lady Mary took another look at the mixture in the bowl. 'I think I'll leave that and have a go at it to morrow. It might mature overnight into something good.' Then she let Charmian have it. 'You won't get anything out of her, Emily Grahamden zoomed over plus her favoured pet medic, and he plugged her full of sedatives and they took her back to Chantrey House.' Mary turned back to the window. 'I'm told she was carried out to the car, screaming her head off, nasty picture, isn't it, but I expect the sedatives have worked by now.'

'Yes, thanks for telling me. I will go and see her though. Do you think they will let me in?'

'You're joking . . . Who can keep you out?'

When Charmian got home, Muff was sitting on the step waiting for her. 'Oh, there you are. Coming in?' Muff moved forward so that her mistress could stroke her head. 'Good cat.'

Muff stood for a moment, then tossed her head and leapt away as if she had heard something. She sprang on to the garden wall, always go high if alarmed was her philosophy.

Charmian looked around, she had a sense of movement, of a presence. Someone in the garden? There was nothing to be seen but the river mist was hanging low over Maid of Honour Row. The trees that lined the empty ground across the road were festooned with it as were all the bushes in her small garden. She moved towards the hedge that sheltered her from the road: nothing to be seen.

In the past several sad souls had tried to reach her here in this garden, the past was polluted all right, no doubt some murderous ghosts hung around. Muff would claim to have seen one.

Inside the house, there was a message from Humphrey on the machine.

'I'm staying in the clinic one more night. Sorry not to have got in touch before, but it's not as easy as you might think. You ring me. Only not tonight because they've given me a big blue capsule that is supposed to put me to sleep. Try later tomorrow. All my love.'

So Humphrey was comfortably in bed, tucked away inside his comfortable and expensive clinic.

Chapter Thirteen

'The place through which he made his way was
one of those receptacles for old and curious things
which seem to crouch in corners of this town . . .
There were suits of mail like ghosts in armour,
rusty weapons, fantastic carvings, figures in china
and wood, tapestry and strange furniture.'

The Old Curiosity Shop

Mr Madge, whose given name of William seemed to get
forgotten in the public figure, was at home in his shop,
sitting in his big chair and at intervals walking around
in the flat above, where he lived surrounded by old and
valuable objects. Up here were his special favourites,
the chair in which Charles Dickens had sat, the old
teapot which might have come from Dr Johnson's establishment, and the oak table . . . well, the table had no
special history but it had legs like a small oak tree and
he liked it. He was resting in an armchair close by it
now, with a glass of brandy and a cup of tea, together
with a slice of rich fruit cake placed lovingly on a plate
which he fondly believed to have come from Versailles
before the Revolution. It may have done but there are
many fakes in this world.

Tea and brandy mixed well inside him, allowing his
thoughts to roam free. He was considering his position;
he was a well-known local businessman who did not
like talking to the police. He had standing, contacts,

belonged to all the right associations and had presided at some but still he found dealings with the police awkward. He could talk to Dan Feather, but past relations had not made him fond of the police. —He could imagine their reaction. 'What's he on about, the silly old bag?' He had heard comments like that before.

When a crime of this sort happened in the community, he knew that he would be talked about in certain circles. Everything he did was always for the best, always had been, youngsters needed help, youngsters such as Joe, you gave it to them, no questions asked.

But evil minds, wicked tongues did ask questions.

All was well in his own mind because his heart was innocent, but innocence, like a negative, can be hard to prove. It is a negative, the absence of guilt.

I am fond of the human race, he told himself, especially little bits of it with pretty eyes and taking bottoms. No harm intended, none done.

As a rule.

One must not generalize but this was usually the case. A truly good man can do no wrong because what he intends must be good.

He poured some tea and bit into the slice of cake which was moist and fruity, just how he liked it. Food helped, no doubt about it, his mother had taught him that and he had followed what she said. 'Never miss a meal, William, and if you have a problem, eat on it.'

There was so much insecurity around that even he sometimes felt he was on the edge of an abyss into which he might fall at any moment, so what must the young ones feel like?

He considered his problem while he sipped his tea. It gave him great comfort that he could drink from porcelain, not a particularly old piece but a very nice little cup and saucer of Late Victorian Worcester china, decorated in the deep rich blue, red and gold that so pleased that period when gold was king and the old Queen reigned. He liked the idea that generations of lips had taken tea from this cup. He had the complete service, unusually lucky in that, purchased from an old lady who had it from her mother, not a piece had been broken.

Today, his problem was not quite solved by lip contact with cake or cup, and he grumbled away inside himself. In sexual matters he usually put the blame on the female, but in this case, he could not.

'I am an honest man,' he said to himself, which was true, all accounts were paid on the nail and no customer was overcharged. Honesty told him now that confession was the right way forward. He knew he should speak to Dan Feather.

But he did not want to, he feared to, that was the truth of it. It was strange the urge to punish, but it was there in men like Feather and strong, he admitted it, in himself. His manifestation had been reined in, and thus came popping out in various ways, while Feather was allowed to operate his lawfully as a policeman.

The truth was he did not want, in any way, in anyone's mind, to be associated with the death of Joe.

Especially in the mind of that censorious twit Dan Feather whom he had taught in Sunday School and found to have a sharp temper and a great sense of his own worth. People said now that he beat his wife but William Madge did not believe it. People like Dan Feather did not do such things.

They got their punishment-pleasures in other ways.

His mother was right, the fruit cake, the hot tea in

the thin china were clearing his mind. There was inside old Madge, who had been young Madge as long as his father had lived, a streak of courage. Some generally brave people had streaks of cowardice like thin strands of fat in a piece of bacon, with him it was the other way round: he had, just here and there, a solid wedge of courage.

He could telephone Dan Feather. The telephone did protect you in a way, he needn't see Dan Feather's face, see the look in his eyes. And it wasn't as if Dan had an expressive voice.

He finished his tea, then went down to the telephone in the shop. He could face a situation if he had to, that was what it came down to.

He imagined what he would say: I have something to tell you about Joe. First of all, I knew Joe. I may not have mentioned that? No. Not by name, of course, but I knew him. He was well known. He was not, in some respects, a good boy, but I expect you have discovered that by now. Not above the odd lie, the odd theft or the little hint of blackmail. Yes, I gave him chocolates and the odd present of money. But I sent him on his way.

He put his hand out to the telephone, he could ring Dan at home, that'd be a start.

Then he let his hand fall away. Leave it a bit. Drink another cup of tea? Take some more brandy with it.

Perhaps talk to Lady Grahamden first, he certainly had something he could tell her. And then, he had ways of dealing with his problem, friends (if you could call them so) to whom a little gift of money might do much. He could tell such friends, and he could think of two, what to say.

But oddly enough, his hand, as if it had a mind of its

own, dialled the number of Dan Feather's house.

An elderly female voice answered him. No, Dan was out, this was his mother, she was staying with him for the time being. Dan was very busy this week. Could she take a message?

'No,' he said. 'I'll leave it for the moment.' Did he feel relief? Or a sense of disappointment that he had not got something, anything out.

What name should she say? fluted the old voice.

'William Madge.'

Will Madge? She remembered Willy Madge and had known his father, she showed every sign of embarking on a long historical survey of how she had known him.

He put the receiver down with a muttered goodbye. He was in no mood for memories, he had more than enough of those to keep him going at the moment.

Lady Grahamden? No, somehow his hand would not dial Lady Grahamden's number, it was getting really obstreperous and he had to hang on to it.

There was someone else he could telephone, a person whose integrity and yes, compassion, he felt he trusted. His fingers allowed him to try this call and the telephone rang inside Charmian's house, but only her answering machine responded. This was no good, so he hung up without talking to it.

As he was going back upstairs, he thought he heard someone at the back door which led to the cobbled yard where his van had its garage, a plain white van, small, dirty, and anonymous as suited his trade. He went to the window on the back stairs to look. The police did come around occasionally to check, and once or twice they had reported to him that he had left the door unlocked. There would be a certain irony if this was one of those nights. But there was no one to be seen, no noise, all was dark and still. Then he saw someone in the shadows.

'You?' He felt his hands tingle, as if they were anxious to touch this person. Or strangle. 'Come on in.' And they went upstairs to the cosiness of his warm sitting-room.

Chapter Fourteen

'We are so much in the habit of allowing
impressions to be made on us by external objects,
that I am not sure I should have been so thoroughly
possessed by this one subject but for the heaps of
fantastic things I had seen huddled together in the
curiosity dealer's warehouse . . . These, crowding
on my mind, in connection with the child, brought
her condition palpably before me.'

The Old Curiosity Shop

Dawn comes late to Windsor in winter when the mist
and rain hang over the town, covering it like a shroud
from river to Castle mound, but Charmian awoke later
still that morning; she refused to admit to a hangover
but something uncomfortable was banging away at the
back of her head and it felt like a headache. The heavy
curtains were drawn at her windows keeping out what
light there was. Not sound however, so she could hear
cars passing and the planes from nearby Heathrow roar-
ing overhead. Usually Charmian did not mind the noise.
She liked to feel that the world was full of people, awake
and getting on with their own business, even if some of
that business was criminous and would bring them her
way, they were alive and active and that mattered most
to her. But this morning she muttered crossly as a jet
rumbled towards its landing and reached out for her
dressing-gown.

Muff had got there before her and was sleeping happily upon it. 'Off.' She deposited Muff on the floor and went downstairs.

A pile of post on the mat, the newspaper, and in the kitchen some stale coffee still there from yesterday. She considered making a fresh pot but decided to use what Amy Mercer had left behind.

No sign of Amy as yet, but perhaps she didn't mean to come every day. 'Suits me,' Charmian decided, as she warmed up the coffee and buttered a rusk, she could tell already that today was going to be a stale coffee and cold rusk kind of day and you might as well start as you will have to go on. Muff came loping into the room with a gentle, cross-eyed look and drooping tail, as if her day was now going badly too.

Before anything else, there was one thing to be done, one telephone call to be made.

Charmian tapped out the number of the clinic where Humphrey was, and asked if she could speak to him. She had to wait a minute before an answer came back and then it was a refusal. No, it wasn't possible just yet, but she could leave a message?'

'When can I talk to him?'

Another gap, another off-stage consultation, this time the answer was more pleasing to her: late this afternoon would be a very good time.

Half exasperated, half relieved, he wasn't dead, didn't appear to be dying, was clearly undergoing tests or treatment of some sort, but they could speak later.

She felt better, more forgiving, more hopeful as she put the receiver down. People like Humphrey were never seriously, mortally ill, they were indestructible, that was what she liked about him, he wasn't going to die. She drank some more coffee and waited for the caffeine to produce its usual uplift. Even stale, luke-warm coffee was better than nothing.

Presently she felt better. No one was going to die. The graveyards were full of the careless and the unlucky, she did not intend to let Humphrey join them.

Without meaning to she had signed herself up on his side, all misgivings gone.

He was going to live, whatever happened, whatever the diagnosis, he would survive, she was willing it. Someone else could go in his place.

She rang back: 'I've changed my mind, I will leave a message. Just say: "Love from Charmian." '

Then, before anything else, she went to see Kate. Going, as she said to herself, her radical, egalitarian streak, product of a Scottish working-class background showing itself, from one expensive place of sickness to another. For neither Humphrey's London clinic nor Kate's hospital was free. As she drove there a sense of urgency came over her, it was so sharp that it was akin to fear.

So it was a relief to see that Kate was up, dressed in a loose wrap which hung from her now very thin shoulders, but wearing make-up and striding around the room with almost something of her old manner.

'Darling child, should you be doing this?'

'Oh yes, I'm allowed. Movement is now decreed.' She spoke gaily, cheerfully. 'Mum's coming in later, so give me strength.' There was a bright red spot under each cheek. 'I am absolutely empowered to walk around and be active.'

'If you say so.'

'I do, I do. Ask Sister Peters, she's the boss figure round here.' I might do that, thought Charmian.

'How do I look?' Kate swirled round in front of the

very small looking-glass on one wall. The yellow robe was pleated from the shoulders, an angel could have sung of joy in it. Without doubt it had come from a major couture house, probably in Paris.

'Lovely, darling,' said Charmian doubtfully.

'Anny sent the robe and she will want to see me in it.' Sometimes she called her mother Anny, said in slightly ironic affection. Of her two warring parents, she probably loved her father most. 'Might take her mind off the fact she didn't approve of this pregnancy anyway. Well, it's a baby now, you can't really call this bump a pregnancy, it's gone beyond that. Pregnancy is latent, this is bloody obvious.'

She was talking too much, her eyes too bright, her voice too loud.

Sister Peters swung into the room with a tray, on which was a glass of water and a round pill on a saucer. 'Come on, my dear, sit down and take this pill.' She offered the pill, smiled at Charmian, and took Kate's pulse all in one smooth professional motion.

Charmian wanted to ask: And how is she really? But she knew she wouldn't get a straight answer so better not to ask.

'Terrible day, isn't it?' went on Sister. 'I'm going off duty soon and Sister Johannes will be on in my place.'

'She's the Dutch one?' said Kate.

'You like her, and I'll be back this afternoon. You'll see me then. Now I expect you two would like some coffee, I'll send some along.' As she left, she fired the first warning shot: 'Don't stay too long, Miss Daniels.'

I ought not to talk about death and murder, but I must, thought Charmian.

She made conversation and watched Kate's face until the coffee arrived. Twitchy and too flushed.

When the coffee came, she poured a cup for Kate, then took her own over to the window to look out.

The area of the two burials had been covered with yellow plastic and a solitary policeman still stood on guard under a tree. So Dan Feather had not abandoned the site? Work was still in progress, he hadn't mentioned that fact.

She sipped the coffee as she stared out. You could see the road easily enough, and, it being winter, the bare trees did not obscure the view. A police car was parked at the kerb, clearly visible even through the mist.

'You can see the road,' she said aloud. Aware and slightly guilty of what she was doing.

'Of course, you can. I told you so.' Kate bit into a biscuit. 'I saw the yellow car. I haven't forgotten.'

'Did you see anyone in it?'

'You've been talking to Dolly . . . You know I actually feel hungry again, that must be good. Yes, I think there was a woman sitting there. Looked like one. There's a kind of female way of sitting over the wheel, isn't there?'

'Sometimes,' observed Charmian. 'He or she was driving, then?'

'Oh yes. Sat there, looked out, then drove away . . . Never stayed long. The van was parked longer . . .'

'You never mentioned the van.'

'I thought I did . . . said a van, didn't I?' She was losing interest, tiring, her godmother decided. She was no longer touched by the shadow of death outside as she once had been, she moved on, further and further into her own future.

Charmian kissed her and said goodbye. 'I'll call again tomorrow.'

'I hope you don't run into my mother on the way out.'

'I hope not too.' Anny was her oldest and best friend,

but she didn't feel ready for her just at this moment, you had to be strong to take a fall with Anny. Anny about to become a grandmother was a formidable figure indeed, and not one you could laugh at, a sense of humour not being one of Anny's strongest qualities. She was a very good artist, whose work, both in oils and watercolour, commanded the respect of critics and a high price in the market, but even here she was taken seriously and made no jokes. If she did your portrait, you had to watch what you said.

She had offered, nay commanded, to do Charmian. But Charmian had said: 'No, thank you, Anny, I don't think our relationship could stand it. Either you'd quarrel with me, or I would quarrel with you.'

'We've often quarrelled.'

'So we have. And don't tell me that you want to do me because I have an interesting face. I would not take it as a compliment.'

Anny had laughed. She could laugh at herself sometimes, she knew what she was like, knew that life had spoiled her, and did not make excuses for herself.

Nor for other people, so Charmian was grateful that she did not run into her dear old friend Anny on the stairs or on the way to her car.

She drove straight to her own office where work for the day had already started. Amos Elliot was standing by her desk on which he had just placed a pile of folders. He grinned at her, he was a cheerful young man with a broad smile. 'Here you are, ma'am, today's contribution.'

'Thank you.' They were always polite to each other in this office and Charmian was so now even though she felt depressed at the size of the pile. Reading, reading, and rereading reports and surveys, which made up a lot of her work these days, necessary valuable work, but she liked to be active, out in the field, doing the real task of investigation. Then she pulled herself together; what she did at SRADIC was valuable and just as much detection as gathering evidence on the doorstep.

'I've done all that bit,' she said silently to herself as she hung up her coat. 'That's in my past.' For ever in the past? came a question deeper down, you interfere, go out looking and always will do, you are doing it now. What about the dead baby's bones?

'Nothing much there,' said Amos, patting the pile. 'All ticketyboo, but one or two other cases fizzing along nicely.'

Every office needs a joker, even if you feel like shooting him on occasion, and Amos did this service here. Charmian thought that unconsciously she had probably chosen him for this very gift. He was also very clever and sharp, and very good looking but she would hate to think that was a factor.

'Quieten down, Amos,' said Jane Gibson from the door. Jane was sturdy and quiet, the antithesis of her colleague, but they matched and complemented each other. She had none of his flair, his capacity for seeing at once a gap in the evidence in a case, a crucial flaw that the initial investigating team had missed, but she could patiently and doggedly repair the hole. Amos might plant a waving flag by an omission but it would be Jane who knew what to do or even if there was nothing that could be done, and that a case must either fall by the wayside or start again. Many a CID team had cause to be grateful to her, and the Department of Public Prosecutions most certainly had. Jane loaded herself with work and bore the load without complaint. She would go high, perhaps higher than the brilliant Amos.

These thoughts moved through Charmian's mind as she sorted the papers.

George Rewley, who was a generation ahead of them, and who had qualities neither of the two shared, might very well end up top of the heap. Once he and Kate had their baby and their life settled down, then she ought to smooth his way to working in the Met. He needed a bigger pool to swim in than she could provide.

She would miss him, and Kate, but life had to move on. After all, she would be marrying, her life would change, it was exciting even if alarming too. Lady Kent it didn't bear thinking about, all her radical feeling rose to the surface, she would never use the name professionally.

'Doesn't look too good about the missing girl,' said Jane in a sober voice. 'I think she's had it, poor kid. No more sightings, I never trusted them, and I hear the response to the TV appeal was meagre.'

'Pity.' They were looking for a dead body now.

'Bit more on the boy, Joe, however, witnesses coming forward here and there, admitting to seeing him.'

'Under severe prompting,' said Amos with a grin.

'Yes, not very reputable gentlemen some of them.'

'Although it's amazing how high up the social scale pederasty can go.' And Amos started the national anthem.

'Shut up, Amos.'

Charmian shook her head.

Amos laughed. 'My joke, I just like to smite the social structure every so often.'

Jane said in a severe voice: 'You're paid to support it.'

'I do, I do. In my way.'

'There are ramifications in this affair that we can't see as yet,' said Jane. 'You know, the families, the names.'

They were both old enough to remember the Loomis murder case, and they were interested, they thought there must be a connection but they couldn't see how.

'No one can.' Charmian wondered if any of them had given enough weight to this factor.

They knew about Lady Grahamden, she was much photographed and she was celebrated for her wealth and position, the local papers made much of it. They were doing so now in a quiet style, aware that they had to be cautious as Emily Grahamden had efficient lawyers with the money to pay them.

'I wonder if who they are, the family connection is keeping people quiet,' she said thoughtfully.

'Sure of it,' said Amos.

Jane was more cautious. 'I'm not so sure. Might draw people in to talk. Not everyone loves Lady Grahamden . . . and this does involve a child, people like to help.'

Not helping much in this case, thought Charmian.

'I heard on my way in that there was a search going on in Warrior Woods.'

Warrior Woods was an ancient piece of woodlands on a hill beyond Windsor, near the village of Parsons Green. You could take your pick on what Warrior was meant: Celt, Anglo-Saxon, Dane, or Norman.

Charmian was surprised. 'That's some way off. Must have a strong lead to go that far.'

'Got the full equipment out there, so I've heard.'

'Digging?'

Amos nodded. 'Digging.'

The news quietened them all for the moment.

'Sickening, isn't it,' said Jane, 'when you hear of a kid going that way? God, I hate this job sometimes. Glad it's not me out there at the dig.'

Amos kept quiet, no jokes now, they both knew that he had been at such a dig. One year ago, before joining Charmian's outfit, he had worked with a team investigating the disappearance of a thirteen-year-old schoolgirl. Deborah Hendon had been missing for thirteen weeks before her body was found, hidden near a hedgerow in a Berkshire field.

'It wasn't so much the stench,' he burst out, 'although that was bad enough and I wasn't prepared, but the utter disappearance of all human identity. Nature had just taken over and was converting her for its own purpose, she'd just become a food for a lot of other organisms.'

'Shut up, Amos,' said Jane again, but this time she said it with sympathy.

'Sorry, sorry, ma'am.'

'Let's all have some coffee. I can smell you've got it brewing, Jane'—and then go away both of you and let me get on with work, was the unspoken addition.

Amos took the hint, disappearing through the door, and not coming back. Jane came in with some coffee for Charmian.

'Forgot to say: a message on the pad from yesterday. Came in late in the afternoon. I should have told you but I forgot. Sorry. Mr Madge telephoned. He would like to see you as he has something to show you. Or tell. Both, I think.'

'I'll do something about it. I have a lunchtime meeting in London but I'll go into the shop on my way home.' But before that I will have telephoned Humphrey. Or, with luck, have received a call from him myself. Perhaps even here.

Jane still hesitated. 'Mr Madge said he's been thinking of telephoning you for days. He didn't leave a message

because he wanted to talk to you. He sounded agitated.'
She still stood at the door as if there was more to say.

'Did he mention what it was about?'

'A locket. Something about the locket. He's a strange man.'

'You know him?'

'Well, everyone knows him. You used to see him at jumble sales and sales in private houses, picking over the bits to see if there was anything worthwhile. He has a marvellous eye. He used to teach my mother in Sunday school, but she never had any trouble. Some did. Boys mostly, nothing really much . . . thought I'd just mention it.'

The words were not quite a surprise to her, she had information like that filed away inside her, but she had learnt not to draw it out into the world of friends and neighbours unless it was necessary.

She drank the coffee, then bent to her work. She could hear voices in the next room for a time, then they fell silent.

She stopped work and sat there thinking, hard, painful thoughts with a dark picture behind those thoughts.

She always dressed for London in a certain kind of way, a dark suit, very quiet but elegant, silk in summer, fine wool in winter. Her meeting in London, in that office off Bond Street, close to an exceedingly smart art gallery, was short. At such meetings, as always, she received certain information and in her turn, she passed some back. This side of her work was not pleasing to her, she did not like the insights she got into the lives of others whose privacy was thus invaded. Unknown to them, as well, in some cases. They might be security risks, she was never sure.

She was never quite certain, either, at what point in her relationship with Humphrey she realized that he had information on her and had had before they met, and for all she knew, might be continuing to receive it. The observer, observed.

She had a shrewd idea that if she so cared she could obtain information on Humphrey, and in some of her angrier moments she had considered doing this, but it is not how you behave to someone you love.

Before leaving London, Charmian made her way to the Royal Hotel in Piccadilly, ordered some tea, and used the telephone to call the clinic where Humphrey still was. He answered at once, and cheerfully.

'Hello. I knew it would be you.'

'How are you?'

'You'll see me tomorrow, I'll come straight to Maid of Honour Row . . . as to how I am, I feel splendid and very optimistic.'

A coldness cut into Charmian: if you were optimistic the implication was you could have been pessimistic. 'You're sure?'

He caught the wobble in her voice. 'Yes, cheer up, the gods here give judgement tomorrow. You'll know.'

'I shall look forward to seeing you,' she said gravely.

'And what about you, your day?'

'Meeting in London. I'm going to see Mr Madge the jeweller, he's been doing my ring . . . And I've been asking his advice about a bit of jewellery, a locket, that might hold a clue to the poor little bag of bones that was found near the dead boy. If it hadn't been for Joe, they would never have been discovered.'

'Old Madge is a good craftsman, he'll see the ring is well done and may be able to help you with the other, he knows his jewellery.'

'People seem to have reservations about him.'

'Oh well . . .' There was an amused, dry note in his voice. 'I can understand that. He's the archetypal old English bachelor and clubman, they put up with them better in the days of good Victoria. Comparisons with Lewis Carroll spring to mind.'

'You remember what's going on down here?'

He was silent and when he spoke again, his voice had changed, the amusement had left it. 'You mean he's being mentioned in connection with the missing child and the dead boy? That does change matters.'

'It's tough being Loomis, the first child died, you know.'

'Was there one? I'd forgotten.'

'Yes, he and the wife had one child which died at a few years old. Too much intermarrying in that circle: he and his wife were cousins and so is Biddy for that matter . . . Sure the child's death had something to do with what happened later. I've always thought the wife killed herself. Fell, or jumped, that sort of thing.'

—Dan Feather certainly knew about the death of the first child and had kept it to himself. No wonder he eyed Peter Loomis with some scepticism as a parent, too much death hung around him. But she ought to have found out for herself.

'Of course, there can't be any connection with this later business,' said Humphrey.

'You think not?'

'Oh no, it was natural death, of that I'm sure.' He sounded confident. This was where all the close connections of the group came in and influenced judgements, she thought.

'Any advice about William Madge?' What she really

227

meant: Have you anything else to say, any little secrets you could pass on?

'I don't know there, you must use your own judgement.'

'Oh, I will. I'm going to see him, see what he has to say.'

She went home, changed into black jeans, acknowledged the existence of Muff with a meal, which was the form of acknowledgement that Muff desired, checked her answerphone, which was quiet, and drove towards the road downhill and beyond the Castle Mount where Mr Madge kept his establishment.

It was a dark night. Winter had come early this year to Windsor, bringing with it more damp and mist than usual. The Castle as she drove past it was shrouded and remote. You could see lighted windows above the towers and battlements but it didn't look friendly. It was too misty to see much sign of the fire, which had destroyed several great halls, but distantly she could make out scaffolding.

She had not telephoned ahead to say that she was coming, which was deliberate because she wanted an element of surprise. She might be able to read more clearly if she got a moment when he saw her without being prepared. She suspected that he was an accomplished dissembler, a man with many masks and who knew how to slip them into place. A different face for each person.

She had seen Mr Madge, the charming old jeweller, the great craftsman, in love with what he did. She saw now that he also played out for her the man of tradition, the tradesman who could look back with pride on his forebears, generations of men who had been the respected owners of this shop. The portrait of George III played its part here.

He played the courtly old man who bowed when she arrived and opened the door for her, and whose bills were always written out in a flowing long hand as if the age of the typewriter and the computer had never arrived.

She wanted to see what was underneath this mask, because there was another man, one who taught in a Sunday school and liked little boys, who might have a darker side. He might be a man who walked the streets at evening and knew the side alleys and hiding places of the lost boys, might have a secret, hidden life.

She wanted to rip off William Madge's mask. She felt no compunction in not talking first to Dan Feather because she knew he kept his own secrets, and if there was anything to tell, he would learn later.

She drove across the cobbles to the shop which was dark and closed, which was to be expected as it was six o'clock. The shop normally closed at five. He had kept it open once especially for her, but that had been by arrangement.

'No arrangement this time, my dear Mr Madge,' she said as she locked the car. 'But I shall get in. I'll huff and I'll puff and I'll blow your house down.'

Her little joke amused her mildly as she walked round to the back where the door to the living quarters was to the right of the archway into the courtyard. The court-yard had once been home to a carriage and pair, with the coachman living above the stables, there was still the feeling of horses about the place but now it was used as a garage. It was lit by a standing lamppost.

A light shone above the door, and in a room upstairs. A brightly polished bell-pull shaped like a tassel on a brass chain hung beside the door. An antique in itself, the policewoman inside Charmian marvelled that it had not been stolen.

Maybe that very thing said something formidable about Mr Madge's standing in the Windsor subculture.

She gave the bell a brisk pull, and then to make sure, another. Distantly within the dark house she could hear a bell tumbling away. In what had been the kitchens of the old house, where servants lived, she imagined, but she felt sure Mr Madge could hear.

She took a pace backwards to look up at the lighted window. She saw a curtain move as a face looked down. 'Saw me.' She knew she could be recognized in the light from the lamp which was an object of historical interest in itself; ornate and elegant, it might have lighted the Prince Regent himself on his way.

She waved a hand at the face, which disappeared behind the curtain. Some minutes passed before she heard feet coming down towards the door and heard the chain loosened and the lock turned. She understood the delay when she saw her host: Mr Madge was wearing an elaborately frogged and corded velvet dressing-gown which must have formed part (and an expensive part) of some Edwardian gentleman's evening-at-home wardrobe.

'Ah, it's you, my dear lady.' The courtly manner was well in place. 'How good of you to call. So late too, I am afraid the shop is closed.'

She ignored the glossy smooth impertinence, taking it as a sign of some sort. 'I knew you wanted to see me, so I was anxious.'

The door was wide open and he was bowing her inside. 'Do come in, my living-room is upstairs . . . but you know that.'

'I did see you at the window, yes.' He'd been drinking, she thought.

He led her up the stairs, murmuring platitudes about the size of the house and the difficulty of getting domestic cleaning and for her to watch the bend of the stair just there, so dangerous, puffed out on breaths of brandy. The smell caught up with her as she followed behind.

The living-room made her draw in her breath. The fire in the grate and soft light from several small lamps made the room a mysterious cavern filled with handsome, interesting pieces of furniture and some objects so strange she did not know what to make of them. Was that huge object on the wall a stuffed capercaillie and had he shot it or just collected it? She banged against a brass lectern on which lay a large opened book. Not for prayers, she thought.

'Sit you down, my dear.' Now he was being the kind Victorian grandfather. Well, he could have played that part to good effect with poor Joe.

She took her seat in a big leather armchair with embroidered armrests. Surely that was a crest embroidered there?

'The Duke of Southland's armorial bearings,' he said, seeing her eyes. 'Picked it up at the sale of Southland Great House. He'd been broke for years, poor fellow, but Christie's and an American buyer got the best of it. Ah . . . I wasn't looking for the best, not for my little place, just what I could pick up.'

She refused brandy. 'I have to drive home. You wanted to see me? Was it about the ring? It's ready?'

'It is ready certainly, a beautiful ring.' An honest note in his voice at that, he could speak truthfully about his trade. 'You will enjoy wearing it.'

'I hope so.' Without meaning to, a note of anxiety, of doubt must have crept into her tone.

'A family ring, of course, but Sir Humphrey will be all right, he'll pull through, good stock there.'

The breath was fairly knocked out of her. 'How do you know about that?'

He shrugged, drew his mouth down, and shook his head from side to side. He wasn't going to say. 'Just take my word for it, my dear lady. Are you sure about the brandy?' He looked wistfully at the decanter.

'No, I wanted to see you about the locket.'

'You found something out?'

'Yes, most interesting. You remember I told you that my grandfather had stocked such lockets . . . of course, it must have been that many jewellers at that time stocked the trinkets, but this one had been engraved by him. So we knew the locket came from this establishment.' He paused. 'But I have discovered something more.'

'You know who bought it?' It seemed incredible; she might have an identity for the dead child. Or at least, a trace, a clue to a family name.

'Er . . . I know who bought it, I found the record in my grandfather's books, he kept very complete records always, and in his own hand . . . but let me go downstairs, find the book in question, and bring it up.'

He was out of the door before she could say anything. There was a pause which she filled in by looking round the room. A great bowl of pot pourri rested on a lyre-footed sofa table by her side. She could smell roses and carnation but it smelt sickly like decay. She turned her head away.

She heard him coming up the stairs, slowly, heavy footed, and when he came in the room, he was carrying a big red book, opened already. He had put something in his pocket at the same time which she eyed speculatively.

He laid it on her knees and pointed.

In a beautiful clear hand, pale now with age, she read: 'Nine gold lockets at a guinea a piece, sold to Lord Grahamden, and delivered by me personally.'

Nine gold lockets sold to an earlier bearer of that name? 'He bought nine?'

William pointed. 'Look at the date.'

At the top of the page, where the first entry recorded the sale of a diamond brooch, to the same lordship, was written: December 22, 1901.

'A Christmas present.'

'Yes, to members of the household, senior servants and such . . . But they were old stock, so he got them cheaper . . . And look underneath.'

Another sentence said: All to be engraved, the price included.

Charmian tried to absorb the information. So, the locket had come from the Grahamden household. She had to assess what that meant.

'Will there be a record of that engraving? So we could know the precise person who received it?' Who might be the mother of this child?

William Madge pursed his lips. 'I may be able to. The record may be there.'

She stood up, handing him back the book. 'Try.' It came out as an order.

'I may find something.' He rested his hand on his pocket. If that is a weapon he has there, then I know what to do, she decided.

'I can get a search warrant.'

The colour left his face in small blotches.

233

'I have helped you. I may need a friend. I knew the boy called Joe.'

He had tried on various faces for her benefit but now the real one was coming out: a thin, frightened old man. Suddenly, she knew what he was about to say and still it shocked her.

'I knew Joe,' he repeated. 'We had been . . . together.'

She didn't react in any open way, she felt hard and cold. 'Get me the locket, please. And let me have the book.' She was watching his hand on his pocket. 'Find what I ask for and I will see what I can do. I have taken in what you say about Joe.' She started to walk towards the door. —I wonder if I'll get away without trouble? was the question inside.

He reached into his pocket and drew out a grey plastic object which he put in his mouth and puffed. 'Will try,' he gasped. 'Asthma . . . Will try. Do your best for me.'

Driving home, the locket resting in her pocket, she said to herself: You know what you have done? You have traced the locket which rested in the soil by the baby and Joe to Chantrey House. You've got to think this out, girl, there's a lot to think about and things aren't always what they seem.

The house was quiet, the cat asleep in her basket. But there was a stream of paper hanging out of her fax machine and a message flashing on the answerphone.

Her eye caught the word 'body', but she listened to Feather's voice first. His message was blunt.

'We have a body,' he said.

Chapter Fifteen

' "Is this true concerning the poor girl?"

He slightly inclines his head.

"You know what you related. Is it true? Do my friends know my story also? Is it the town talk yet? Is it chalked upon the walls and cried upon the streets?" '

Bleak House

Early next morning, when it was barely dawn, she drove through a light drizzle to the woods beyond Windsor where, in an ancient piece of woodland, the police had set up their station in Warrior's Wood. It was not an expedition she looked forward to, but her attendance seemed necessary.

'We've got a body,' Feather had said. 'But it's not the one we expected.'

She was thinking of his words as she drove out into the country with the River Thames running by her side. The rain was getting heavier, obscuring all she could see. It was not going to be a good day.

Feather had gone on: 'You've got to take a look.'

Before she left home she had spoken to Rewley on the telephone. 'I know it's early.'

He sounded wakeful. 'I'm around. Life's hotting up round here . . . you know about the body?'

'I'm on my way.'

'It's not good news.'

She had come to the same conclusion herself last night and been thinking about it in the darkness with not much sleep, and what sleep there was had been dominated by dreams whose stories she could not remember.

There were a lot of facts to put together and among them was the behaviour and confession (if that was what it was) of William Madge, and the information he had passed on (if it could be trusted, but she had the ledger of sales and it would be tested) about the history of the locket. The locket itself now lay, uncovered as if she could make out its secret if she kept looking at it, on her dressing table.

But she had had a more personal reason for telephoning George Rewley so early: 'How's Kate?'

Rewley said: 'I thought she seemed quiet . . . We spent the evening playing Scrabble.'

'I had a session with William Madge last night . . .'

'Our jeweller friend? What had he got to say?'

'He says he knew Joe, they were, as he obliquely puts it, "together". You can work out for yourself what that means.'

'He must be an anxious man,' Feather had said.

That was an understatement, thought Charmian as she drove up the hill to Warrior's Wood.

Ahead, through what was now a thinning mist with a pale sun beginning to show its face, she could see police cars, and a large black van. A few yards into the wood, an area had been taped off and inside this area a tarpaulin cover had been erected.

She sat in the car for a moment, watching. Not much seemed to be going on, then she saw Feather emerge from the tented area in company with two police photographers. He saw her and waved to her. 'Come over here,' the wave said.

She got out of the car and walked towards him. Even at a distance she could see that he looked cold and tired as if he had been rained on all night.

But he had his head up and walked briskly. 'Good morning, ma'am.' Politeness was on form this morning. 'I was going to get some coffee. Would you like some before taking a look?'

Her head ached and her mouth watered for coffee, the mugful drunk before leaving Maid of Honour Row seemed long ago. Also she thought he needed a hot drink, and perhaps had some reason for asking her other than politeness.

'Oh good, I'm perished.' He rubbed his hands together. 'And so will you be after a few minutes out there.' He led her towards the big van. 'Besides, you might not fancy the coffee afterwards . . . it's not too nice outside.' Just kindness then as a motive? She made up her mind to have nicer, more trusting thoughts about Dan Feather. Not too trusting though, Charmian, she told herself.

Two steps up to the open door of the van and then inside to a warm, well-lit inside crowded with large men. The air was smoky and possibly someone had been eating a bacon sandwich, but she was handed a mug of hot coffee with a smile.

The coffee was good and strong, the smile welcome, so that she could forget for a moment what she was going to look at, and how much she might be to blame for what lay there. Some things in life got better and other things worse.

Feather stood by her, gripping his mug of coffee, feet straddling the floor, taking up more than his fair share of what space there was and looking cheerful.

He's enjoying it, damn him. Then she immediately corrected herself. No, not enjoying it, it's professional satisfaction, he's realizing he's got a break in the case and senses he'll see the end of it. I suppose I've had that look on my face sometimes and probably it's looked heartless enough to others.

She knew most of the men there but none of them spoke to her, the one uniformed WPC present was called Jessie Armour, she remembered that much, but Jessie was occupied with brewing the coffee and washing dirty mugs which this group of men had decided was women's work. Jessie looked cheerful enough even though she was banging the mugs together.

Charmian finished her coffee and looked at Feather. 'Now?'

He nodded. 'All right with me. I've warmed up a bit.' He looked up at the sky as they walked. 'I think the day's going to clear. Well, we found her yesterday . . . A woman in a house over there' – he nodded – 'saw a van in the small hours and didn't like it and called us in the morning. Not as prompt as we would have liked, but there you are.'

He led the way forward and held back the curtain of the tent. 'It was pretty murky up here by the time we found her, so we decided to leave her here overnight and do the measuring and photographing this morning.' The ground was squashy with mud and layers of wet leaves under foot, their shoes sank in.

Charmian looked down at the body. 'I see why you wanted me here. Yes, that's Amy Mercer.' She turned away. She had expected to meet Amy again, but not like this. 'What happened to her face?'

'There wasn't much attempt made to bury her, and there's wildlife up here. Been a hungry winter, I'd say,' he said, turning away. 'Might have been a fox at her, we'll know more later on.'

'And exactly how she died?'

'That too. But you're sure it's her?'

'Oh yes, there's not much of the features left, but enough, and the hair. Yes, I recognize her . . . That looks like an apron, what I can see of it.'

'Yes, she appears to have been wearing an apron when she died.'

—She must have gone straight from my house. Or been dragged away. No wonder she never had time to put everything away in the kitchen. Either she had got in touch with her killer from the house, or she had been followed. There had been a look on her face, perhaps she had telephoned and made threats to someone? To whom?

'She worked for me, just that one day, I tried to get in touch, she gave me her phone number but now I know why she never answered . . . It may have been because she was working for me that she was killed.'

Feather waited for her to go on. 'I had talked to her about seeing the girl Sarah running up and down Peascod Street, and although I definitely didn't offer her the chance to work for me, she assumed I had, or pretended to . . . I think she still wanted to talk to me.'

'Did you believe her story?'

'Not exactly and now I am sure she was lying, but she wanted to draw attention to herself . . . she had something to say, and that was perhaps why she was killed.'

'It could be the motive.'

'I think her killer may have come to my house and that Amy left with him.'

It was damp inside the tent and full of the smell of death. Charmian remembered the woman at the checkout desk in the supermarket, and the way she had sat talking over a cup of tea. Or had it been coffee? She remembered the bright, hopeful face of Amy as she had reported for work.

She came to me for help, she wanted to tell me something, and I let her down.

'You couldn't have stopped her being murdered,' said Feather, who seemed to read her thoughts. He covered up what was left of Amy Mercer. 'Let's go back . . . the photographers and the forensic lads are waiting to do their stuff, but I wanted you to see first. Don't blame yourself.' It was his habit to say this to the relatives of victims of one sort or another of violence. The words came easily to him.

'I could have tried harder.'

'I suppose you have no idea what she wanted to say?'

'No, she talked about the girl, and her aunt and working at Chantrey House. She may have been leading up to something. Sussing me out, maybe, to see if I was the right person to tell.'

'Given time, you could have been.'

But there had been no time.

'Like some more coffee, Miss Daniels?' He had never called her Charmian, he might have to call her Lady Kent but that would be it.

'No, I must get to my office . . . I had an interview with William Madge last night. I think he wants to talk to you. He ought to in my opinion.'

Feather grinned. 'Yes, I heard he'd been phoning me. Wants to tell me that he knew Joe, I expect. But I knew already. And I'm waiting for him. If he hadn't wanted to come, I would have gone for him.' He had sent a police constable to check the house last night, no harm meant, just to frighten Madge a little.

'You sound really angry.'

'I am angry. Been quite a figure in my life, William Madge. Head of this and president of that . . . a figure in the town. He could pull strings, perhaps he tried to pull a few of mine.'

—And perhaps you let him, thought Charmian. A little pull, anyway, and now you are ashamed and angry.

'I'm telling you: a white van was seen here, where the body of Amy was dumped, for I won't use the word buried, buried it was not, just dropped here like a bit of rubbish. And a white van was parked in the road overlooking the rough ground where Joe was buried.'

'So you know about that?'

'Certainly I know, I take it you do too? Well, William Madge drives such a van, and I'm going to take him in for questioning and have that van examined for forensic traces.'

'I'd like to question him myself, if that's all right by you. Will you ask him about the girl, Sarah?' she said. Feather nodded, he would, of course, the two investigations into Joe's death and Sarah's disappearance had become one. And were now joined by a third: the death of Amy Mercer. 'But you can have first go.'

Her office was empty when she got back, Jane and Amos had gone about their own business. She searched around for the spectacles which she sometimes wore when no one was about for close work – to use her grandmother's term.

She sat back, reminded of that difficult old lady who had been old when Charmian was born. Contemporary grandmothers were young and jogged and swam or wrote poetry or best-sellers, but Charmian's grandmother had been professionally old. Also somewhat frightening. She frightened me, at any rate, and Charmian went to work. Work blotted out a lot of grief and pain and worry. At this moment it did not succeed in wiping out Humphrey nor Kate, but it did for Grandma. Deleted you, Gran.

It was a quiet day in which she got through a great deal of paperwork, she didn't stop for lunch, intent on clearing the backlog. The telephone stayed quiet, and she kept her head down until hunger drove her out to the delicatessen round the corner to buy a sandwich. When she came back, the tuna and mayonnaise on her lips, the telephone was ringing. Would she like to come across to the Incident Room?

A misnomer now, Incident Room, she thought as she approached on foot. Incident Suite would be more like it. Dan Feather was standing outside, smoking a cigarette.

'He came in of his own accord and I've been keeping him waiting. He's in that state that he would confess to killing Jesus Christ if I gave him the opportunity.' Feather was full of bitter mirth. 'I respected that man, all right I knew the way he went on, but he was good to my family when I was a kid, and I liked him . . . Now . . .' He shook his head. 'Poor old bugger, I don't know whether to laugh or cry. Yes, I do, he's doing the crying for us both. He's beating his breast because of the scandal and the what will people say syndrome, but I swear he's enjoying it too, the old creep.' He ground out his cigarette and deposited it neatly in a rubbish bin. 'Still, the state he's in, I'll get him to tell me how he killed Amy Mercer, the boy, and what he did with the girl.'

Charmian wondered if she ought to stop Feather handling the questioning in this mood. A childhood idol had been toppled and he had been forced to face facts that were painful.

He read the doubts in her face. 'Don't worry, I won't

go over the top, and you'll be watching, ma'am. But I'll get him, he'll confess.'

But Feather was wrong. William Madge talked freely about his relationship with the boy Joe. He had seen Joe about the town, he was vague on exactly where, but gave ground when Feather pressed him.

'The old bus station, not the new one, but the one in Fleming Road, kids hang around there. Alma Park, that was popular, I have a dog I walk there.'

'Useful dog,' commented Feather sourly. 'What is it, a poodle?'

Madge flinched. 'A little corgi bitch.' Then he went on searching his memory: 'The amusement arcade in Pennyroyal Street, yes, they met there once or twice.'

'Usual places, don't think I don't know them,' said Feather and Madge inclined his head in submission. 'And then?'

'I gave him a meal, he was always hungry, a little money . . . I don't think he lived in the town, or not all the time, he took a bus to Slough and once to Hounslow, he had places.'

He had driven him out into the country, yes, Joe could have walked to Lady Grahamden's from where he left him, but he would not confess to killing Joe. He did admit to knowing Totty Bow who had offered to tell the story he had told, money might have changed hands, and Totty in his turn and at William's request might have got at another fellow . . . Yes, the bank clerk who came in and said he had seen Sarah.

Charmian could see Feather grinding his teeth. 'And you still say you did not kill the boy?'

'No, no, and no.' And then he went silent.

Feather suspended the interview at this point and took Charmian outside. 'We'll have a go at him about the girl. Do you want to try? I don't think I'm doing too well.'

'Do I mention Amy Mercer?'

'Up to you. But I thought of holding her in reserve until the forensics are in. She was strangled by the way. Probably been dead about thirty-six hours or so when we found her.'

'I'll do what I can.'

William Madge admitted he knew the girl child Sarah by sight. Of course he knew her, the family were old customers. They had been customers for generations.

But he had no more knowledge of her beyond the family connection. He rapped the words out with unusual force. 'No more knowledge.' The accusation had steadied him and given him renewed strength.

However strongly she pressed him and long as they went on, he gave no ground. He had not touched, abducted, or killed Sarah.

'She was a quiet, decent little thing, I liked her. She needed looking after, anyone could see that.'

'What do you mean by that?' said Charmian.

He shrugged. 'Children do need looking after, tender and loving care. Loved for what they are, not for what you think they should be. You should enjoy what you get.'

Charmian studied his face. 'Go on with that, tell me some more.'

In a way, he now had the upper hand. 'I cannot,' he said decisively. 'That is your job.' He put his hand to his face and gently touched the left eye as if it hurt him, he gave a little grimace, but he never took his other eye off her face. 'But I got you those details and I can tell you that the engraving was paid for by Betty Crisp who was a servant at Chantrey House.'

'I didn't do any better than you,' said Charmian after-wards. She was tired and dispirited. 'But he knows or thinks he knows something about the child.' She would have gone on to tell Dan Feather about the locket and what she now knew of what historians call its 'prov-enance', but he was being summoned to the telephone.

'I'll hang on to him for a bit longer. Wait until we get the info on his van . . . And I'll hang on to Totty Bow too. There's bound to be something I can charge that one with.' Feather was still confident as he hurried away. 'I'll keep you informed.'

Charmian walked back to her car, her limbs felt heavy and she sat for a long minute at the wheel before driving off. She was almost too tired to bother with driving, so she opened the windows and drove with the cold, damp wind blowing in her face.

William Madge had been telling her something with that long direct one-eyed look but she didn't know what.

Instead of driving straight back to Maid of Honour Row, she returned to her own office, where tomorrow's work was already assembling itself on her desk as if it grew there like an organic growth without the help of human hands.

She made herself some coffee, abstracted a chocolate biscuit from the furtive supply that Amos kept there, and sat thinking.

On the walls about her was the library of medico-legal books she had assembled, next to a few books on English history, and a whole row of Hodge's *Notable British Trials*. Novels and poetry she kept at home.

Somehow she felt as if she had been bludgeoned. She moved along the red row of trials, chocolate biscuit in her hand.

Some nasty cases: the trial of Mrs Maybrick for poisoning her husband when she probably had not done, and the trial of Adelaide Bartlett for poisoning hers, a death of which she was almost certainly guilty. The trial of the Stauntons . . . very nasty, the simple-minded girl had been starved to death. Then there was Constance Kent who had killed her little brother, or said she had done, but perhaps her father was the real murderer.

She went back to her desk, finished the coffee, and sat thinking.

She knew what she had, and William Madge had given it to her: she had the locket.

To her, in the beginning, the locket had been associated with the bones of the dead baby. A locket left there as a memento with the buried baby.

The locket was old enough, but now she thought about it the clothes of the young woman whose photograph was in the locket did not quite match the age. When that photograph had been slipped inside the locket, the locket itself had already been old.

Old Lord Grahamden had given that locket to one of his servants, Betty Crisp. That servant had passed it on in her turn. And as the century had turned onwards, a girl's photograph had been inserted. The photograph and the locket were not of the same age. From what Charmian remembered of the clothes and hairstyle, the girl in the photograph had been young and pretty in the decade before the First World War.

The baby had been buried before she was born.

Yet she herself, if still alive, could be someone's grandmother or great-grandmother. She was probably dead.

But someone had worn her photograph. And lost her photograph.

It wasn't buried with the baby, but it was buried near Joe. Lost near Joe.

Charmian looked down at her hands. 'I was trying to find out who the baby was. Perhaps I will discover through another route, but the locket had nothing to do with the baby.'

Jewellery gets lost all the time, nothing can be taken for granted. But there was the locket and there was Joe.

You had to make a connection. There was an arrow pointing towards him, and then the arrow pointed onwards to Chantrey House.

She leaned back. She ought to tell Dan Feather, but that could wait till tomorrow; he might have more positive evidence against William Madge by then. Something detached like forensic traces from Joe and Amy on or around William and his possessions.

And William might have had his own reasons for lying about the locket.

She drove home, and there was Humphrey's car. He was there, truly there.

She ran into the hall. 'Darling, you've come home.'

Humphrey appeared at the kitchen door, he had Muff in his arms. 'Here I am. I was cooking something for dinner. I brought it with me.'

'How are you, tell me?' She looked up at him. 'They've shaved your hair.'

He put Muff down and came up to her. 'Only a strip and they wanted a closer look, my hair got in the way . . . I'm all right: the last scan cleared me of a benign brain tumour, they had already ruled out malignancy. I am to have medicine for high blood pressure, I will certainly have to wear spectacles, and I may get a bit cross-eyed.'

Charmian gave a small, horrified sound.

'Joke,' he said gently.

*

They spent the night in each other's arms. Humphrey slept the happy sleep of someone who has come in out of the dark. Charmian dreamt, another nightmare, and this time there was an old woman in it.

Whispers from the Past

The old voice had lost some of its softness but was anyone listening to her? 'Now hear what I say, will you? Listen to me, dearie, and see you make the girl listen.' The old voice sounded cross. 'She looks at me but does not hear.'

But the child did hear.

'She's over young to hear what you say, Granny Niven.'

'Ye canna be too young to learn the good ways. You must instruct her and it's never a day too young. Keep herself clean, untouched. Good girls don't have babies.'

'But you did, Mistress Niven, didn't you, although you don't like to talk about it now. We don't hold it against you.' But this was not said aloud just breathed beneath by the woman who held the child on her knee. No one thought the worst of Granny Niven for that little episode in the past. Village communities in Angus always had their little secrets.

'What's that you say?'

'Nothing, nothing . . .'

'She heard, she heard.'

'She won't remember, Granny Niven.'

But the child did.

Sarah Allen had been forced to leave her serving position at a Westminster public house when she became pregnant: she suffocated her infant in the workhouse.

Chapter Sixteen

' "A heavy weight has fallen upon my spirits, and the sadness that gathers over me, will yield to neither hope nor reason." '

The Old Curiosity Shop

Charmian was up at first light, bits of her nightmare still hanging round her shoulders as if she was wearing it like a veil, it was wispy and torn but still there, inducing a sense of fear. How could phantoms walk through her sleep at night?

She took a look at her sleeping companion: Humphrey was lying on his side, one arm outstretched. 'Oh darling, darling.' It was all she could find to say, waves of love swept over her, wiping out the nightmare. She knew how important he was to her.

She crept downstairs unwilling to disturb the sleeper; she moved about the house, tidying the debris of yesterday. They had eaten soup and sandwiches on a tray by the fire; the tray was still there, the empty wine bottle and the glasses on the floor. They had talked and talked and then gone to bed.

She deposited the dirty china and glass in the machine and began to run it through, closing the kitchen door so that the noise would not travel. Muff sat on the kitchen window sill, lashing her tail and demanding food. Fed, she disappeared on an errand of her own.

Charmian picked up the post, and the newspaper,

then checked the answering machine which she had ignored yesterday.

There was a call from her sister: 'Hello there, this is Imogen. You're out as usual. Call Mum tomorrow. It's her birthday, you forgot it last time. Message ends.'

Charmian tied a mental knot: Right, Imogen, right. When I come home. She looked at the clock. Not the time to ring, as her mother would be comfortably sipping her first cup of tea of the day which was definitely a Do Not Disturb Me time. Her mother had recently started doing a degree in English, specializing in Shakespearian studies, from the Open University, she worked late at night, and said she needed her rest. Her mother, who wished now to be called Maggie, was an independent lady who really hardly thought about her daughters at all these days ('Out of the nest, weren't they?'), but Imogen had the idea that she needed to be cherished. Although Maggie, nearly six foot, with flaming red hair, expensively tinted once a month, was fully capable of looking after herself. Indeed, she preferred to do so.

Imogen lived twenty miles from their widowed mother and made it part of her job to see that Charmian behaved like a member of the family instead of an alien who occasionally winged in from another planet. The sisters had an affectionate relationship which allowed Imogen to do what she called 'keeping Charmian up to the mark in family matters'. She never called her mother Maggie while Charmian did her best: it marked the difference between them.

Before she dressed, she wrote a short report on the locket, passing on what she knew, then she put it in a thick envelope, and addressed it to Dan Feather. At the same time, she took the photograph of it into her bag, between other papers.

252

Charmian carried a cup of coffee and some hot toast up to her sleepy lover, kissed him, told him to rest and that she would be back.

She drove briskly to her office through rain-washed streets still empty of traffic, down Maid of Honour Row, up River Street, past Peascod Street, into Hanover Road, then on to her office. Here, with no one to disturb her, she did two rapid hours of work, cancelled two appointments by fax (one was with the Chief of Command, there would be an angry response but she could deal with that later), and kept an eye on the time.

Nine a.m. A reasonable time to make a call, even to a hospital. In any case, Kate's luxurious establishment allowed visiting at all hours.

Before she did anything else that day, she had to see Kate.

The nurse outside Kate's room was one she did not know. She was plump and cheerful, wearing a very pretty starched cap. 'I'm Mrs Rewley's special,' she said with a friendly look, and as Charmian raised an alarmed eyebrow. 'Her mother insisted.'

Yes, that sounded like Anny.

'May I see her?'

'She hasn't eaten much breakfast, so it might be a good idea. Cheer her up. But don't stay long.' She looked at Charmian as if she could say more.

Inside the room, the bedside lamp was on and Kate had a newspaper on her lap, but her eyes were closed. She looked pale but the two red patches beneath her cheeks were more marked than before.

'How are you feeling, dearest child?'

Kate opened her eyes. 'So so. Lovely to see you.'

Charmian kissed her cheek, and sat there for a moment, holding the girl's hand. The vibrant, energetic

Kate she had known seemed to have disappeared into a frail stranger. Was it worth it? she asked herself.

'I hate to bother you with questions.'

'But you're going to . . .' Kate's eyes were the same, full of amused comprehension. 'Come on, Godmother, when have you ever let human frailty stop you?'

'Are you feeling frail, Kate?'

Kate hesitated. 'Strong enough.' She closed her eyes for a second, then opened them wide. 'So ask away.'

'When you saw the yellow car, you told me you saw someone sitting in it, are you sure?'

'Yes, it was a long way off.' She thought about it: 'But it was parked under a street light . . . I could see a bit. Yes, there was someone at the wheel. Sort of hunched over the wheel, you know.'

'Kate, and you thought it was a woman? Are you sure?' It could be so important.

'Ah, sure? That's more difficult . . .' She shook her head. 'I thought it was female.' She took a deep breath.

'Thanks, Kate . . . There was a white van parked in that street as well, I don't suppose you could see who was in that?'

'No, nothing. Sorry.'

'I shouldn't have bothered you really, but I wondered if there was anything else you could say.' She waited.

'Only that in my mind they were part of the burying of the boy. Imagination, I expect. Once again, sorry.'

'No, love, you've been very good.'

Kate let her lips curve in a small smile.

'I'll go now.'

Kate hung to her hand. 'Stay awhile.' They sat for a moment or two in silence. 'I think the baby's started.'

Charmian moved her hand. 'I must tell the nurse . . .'

'No, no, I think she knows. I thought it had begun

yesterday, but I was wrong . . . false alarm.' She moved against her pillows as if in pain. 'But not today, this is it.'

'I'll stay,' said Charmian, abandoning all plans for work.

'No.' Kate released her hand. 'You can go now. The nurse will be in, you'll see. Goodbye.'

Charmian stood by the bed, not sure what to do, but Kate gave her a little push. 'Go on. Time for you to go.'

Outside the door, the nurse was already hovering. 'I think you ought to be with her,' said Charmian. 'Things might be moving.'

'I thought as much.' Charmian watched as the nurse opened the door and went in. She walked down the corridor, then stood there watching. But the door remained closed. Presently, the nurse came out and went to a telephone and made a call, then she came over to Charmian. 'Everything will be all right. The doctor is on his way. I'll tell Mr Rewley and he can tell Mrs Cooper.'

'When can I telephone?'

'Later, later.' She was noncommittal, already turning her attention back to her patient. 'I must go. Don't worry, Mr Green, her obstetrician, is very good.'

—Don't worry, thought Kate as she drove away. Of course one worries.

She drove first to the Incident Room where activity had been ticking over in a quiet way for some time. Dan Feather must also have risen early because there was his car.

Was William Madge still there? It seemed very likely that he was being questioned again by Dan Feather. She delivered the envelope, with the message it was to be given to him as soon as possible.

Charmian drove off once more, with no sense of personal danger. She wanted to get this over, then pass to Dan Feather any evidence she might have turned up, together with any conclusions she had come to, and take a few days' leave to concentrate on Humphrey and Kate.

Now, deliberately, she put those loved figures aside, deposited them at the back of her mind, to concentrate on what she wanted to do now.

The road out of Windsor was now heavy with morning traffic, but she used the slowness of the journey into the country to think. What had she got? The initials on a locket, the discovery of this locket near the baby's bones, but also near Joe.

Amy Mercer had known something of that death and Sarah's disappearance and been killed because of her contact with Charmian. The killer, or killers, because she had to reckon with that concept, had no notion how much was revealed by the very act of this second killing.

Charmian was known, her address was known, and Amy's contact with her was known. Only someone close to Amy and knowledgeable about Charmian could have been in action.

That conclusion took some thinking about and as she drove she wondered what Dan Feather was making of it all and if he had looked at the locket and questioned William Madge on the subject.

She knew where her own thoughts were taking her: out to Chantrey House, but she was also making a detour. The car took the way almost without consulting her.

Once again she parked on the grass verge near the Vinery. There it was, that long grey building humped into the ground, and on which no vines grew, nor ever had as far as she could see. Perhaps the Romans might have had a vinery here and folk memory had preserved the name, but if so the climate had changed, she thought, as she got out of the car, to walk on the muddy turf.

The path to the house was already overgrown with trailing plants that had spread out from the flowery border to settle on the paving stones. Biddy would have cut them back but now they were free to advance. Charmian found the sight dispiriting. If the whole of the animal world disappeared plants and insects would take over in no time at all. Nature did not really care who survived, she could always start again.

The Vinery was empty, had been for days and it showed. The curtains were drawn upstairs and the brass knocker on the front door was unpolished. Biddy might not have been much of a housekeeper but Charmian remembered that the knocker had been bright the day she had come before.

Before what?

Before Biddy was taken to Chantrey House, before William Madge gave me the news about the locket and before Amy Mercer was killed.

'Amy knew you, Biddy, and she knew Sarah, I think she was going to tell me something.' Charmian's foot slipped on a frond of wet greenery and she slid into the mud. 'Damn.' She stood up, leaned on the front door, and rubbed her hands on a tissue.

The window to her right was uncurtained so she could see through: straight ahead of her, in full view, was a row of little dolls. They were seated primly on the sofa, except where one or two had fallen over and were leaning fondly or drunkenly on each other. The silent, still brood stared back at Charmian.

Dolls, she recalled, were once given to women who had lost their babies to place in the cradle as a substitute. What a lot of substitute babies there were in this house.

The Vinery was empty except for them; the dolls were alone in the house, which they ruled.

Charmian went back to her car, avoiding the slippery bits of the path, and drove away from the dolls' house. She had got what she had come for.

The mother and daughter who had lived in this house had been disturbed people who had put on as good a face as they could for the outside world, and since children take the atmosphere from the parent, then it had to have started with Biddy. The row of dolls, still in place, was a dead giveaway.

No average well-balanced mother would have let such an obsession with the same little plastic objects develop in a child who was not much more than a baby herself.

Charmian, like most police officers, was one of those who strongly believed that parents are responsible for nearly all that goes wrong with children. Of course, some parent behind that parent was responsible too but she didn't believe in going more than one generation back. You had to stop somewhere.

She turned the car to drive fast towards Chantrey House.

The Chantrey was a big place, she moved into the drive and the house surrounded her. Lady Grahamden's Rolls was parked in front of the house where it was being cleaned by a man in overalls; Kleankars, said a name across the front.

'Is Lady Grahamden in?'

'Might be, love.' He did not pause in his polishing. 'Try the front door.'

'Is that car kept out here or is it garaged?'

He did look at her then, as if he wondered what all this was about. 'I dunno. It was left out here for me to work on. I've never been here before . . . I reckon the garages are over there.' He nodded towards the grey-roofed range of old stables and coach houses.

'Got more than one car, have they?'

'I don't know. I expect so, they're gentry, aren't they?'

Charmian walked over to the stables but the ironwork door leading to them was locked. Inside, she could see a cobbled yard with several buildings with neatly painted white doors and windows, all closed except one. Through that one open door she could just make out a yellow car.

They liked things private at Chantrey House. Money was spent here, all was in good order, but display was not allowed. No doubt someone, probably Peter Loomis or even Emily Grahamden herself, would put the car away and then lock it up. But someone had forgotten this time. One of those crucial lapses that tell so much.

She rang the bell, and was admitted by Peter Loomis himself. 'Can I see Biddy, please?' The please was an extra as she was determined to see Biddy Holt.

Peter Loomis stood back politely. 'Do come in, but as to Biddy . . !' He shook his head. 'I don't think she's up to it.'

'It's important.'

'Better not try. We are trying to keep her calm.'

—Dosed to the teeth had been more or less what Lady Mary had implied. Charmian was unmoved. 'Please,' she said again. And this time the please was more threatening than placatory. Loomis looked worried as if he didn't know what to do.

Then Emily Grahamden appeared at the end of the hall. 'What is it?'

'Miss Daniels' – he had her name off pat, Charmian observed – 'she wants to see Biddy.'

'Well, let her, let her.' Emily advanced down the hall. 'She not quite herself but you can see what you can do with her.'

'I want to ask her some questions.'

'Of course you do. So do we all . . . We've had another shock here, you know, the niece of my old servant, friend, I must call her so these days, has been found dead.'

'I expect Miss Daniels knows all about it,' put in Peter Loomis, who seemed embarrassed by his mother's flow of talk.

'Poor Moucher's quite destroyed by it. No one can see her, that's certain.'

'She is someone I might want to see.'

'Is this an official visit?' asked Lady Grahamden.

'Oh don't, Mother.'

'It always could be,' said Charmian, noting Peter's ill ease. She decided to push her luck: 'Who owns that yellow car in the garage?'

'Moucher,' he said, after a pause. 'Mrs Moucher, it's her car.'

'Then I shall have to talk to her. And the car will have to be examined.'

'What's all this about?' Emily Grahamden again, being the great lady more than ever, and this time her son did not try to quieten her.

'I can't say.'

—I'm just guessing, but I think Amy was killed because she knew something about Joe and Sarah, and Joe was killed because he knew or had seen Sarah.

'You know we have a lot to grieve us,' said Emily with dignity and conviction, 'much, and we are bearing it as well as we can.' Her breathing was fast and shallow, but she was under control.

Charmian kept quiet, an instinct told her to say nothing more at that moment when Emily Grahamden was face to face with black thoughts.

'Oh, let her see Biddy,' said Emily Grahamden, turning away. 'Take her up there.' As she moved away, her shoulders sagged as if she was past bearing what she must bear.

Charmian heard her mutter: 'One protects, one protects, but it is past protecting.'

Peter turned to Charmian. 'Biddy's upstairs. I'll show you, but don't hurt her . . . Biddy's a good person, who's always tried to do her best.' His voice was full of pain. 'I don't trust you, you know.' Charmian made a slight kind of bow, letting him know she regarded this as a compliment if a sharp one. 'And Biddy hasn't, couldn't, kill anyone, if that's what you are thinking.'

—Well, William Madge is lined up for several killings at the moment, but you don't know that, nor shall I let you know, just yet, maybe later.

Biddy was in a soft chair by the window, through which she was looking, with a cat resting on her lap. The cat leapt away as they came but Biddy did not move, the window had all her interest.

From it she could see lawns and the roof of the stables as well as the outline of a low grey building like a chapel.

'Are you up to talking?' Peter asked, his voice gentle. 'Say if not.'

'I can talk.' It was the voice of a polite, good child.

Peter stood by the door. 'Shall I stay, Biddy? Want me to?'

Charmian said: 'You can stay if you like, listen. I don't mind.'

'Please go,' said the good little girl who was Biddy now.

As he slowly and doubtfully left the room, Charmian said: 'Do you want to stay here, Biddy? I can get you out, you know, you can come with me. Lady Mary will put you up.'

'I might as well be here . . . What else is there? I can't have Sarah back, they said so. I wanted her back. Very much. We could have stayed together, I would have managed, somehow. I suppose you think I couldn't?'

'I'm not thinking anything about that, because I don't know and can't imagine.' My imagination is stretching wider and wider but I don't know if it can take in all I begin to sense here. 'What I want you to do for me, if you will, is to tell me again about the day Sarah was taken away.'

Biddy began to trot out the first story: how the man had come to collect Sarah, how the child had run to meet him, and how she had thought it was the expected father. 'I thought it was the father,' she said. 'Although I didn't know his face. His face was a blank to me.'

'But later, you changed that story and said that perhaps you had seen the man before, wasn't that so?'

'Yes.' Biddy nodded. 'I think I did.'

'I assure you that you did . . . so his face was not quite a blank to you?'

'It's what I remember,' she faltered. 'How I remember it.'

They went through it all again, but all Biddy could say was that this was what she remembered.

Charmian leaned back in her chair and looked at the young woman with sympathy. What can she remember?

She has blacked out the truth; she is remembering a lie.

But it is her memory; she is telling the truth as far as she recalls it.

Does memory always tell the truth? And Charmian knew it did not.

'Thanks, Biddy,' she said, patting the girl's hand. 'You've done well. I think you might be able to go home soon, if you want to.'

She walked down the stairs, feeling more tired than she had ever been, weights seemed fixed to her legs. I must have been tightening every muscle in there.

She guessed she ought to telephone Dan Feather, her mobile phone was in the car, but at the foot of the stair, Peter Loomis was waiting. 'My mother would be glad if you would come and see her before you go.'

Charmian followed him into the large room furnished comfortably with the chintz and elegant pieces suited to a wealthy spoilt woman. There were long windows on two walls from which much the same view of the grounds could be had as in Biddy's room on the upper floor.

'She's just above,' she told herself. 'They can probably hear if she moves around.' Not that Biddy had shown much sign of it.

Emily Grahamden was standing at the window, staring out at the rain-sodden grounds. Charmian followed her eyes. 'What's that row of buildings over there?'

'The old stables,' said Peter. 'Used as garages now, of course. We don't keep any horses.'

'And that building over there?' She pointed to a little gothic structure.

He looked at his mother, who was still staring out. 'A folly,' he said briefly. 'Mama, Miss Daniels is here.'

'It's hard on creatures when they are rained on,' his

mother said. 'I am always so glad to keep warm and dry . . . I want her to go.'

'Lady Emily,' began Charmian.

'You can call me Emily, or Lady Grahamden, but Lady Emily I am not.' Her voice was austere. 'I am a baroness in my own right, the barony being one of the few that can descend to an heiress, but the daughter of an earl or a duke I am not.'

'I must see Mrs Moucher.'

'Why should I take any notice of you?'

'I can order her down to the police station. You too, if I must.'

Peter went to the door. 'I'm getting her. Be quiet, Mother.'

Lady Grahamden went back to the window to continue her study of the grounds. She seemed to be shrugging off any responsibility.

She heard Peter shouting: 'Mousie, we want you in Mama's boudoir.'

They both came into the room together, Peter poker-faced, but the woman was red eyed; she had been crying.

'I'm sorry about Amy, Mrs Moucher,' said Charmian.

The woman looked at her, looked at Lady Grahamden, and said: 'I'm not Mrs Moucher, the name's Morgan. Her ladyship gave me that name as a joke, she said I reminded her of something out of Charles Dickens, and she kept on with it. Even Mr Peter probably thinks it's my real name, but it isn't. I used not to mind.'

'But now you do? I understand.'

'Do you?'

'Yes, I believe I do.' I hate this house, Charmian said to herself, all her professional shell cracking away. I want to get home to Humphrey and Kate, but I'm on to something here and I'm going to hang on.

She produced the photograph of the locket from her bag. 'Will you look at that . . . do you know it?'

Peter could see it, and she saw from his expression that he recognized it, but his mouth closed.

'I thought it might have been yours.'

'I don't know why you should think so.' What a fierce, wild, angry face she had. She was a character out of Dickens all right, and one of his more violent ones.

'Mr Madge told me that six or more of them were ordered and given as presents to senior servants in this house.'

'Well, I wasn't one, I'm not so old.'

'I don't suggest that . . . but your mother?'

'The photograph might be Mother,' Mrs Morgan said grudgingly. 'It has her look, but I couldn't say.'

'There are initials on it . . . they were paid for by a Betty Crisp.'

Mrs Morgan said: 'My mother's great-aunt, she left it to my mother. She never had any children herself. It's Mother's photograph.'

'So the locket is yours?'

Mrs Morgan turned away without answering.

Charmian took back the photograph. 'The locket itself was found near the dead boy, Joe.' She saw Peter make a quick movement with his hand, instantly controlled. He didn't like hearing that, she decided.

'So that's what all this is about,' said Emily Graham-den, swinging round and facing the room.

'In part.'

The room was silent, she could see through the window that the rain was falling more heavily now.

'But the finding of the locket near Joe's body points to this house, and less directly to Sarah and Amy. I want to know how the locket got where it did. At first I connected it with the bones of a long-dead baby. I think I was wrong, it was dropped when Joe was buried.'

'And what about William Madge?' asked Emily Grahamden.

Charmian was taken aback. 'How do you know about that?'

Lady Grahamden laughed. 'Windsor may be a royal town, but it is also a small town. Stories get told.' She did not go on.

'I shall need to see the yellow car,' Charmian said. 'A yellow car was seen parked in the road near where the boy was buried.'

'It's my car,' said Mrs Moucher. She shrugged. 'Look if you must.'

I wonder if I will get out of this house, thought Charmian. Someone here would like to kill me but I'm not sure who. Possibly all three.

'I'm going out to see the car, will you unlock the outer gate?'

Peter Loomis stood up. 'I will . . .'

He led the way out through a side door. 'As a matter of fact, it's not locked on this side, you can get through.' He walked out with her, then turned back. 'You may find this hard to believe, but I can't comprehend all you are saying. Mousie couldn't have killed the boy and would never have killed her niece, she was fond of Amy.'

'They had quarrelled.' Charmian was already walking towards the garage with the yellow car.

'That didn't mean anything.'

'Amy was a threat.'

He stood with her while she opened the door of the yellow car and looked inside. The interior smelt of cigarette smoke.

'Mousie sits inside to smoke, so do I some-times, Mother doesn't care for smoking in the house.'

In the depths of the garage, hard to see, was another vehicle. A white van.

'Go back to the house,' said Charmian. 'And stay there. Don't go away any of you. I shall be outside.'

She walked to her own car, where she had a telephone.

As she sat in the car, she got through to Feather in person. He was grouchy. 'I can't get that bugger Madge to confess to anything. God knows I've tried.'

She ignored this sally. 'I'm at Chantrey House. Get out here, will you? Bring the full complement, a woman, a calm, kind one.'

'Are you all right? You sound sick.'

'No, just a bit frightened. Although I don't think anyone here will kill me.'

'What have you turned up?'

'I'm not sure what I've turned up,' she said wearily. 'But we'll see when you get here.'

She sat for a while, thinking. Biddy was still visible at the window, her eyes focused on the distance.

'Not so,' Charmian saw. 'Not so far distant.'

She got out of the car and tried to follow the line of vision that Biddy was staring at.

The Folly. But it was not a so-called folly, it was a chapel. The door opened at a push. She walked inside a square dark building with one window above a small altar on which were flowers. Behind an iron grille was the ornate marble tomb of a woman with delicate carved features. Across the way was another similar tomb with a man carrying a sword.

Although it was cold, and it felt damp, the air was

sweet with flowers arranged around both tombs, lilies and carnations, freshly done.

In hollowed recesses of the chapel or mausoleum were stone seats covered in velvet cushions. An antique Persian rug lay before the altar. Charmian thought it was a family god that was worshipped here.

A small silver gleam attracted her attention to one cushion. A piece of chocolate paper. She moved the cushion, more chocolate papers underneath, even one unopened packet.

Surely the child Sarah had not been imprisoned here? She picked over the papers. Joe, she thought, he was here. Perhaps he lived here, secretly for a while, she could visualize it. He might have liked it here once he had crept in. Who had told him about it? William Madge.

Charmian stood there, her feet on the cold, flagged floor. The door behind her closed, and something tight came round her neck. She pulled against it, half turning round in her struggle.

A woman cloaked and hooded was behind her. 'Mrs Moucher, for God's sake,' she managed to gasp, 'don't be a fool.'

'We bury our dead here,' said the woman as her grip tightened.

Chapter Seventeen

'The greater part of the house is shut up, and it is
a show house no longer . . . with so much of itself
abandoned to darkness and vacancy . . . no rows of
lights sparkling by night . . . no family to come and
go, passion and pride have died away.'

Bleak House

At last the sun was shining in the living-room in the
house in Maid of Honour Row. It was the evening sun,
full of golden light.

'She didn't want to kill me,' said Charmian to Humphrey. 'Just to stop me seeing. She said – it was quite
mad, as she is, I think – "Our dead must not be
unburied." '

'What made you believe it was Mrs Moucher or
Morgan or whatever she was?'

'The smell of the cloak, I'd noticed she was a smoker
and I could smell it on the cloak. And the locket, I
thought she owned it, but it wasn't her, of course. She
didn't own it, and it wasn't her.'

But Emily Grahamden herself.

He had had a meal ready, and was feeding her soup
and omelette and wine by the fire. And the first thing
he had said, after greeting her with relief, was that
Rewley had telephoned but there was no news yet of
Kate.

'This is so cosy.'

'I thought you needed comfort, sheer physical comfort.' She had looked driven, spent when she had come into the house. But she was reviving, she had marvellous resilience.

'How did you know? Because you did know a great deal, even before you went to Chantrey House?'

'No, not know just had a feeling, I was guessing . . . But they told me really, William Madge told me a bit, Amy Mercer, she must have guessed or even known, Biddy, by her very lies, what she'd forgotten. She knew, you see, helped the grandmother, and the terrible thing she had done blacked out her memory . . . I could feel the gaps in what she said and fill in the pieces like a jigsaw. But I didn't know until we opened the tomb and there was the child.'

Charmian reached out to take her lover's hand. 'She was on top, shrouded but not in a coffin and her face was uncovered.'

Dan Feather had helped raise the stone lid of the vault himself. It had moved easily enough. It was heavy but it could be done by two careful people. You needed two, and there had been two.

'The father, Peter Loomis, was there, Feather insisted, and he fainted as he saw the child's face.'

'Did he know about it?'

'He says not and I believe him, but only because he kept his eyes shut, as I guess he always did. Afterwards, he must have guessed about Joe and about Amy. Mrs Morgan, Moucher, may not have been the killer, but knew, and helped in the buryings. She'll never admit to it and I'm not sure we will ever get her for it. She says she helped Emily Grahamden inter the child, but she did not kill her.' She added, 'The locket was Emily's, it was she who dropped it. I didn't know that Great-Aunt Crisp had been Emily's nurse.' —Childless herself, that

270

lady, so Mrs Morgan had said, but had this been true? A speculation remained.

'Isn't is strange that they buried Joe where they did? why not at Chantrey House?'

'That was holy ground to Emily and she certainly wouldn't want him near the dead Sarah . . . and then, it was Baby Drop territory where they did bury him. I guess Moucher knew that name, and . . .' She hesitated. 'Perhaps she had a childish memory of hearing talk about a great-aunt or great-great-aunt who had put away a child there.' She thought of her own memories. 'I remembered a snatch of my own grandmother's talk.' Perhaps there would be no more nightmares now the memory had worked to the surface of her mind. 'Amy, of course, was another matter, she was not a candidate for Baby Drop territory. I think I'm lucky they didn't kill her and leave her in this house. She was certainly captured here . . . Yes, I do use that word, the two women together must have been like a hostile army.'

'Why did Amy tell that strange story about the child running up and down Peascod Street?'

'I've wondered about that, we shan't ever know, but she was very angry with her aunt for hitting her in the face, and yet at the same time there was a great tug of loyalty. Even when I did not believe her, yet I felt she had convinced herself that she had seen the child in the street. And of course, she probably had seen Sarah running and laughing and crying too at Chantrey House, she just transferred the story. I think she wanted to attract attention to the Chantrey and her aunt and Lady Grahamden and yet she didn't want to accuse them openly of what she guessed had happened.' Speculation, they might never know, but Amy's very death was a mute testimony to the truth of it.

'I know what Emily Grahamden was like: God and

her family were what she lived by and she was inclined to identify with God. I can see she dominated the lot of them, but even so it's hard to think of Biddy agreeing to the killing of her own child.'

'A mercy killing, you see, that's what Emily called it, was still calling it to Dan Feather. And you have to remember that Biddy had seen the other child.'

Peter's first child by his first wife, his cousin, as Biddy was too.

'She knew what Batten's Disease can do . . . she saw that first child lose first her sight and then die from renal failure. When she saw that one of Sarah's eyes was swivelling, so that she was becoming what people call cross-eyed, she couldn't bear the terrible future she thought she saw for the child. She knew that she and Peter had the same genetic relationship, it's what's called autosomal recessive. The tragedy is that she let Emily Grahamden take control. Emily said it couldn't go on, they couldn't let this child suffer, it was up to them.'

'Biddy always let someone else take control.'

'She let Emily take the child away and told the story that we know she told . . .' Charmian shook her head. 'I think the shock blacked out what really happened so that she truly hardly knew herself.'

But she had sat at the window looking towards where the child was buried, and had wanted her back.

'Quite likely there could have been a cure, but the real desperate thing is that the police doctor who first looked at Sarah, the dead child, says he thinks it's quite likely all she had was this eye problem which could have been operated on, that she was a perfectly normal child.'

Dan Feather had had tears in his eyes, that tough, experienced man, as he had walked out of the tomb.

Charmian said: 'You have to ask who killed Peter's

wife and why. Feather thinks Emily did it, so no other child would be born of that marriage.'

'If she did that, then I suppose it's easier to accept that she killed Joe and killed Amy.'

'Yes, Joe had been hiding in the chapel . . . the stone and dust on his clothes came from there . . . There were traces of him. He may have been hiding there when the child's body first rested on the tomb, perhaps unburied for some hours there, and that was how her hair and other traces got on to his clothes. He probably picked up the little doll then and put it in his pocket.'

'I wonder they didn't see him.'

'You could crawl behind the other big tomb and not be seen . . . And then Emily Grahamden came back and found him, she admits as much. She says he was looking at Sarah. Well, we know from William Madge that he wasn't the sort of boy to walk away without getting something for himself.'

'You'll have to trace his path out there.'

'I think William Madge may have had something to do with that. He told us that he drove the boy into the country and dropped him there. He didn't want Joe in his own place.' —Hide out there, William could have said, I'll come and get you. 'I don't suppose he will be charged, although Totty will go down for something if Feather gets his way, but I think Madge will be advised to quietly retire and let a nephew – I believe there is one – run the shop.'

Humphrey put his arms round her. 'The gene pool is very dangerous, isn't it? At least we haven't got any children.'

Charmian said: 'Oh God, my mother, I was to have telephoned, I forgot.'

'Do it later. Drink the wine.' He put another log on

the fire and Muff rolled towards the blaze luxuriously.

'I did have a pregnancy once, and I had an abortion . . . it seemed right at the time.'

He smoothed her hair. 'I know, you've told me . . . But I think it worries you and this case has stirred things up.'

'I'll never know now who that skeletal baby was . . .'

But perhaps Mrs Morgan could guess. A relation of long ago who had worked at Chantrey House? A family story handed down so that when the burying of Joe was necessary, that was where she went.

She didn't admit it, but she had driven the yellow car and Emily the white van. Each time to a burying.

'It's such a sad terrible story.' Charmian put her head on his shoulder. 'What people those two women were . . . Do you know, I think they were related way back . . . One of those servant-master seductions. And do you know, I believe Mrs Moucher is related somehow to the skeleton . . . the baby had an extra finger, and I noticed that on Mrs Moucher–Morgan's left hand there was a kind of stump by the little finger where another finger might have been . . . they were kin, those two. The locket was Emily's, it was she who dropped it, did I tell you that? It had been given her by her old nanny who was the girl in the picture.'

'What will happen to them?'

'Too early to know yet. Dan Feather took them both into custody, of course, and Peter Loomis was already calling in his lawyers . . . I think Mrs Morgan went over the edge into madness when her niece was killed. Lady Emily will claim a mercy killing for the child but the killing of Joe and then Amy cannot be explained away like that. Prison for her, I guess, for a spell. Possibly diminished responsibility will be the plea for Mousie Moucher. What I can say is that they will get the best legal aid.'

'It's hard to see how she could do it, she couldn't be sure of what the child had.'

'She claims she could. She holds no brief for Western medicine and she consulted her own Chinese practitioner and Dr Liu drew graphs and consulted the stars and said the child was doomed. And I suppose from that moment, so she was,' ended Charmian sadly. 'Lady Grahamden hasn't said very much, if anything, but she has produced what she calls her Testament.'

'So what's that?'

'She says that she believes in the absolute power of love, and that an act done in love can never be wrong. She also says that we are responsible, one for another, and that it is wrong to let a fellow human suffer as an animal.'

'So she says she killed for love?'

'That's about it. She must have persuaded Biddy. It's not a bad defence, and she may well believe. In fact, I think she does. She says she doesn't believe in absolute forgiveness for every act, but if it is done with love, then you are all right. She'll get a lot of sympathy from certain quarters.'

'As well as a lot of publicity . . . What about Loomis?'

'He claims he knew nothing, but he certainly guessed. Biddy knew and there may be some charge for her, but a lot of sympathy too. I don't know. It will be decided by the legal big-wigs, I don't suppose I shall have a say.'

Humphrey said: 'She'll divorce Holt, he's left her anyway, and she'll marry Peter. The marriage to Holt was never anything but a matter of convenience to both of them. Biddy's very rich, you know. She looks a poor little thing but she inherited millions from her grandfather.'

'Happy ending for those two, then.' I ought to have guessed that Biddy had money, Charmian thought, how else would Mary Erskine know her? 'If you can call it happy and if it is an ending. But they may settle down now and be perfectly ordinary people.' Yet still richer than most and, when Emily died (although it was hard to believe she ever would) a lord and lady.

'Wouldn't be surprised,' said Humphrey. He put her gently back on the sofa cushion. 'I must go and see to the pudding and the coffee.'

'Pudding?'

'It's a kind of apple tart,' he said carefully. 'Lady Mary came over and made it.'

'Heaven help us both,' said Charmian, 'I'll drink some more wine to strengthen me for it.'

She sat there drinking strong red wine for a little while, enjoying the rest and the heat. She knew that Biddy had been driven by Peter Loomis to stay with Lady Mary, who was loyal to her friends. There might be a good future for Biddy and Peter, if the gods of the family (who must be related to Hecate and Medusa) let them alone.

She reached out a hand for the telephone: 'Mother, happy birthday tomorrow. How's your work going? Oh good. What would you like for your birthday? Not having one? Don't blame you, darling. I shall give up myself this year, I think.' After a certain age, birthdays were a luxury one could do without. All the same, a present of some sort would travel to her mother. A special note-book, a new best-seller, carefully chosen (what about Donna Tartt?), her mother would like the book even if she never admitted it. 'Mother . . . tell me, if you can remember, was there ever an old lady in my life who kept talking about girls being good? No sex, she meant.'

'Oh' – she could hear her mother laugh – 'that was Granny Niven, she was your great-grandmother really on your father's side, not mine thank goodness, and she was always trying to get me to warn you about sex and babies, you were only about five. She'd been reading a book about the London poor and sad lost girls and I think saw death and damnation ahead for you if I didn't keep you right . . . I caught you looking at the book once and took it away from you. You wouldn't remember.'

Underneath, I did, thought Charmian. 'Thanks for telling me, you've explained something.'

She sipped some wine as she relaxed by the fire, Muff was purring and from the kitchen the smell of apple and cinnamon floated towards her.

The door bell rang loudly, she heard Humphrey answer it and come in with Rewley.

She took one look at his face and stood up. 'The baby . . . tell me.'

'The baby is all right, a boy . . .' He shuddered. 'But Kate died.'

Charmian drew his head on to her shoulder and nursed him against her. She looked towards Humphrey and knew what he was thinking as she was herself.

'You are going to live and Kate is dead.'

That was the way it went.